SERPENT CURSED

WINGS OF REBELLION BOOK 2

BREE MOORE

Serpent Cursed
Published by Innate Ink Publishing
www.AuthorBreeMoore.com

Ebook ISBN: 978-0-9600087-6-6
Paperback ISBN: 978-0-9600087-7-3

PREQUEL NOVELLA

BOOK ONE

BOOK TWO

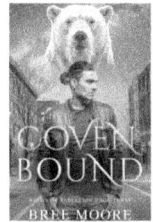

BOOK THREE

BONUS NOVELLA
BECCA + AVAAN

BONUS NOVELLA
IAN + KAMRI

BOOK FOUR

CHAPTER ONE

TYSON

A WEEK AGO, IF someone told Tyson he'd be hitchhiking with a wanted murderer and potential demi-god, he would have laughed in their face. And yet there he stood, thumb up as he squinted in the sun on the side of the road in Nowhere, Oregon.

He sweated up a storm, the moisture mixing with the grime of several days of hitchhiking.

"That one will stop," Harper muttered, angling her head and pasting on a wide smile. "Keep your thumb out."

He obliged, straightening his wilting arm. "Why the crazed look?"

Her smile faltered a bit before firming back up. "Looking human and friendly gets better results. Don't want to look too grim or they'll drive by. Our appearance is bad enough without making them think we're homeless. Smile."

Tyson took a breath in and stretched his mouth in a passable smile. Hunger and heat wore on him, having hiked through the woods for a few hours before reaching the road without any water.

The RV coming up the winding road gave a honk and passed. Tyson dropped his arm and groaned, dejected. Harper swatted his arm. "Stand up!"

Behind them, the bus-like RV had slowed and pulled off the road, parking in the grassy gravel strip next to the pavement. It was cream with strips of faded pink and green color wrapping around the outside, and it looked pretty beat up. Harper headed toward it, gesturing for Tyson to follow.

A woman stepped out from the side of the RV, letting the little white door slam behind her.

"Oh, you poor dears!" She spread her thick arms wide as if she would run and embrace them. Tyson really hoped she wouldn't. Obvious sweat marks stained her blue flannel shirt around her armpits.

Who wore flannel in the summer?

Tyson glanced at Harper, who had a sheepish smile so out of place on her usually scowling face that he actually did a double-take. She had to be acting, right?

"Thank goodness you stopped," Harper said. "We've been hiking all day trying to catch a ride." She elbowed Tyson.

"Yes, thank you." What else was he supposed to say?

The woman beamed. "Well, my mother taught me to never pass by someone in need." She walked up to them and put a hand on each of their shoulders, looking back and forth between them and tsking in a motherly way. "My, my. You look like you've been through the wringer. Let's get you inside before we get some liquid sunshine." Her chin jerked to the right and Tyson followed the gesture, noticing a bank of darker clouds. The morning's overcast skies had cleared up for a few hours, but apparently, mother nature was back for more.

"I'm Wendy, and my husband's Fred." Wendy gestured toward the RV door. "He's driving, you'll meet him in a moment. Who did you say you were?"

"T—"

"Trevor and Jessie," Harper cut in, flashing Tyson a glare.

Right. Fugitives. Tyson clamped his mouth shut and let her take over. Harper had more experience with this sort of thing, no need to get it more mixed up than it had to be. He tried to focus on the story she fed the woman so he could recall the details later.

"You know, we were just on a hike as part of our honeymoon, and we got robbed, if you can believe that! Right on the trail. Thank goodness we were together, and that they weren't violent. They took our keys and our car with most of our belongings."

Wendy's hand dropped from the RV's door handle. "On your honeymoon? Bless you!" She pressed her hand to her chest and teared up. "I'm so glad we stopped. Fred!" she hollered suddenly. Tyson jumped. He gripped the straps of his backpack as the woman flung the RV door open and stormed up the steps. She gestured for them to follow her inside.

"Can you believe these poor dears!" she said as Tyson and Harper climbed the stairs, the RV swaying a bit with the movement. Wendy shook her head. "And you didn't want to stop. They're on their honeymoon!"

"Don't see why we have to ruin it." Fred grumbled the words, but his eyes twinkled. Tyson liked Fred instantly. Fred had a similar squat, wrinkled face as his wife and a mop of grey hair.

Wendy brushed her wispy brown hair out of her eyes, chest still heaving from her charge into the RV. "Where can we take you two? You'll want to report this. Police station?"

"No!" Tyson and Harper blurted together.

"We mean, no thank you," Harper said, glaring in Tyson's direction.

Tyson gave her a desperate "Now what?" look. Harper bit her lip, which somehow changed from suspicious into cute.

Wendy and Fred stared at them.

Tyson waited for Harper to say something, but instead she turned and burrowed her forehead into his shoulder, acting too upset to talk. Tyson patted her shoulder awkwardly. He cleared his throat. "We don't want our entire trip to be ruined by this. If you could get us to the next town, we'll find a hotel and make a call from there. Unless you have a cellphone?"

He winced as he said the words. If they did have one, he'd have to pretend to make a call. Harper's hand gripped his forearm, fingernails digging in.

Wendy frowned. "Oh no, dear. Sorry, but we don't believe in that kind of gadgetry. We'll be happy to take you to the next town, though. It's a few hours." She waved toward the table in the cramped kitchen area. "You just get yourselves settled on those benches and Fred and I will consult the map."

Harper sniffed and turned her head to smile at Wendy. Rubbing her face on Tyson's shoulder had given her a reddened face, almost like she had, in fact, started crying. Tyson didn't know whether to admire or be concerned at her skill.

Harper tugged on his arm, pulling him toward the back of the RV. "Come on, sweetheart." She growled the last word with a fierceness that Tyson thought would surely blow their cover, but Wendy only laughed and exclaimed about young love. Fred grumbled under his breath.

Harper sat on the vinyl seat, pulling down a table folded against the wall. Tyson moved to sit next to her, but she slapped a hand on the vacant spot and gave him a strained smile.

"Tired, pumpkin?" Tyson said sarcastically. He took the opposite bench, clasping his fingers on the table and leaned in. "You make us look like we had an arranged marriage. Would it kill you to act like you like me?"

"It might," Harper replied. "Look, I got us a ride, okay? If I'd left it up to you we would still be wandering in the woods."

Tyson watched her face. There were streaks of dirt on her cheeks and dark circles under her eyes. Her short black hair was tousled. Her hands trembled. Tyson reached out and placed his hand on top of hers to offer a bit of empathy. Harper stared at their hands, rigid. After a moment, she slid her hand out from under his and put it in her lap. She focused on the road moving past the window outside.

"When we get to the next town I can check for any paranormal contacts there." Harper leaned on the table and it tilted alarmingly. She quickly sat back.

"You know that many?" Tyson's behind slid a little as the RV served lanes. He eyed the seatbelt buckle dangling next to him. Something about the way it hung told him it was broken.

"No, but I know how to look for them. We need a ride that can get us over the state line."

"And all the way to Alaska," Tyson finished.

Harper glanced at him. "How sure are you that we need to go there?"

Tyson poked at the chipping surface of the table. "Not at all, to be honest. These... visions. They're confusing, more than anything. I don't know why I'm having them, except they started when I got that knife from my Nana."

Harper closed her eyes. "Remind me again what you saw, exactly?"

Tyson thought the images would have faded, but as he spoke they showed up clearly in his mind's eye. "A raven on a rock, cawing. A serpent coiled beneath it. A mountain standing like an open gate to a wilderness. And just the feeling that it's north."

Harper tapped her finger on the table. "Raven, serpent, and a mountain passage?" She frowned. "Do you think the raven could represent my people? And the snake...danger? Or a threat?"

"Are you dears hungry?" Wendy called from the front. She lumbered toward the small kitchen and wrestled with the door of a small fridge. It looked to have plastic clips holding it shut, but they refused to budge. She finally gave up, red-faced and sweatier than before, and pulled open a cupboard with a jerk. After a moment of rummaging, she pulled out a jar of peanut butter and a slightly squashed loaf of bread.

"No jam, I'm afraid. And the honey's out." She plunked the two items on the table and opened them, placing the bread on napkins she fished out of the cupboard above Tyson's head. She then started going at them with a table knife she had pulled out of a drawer without even having to turn around. "At least you won't starve on my watch." She chuckled.

In such close proximity, the faint stench Tyson had noticed upon entering the RV intensified. A cloyingly-sweet smell, like rotting fruit, clung to the inside of his nostrils, thick and pungent. He choked down a new wave each time Wendy's flabby arms moved. He put a hand beneath his nose and tried not to gag.

Harper's entire face went white when the woman shifted close to her. She wiped at her nose, then dropped her hand and smiled at Wendy with clenched teeth, who smiled back and plunked a chunky-peanut butter sandwich down. A few quick strokes and she had another one. She slid them in front of her guests.

"Now, I know we have some bottled sweet tea somewhere. I'll rustle it up and be right back." Wendy's smile stretched across her face, and she stood there with her hands folded in front of her, as if waiting for something.

Tyson managed to gasp out a strained, "Thank you."

Harper nodded, her lips drawn in a thin smile. Wendy picked up her own sandwich and took a bite, then lumbered to the cupboards above the sofa near the front of the RV in search of sweet tea.

Harper released her breath. "In the name of all... how can a woman smell so bad?" She stage-whispered at Tyson.

Tyson shushed her. It didn't seem like either of their hosts had heard her over the rumble of the engine, but he didn't want to take any chances. "That's rude. You know, they might not have a shower. And if they're only around each other all the time, well, they're probably used to it." He prodded the sandwich in front of him. "Do you think this is safe to eat?"

"She ate some. So probably. Honestly, I'm too hungry to care." Harper took a huge bite of her sandwich, locking her mouth up with the gummy peanut butter. It didn't stop her from talking, but Tyson couldn't understand a word.

"What?" he asked, taking a more reasonable bite out of his sandwich.

Harper scraped the roof of her mouth with her finger, making little choking noises.

Very attractive. Tyson wanted to roll his eyes, but he withheld the urge.

"Nothing human has that smell, Tyson." Harper set her sandwich down. She steepled her fingers and pointed them at him. "Can you think of any magical creatures that might? We need to figure out what we just walked into."

"For the record, hitchhiking was your idea," he pointed out after he finished chewing.

"And your idea was...?" Harper cocked her head.

Tyson took another bite of sandwich in response.

"Ah, lovers' quarrels," Wendy said. Both Tyson and Harper jumped as the woman appeared at their tableside again. She held two glass bottles of iced tea in her hands. "They're warm, but better than nothing. Enjoy!" She folded her hands again.

"Thank you." Tyson reached for a bottle.

Wendy stared, unblinking, at Harper, who froze mid-bite and glanced at the woman out of the corner of her eye. "Oh, of course. Thank you." Wendy turned without comment and walked toward the front of the RV, sitting next to Fred. Harper eyed her sandwich again. "Well, that was weird."

"Weird for her to insist on manners? First you think body odor is cause for alarm, now this? You're paranoid." Tyson managed to untwist the bottle and took a chug of the tepid, sicky sweet drink. It was barely tolerable, but better than choking down a dry peanut butter sandwich.

"Something isn't right about her," Harper whispered loudly. "They're too dumpy to be vampires, werewolves would be weird, but I guess believable. I don't believe for a second she's a witch, there's nothing to indicate that."

"Maybe it's just her. The man might not be anything peculiar."

"Do you enjoy disagreeing with me?" Harper glared at Tyson. "I'm starting to think that's all our conversations ever are."

Tyson took another sip of his drink. "No, I think you jump to conclusions too fast, that you act rashly. Take some time to think about the things we know for sure. Decide whether you will act and how. Slow down, before someone ends up dead."

Harper blinked at him.

"Just a suggestion," he added lamely.

Harper placed her hands on the table, palms down. Tyson's skin prickled at the dead-calm in her eyes. "You're saying I acted 'rashly' when I used the orb?"

No point hiding it. "Yes. You did. You could have waited an hour. Becca and Quinn would have arrived and taken you from the camp, and you would have been none the wiser."

"And I would have left everyone else to continue on as they had. Trapped and brainwashed into believing in your damned system like Fletcher. Look where that got him." The RV filled with silence. Her voice had escalated at the end, and there was no doubt Wendy and Fred had heard, but to their credit the older couple kept their eyes forward and didn't say anything.

Tyson closed his eyes. Fletcher had been his first solo client at Camp Silver Lake. Did Harper think she was the only one grieving his death? He dropped his voice, hoping Harper and her temper would get the hint. "I knew Fletcher for two years. You knew him for a week. Don't pretend you're hurting more than I am."

Harper's entire body tensed like a spring ready to release. She took a fierce bite of her sandwich and chewed viciously, folding her arms and staring out the window. She didn't look back at Tyson, not even a glance. Bite, chew, stare.

Tyson focused on his own food, but his appetite was gone. He finished, more out of desire to not appear rude to Wendy's hospitality, and he drank the too-sweet tea. By the time he finished, Harper's rock hard exterior had mellowed slightly, her shoulders relaxed, her face screwing up with each sip of her tea. He didn't try to break their silence.

After a few miles of passing scenery, Harper reached a hand across to him and leaned in. "Don't think I've forgiven you," she said, "but we're being watched, and we need to look like we're making up." She pasted on a smile so endearing Tyson nearly choked. He let her take his hand and she rubbed small circles with her thumb. He leaned in, and Harper kissed him, then sat back on the bench.

It was just a simple peck on his cheek, but Tyson felt Wendy's eyes boring into the back of his head. She coughed a little.

"No need to be awkward around us, dears. We expect to see a bit of kissing. It's the best way to make up." Her tone increased in pitch, clearly angling for Tyson to respond somehow. If he was reading her correctly, a peck on the cheek wouldn't do it.

Tyson leaned across the table and ran his fingers through Harper's hair, feeling the new growth like fuzz at the base of her neck. His thumb stroked her cheek. It felt awkward right after an argument, the air still heated between them.

Harper cocked an eyebrow, either in a warning or confusion, he wasn't quite sure.

Tyson swallowed. He leaned all the way across the table, bringing her head toward his, and pressed his lips against hers.

The soft kiss lingered. Harper's palm rested on his left cheek, the side facing the window, and she *flicked* him.

The sharp sting of her fingernail broke the spell and Tyson sat back down. Harper smiled that fake, sweet smile.

The reality hit Tyson like a ton of bricks. His cheeks flushed. What had he been thinking? He cleared his throat. Harper gave him a look halfway between murderous and admiring.

"Didn't know you had *that* in you," she muttered as she picked up her tea and took a swallow. Her fingers tapped on the table, and her head darted from side to side, jittery and nervous.

"A lot of things about me would surprise you." Tyson put his hand over her fingers to hide them from the couple at the front. "It wouldn't do for us to get kicked out now. We need this ride."

"Not sure it's worth the trouble," Harper said shortly. She pulled her hand from under his and stood, making her way to the front of the moving RV to start a conversation with Wendy, who seemed all-too happy to oblige.

Maybe it was for the best. He needed a moment to think. Everything was happening too fast for him to make clear decisions. He should never have left Camp Silver Lake. He could have told authorities he wasn't involved in the deaths of Violet and James. But after Violet attacked him and sold Harper out, could he have stayed even if they had lived?

One thing for certain, things would not improve with Lilith in control. That witch had put Harper up to using the orb. She had known it would incapacitate the leaders of the camp, and she had been the one who used magic to bring them down from the window of the lodge. What would Lilith do with the remaining camp residents? Would she give them more freedom, as she had implied to Harper? Or were her plans more nefarious?

And would Tyson ever return to find out?

A deep grinding sound interrupted Tyson's thought process. The RV veered to the shoulder and jerked to a halt. Fred shouted curses as he wrenched at the gear shift, turned off the key, and tried turning the engine back over. It shuddered twice, then died with a depressed hissing sound.

Fred slapped the wheel. "Come on, you overgrown four wheeler. Not now!"

Wendy patted his shoulder. "There now, Fred. Bessie isn't what she used to be. We knew this was coming." She turned to Harper. "I'm just sorry we've gotten you two all mixed up in it." Her look of sympathy melted into a strange smile. "Luckily, we have more than enough room for you to spend the night. We're still an hour or so out of town, but we can enjoy supper and games while Fred gives Bessie a look around inside." Wendy tilted her head at Harper, who gave her a nervous smile.

Harper jabbed her thumb over her shoulder. "It's still light out. We don't want to get in your way. I'm sure we can find someone else to take us to town. You've been more than kind."

Wendy's smile widened further. She glanced over her shoulder at Tyson. "Your man will agree with me. You were lucky we picked you up and not someone with worse intentions. I insist that you stay and enjoy our hospitality. My mama wouldn't stand to hear otherwise, and I won't either."

Tyson swallowed. Wendy's persistence made him uncomfortable, but some women couldn't seem to help being nosy. Was there such a thing as being too nice? Tyson nodded to Harper, who gave him a wide-eyed, panicked expression, but he just folded his arms and smiled reassuringly. Unless Harper could give him a good reason not to trust the over-endearing Wendy and her husband Fred, it looked like they could be staying the night in Bessie the RV.

CHAPTER TWO

HARPER

HARPER GRITTED HER TEETH in a bare resemblance of a smile. Her jaw ached and her shoulders were sore from flying with Tyson that morning.

Just that morning. It seemed like an eternity had passed since the orb.

"More jojos, dear?" Wendy held a plate of wilted, thick potato fries toward her. Harper's stomach clenched at the thought of forcing down more of the wilted, greasy wedges and shook her head. She dropped the over-cooked fried chicken onto her plate, all of it done in the microwave in the RV because Wendy said she had run out of propane for the tiny oven. A barely-chilled coleslaw sat on the table untouched by Harper, as she worried about food poisoning.

Tyson had loaded his plate. How could he eat at a time like this? Stranded on the side of the road with these strange people, forced to pretend to be married, of all things. She had herself to blame for that part of their story, but it had been the most plausible and sympathy-inducing scenario she could create on the spot. Maybe Tyson loved jojos. Harper had never liked them. He seemed like a people person, too, more so than Harper, so maybe he truly enjoyed getting to know Wendy and Fred.

Or maybe Tyson wasn't haunted with guilt over what happened to Fletcher. Or Violet and James.

Harper sat back against the vinyl seat and scrubbed at her eyes. Her chest tightened, and her breath shuddered through her body as she fought off the swell of sadness. The anger lingered too, a slight, fading sting now that she had accomplished what she set out to do—remove Violet and James as leaders of the camp. She hadn't intended for them to be killed, but Lilith had.

"Tired, dear?" Wendy's weedling voice broke through Harper's thoughts.

The door at the front of the RV opened, and Fred stomped up the steps. Wendy held a plate out to him.

"We saved you some dinner, Fred. How is Bessie?"

Fred shook his head, mopping his face with a filthy rag. Wendy squeezed out and offered him her side of the bench at the table and he plopped into the seat, laughing and rubbing his beard.

"Well, Bessie is in need of a rest, it would seem. Not much more I can do for her except wait and see how she is in the morning and call a mechanic if she doesn't start."

Harper's heart stopped. They were stuck here *overnight*. She trained her breathing, keeping it slow and methodical to avoid a reaction. What would an innocent, concerned young woman do? She brought her hand to her chest.

"Oh my. I'm sorry to hear that," she said in a slightly breathy voice, hoping she didn't sound vapid. Tyson gave her the odd look he'd been using ever since she had flagged down the RV. He saw a new side of her, this level of acting and deception—a tool Harper had used to survive since childhood.

"Oh, Fred. I can't believe it." Wendy sighed, then perked up. "On the bright side, we have you dears here to keep us company at least. You know, I think we ought to offer them our bed, Fred. What do you think?"

The man blinked at her, mouth full of jojos. "Why?" he asked, potato bits falling onto his plate.

Wendy wrung her hands, looking distressed. "Why, because they're newlyweds, Fred. And guests. It's the decent thing to do. We can pitch the tent outside."

"No," Fred said flatly. "It's going to rain. We can set up the hide-a-bed in here."

Wendy chuckled. "Of course we can." She didn't look too pleased about it, for some reason.

Harper supposed the woman wanted to give the newlyweds some privacy, but Harper couldn't tell her there was no need. Even if she were spending the night in this suffocating RV with her new husband, Harper wouldn't want to do anything on a stranger's bed.

"That's not necessary," Tyson jumped in, wiping his face with a napkin. Well-mannered even on the run. Tyson didn't have to pretend as hard as she did to be kind and respectful. "Jessie and I can sleep anywhere, as long as we're together." He offered Harper a fake-besotted smile and she returned it with a sarcastic cock of her head.

Wendy exchanged a knowing look with Fred and sighed dreamily. "You two are the picture of new love. I can't believe we're so lucky to pick you up."

Harper itched to slap that wide smile off the lady's face. She didn't buy the act. There was something fishy about the RV breaking down when it did. Something too convenient in their reactions, their willingness to house strangers for the night.

Harper couldn't get rid of the itching in her shoulder blades. Her instinct told her to refuse the offer of a dry place to sleep and run. Could Wendy have heard the news of Harper and Tyson's escape from Camp Silver Lake and decided to hold them until the Stiffs got here?

Harper hadn't heard anything on the radio, and Wendy claimed not to have a cell phone, but that didn't mean the matronly woman wasn't more cunning than she looked. Harper would have to keep her senses honed and be ready to get the hell out of there if things turned south.

"I'll help clean up dinner," Harper said, jumping to her feet.

"Thank you, but I can do it, dear." Wendy reached across to take Harper's and Tyson's plates, and Harper got a full whiff of the woman's horrid scent. An acidic, bitter death smell that made her eyes water at this proximity.

She put her fist against her mouth and closed her eyes, praying her stomach held.

"Fred will get your bed set up," Wendy said.

Fred grunted in agreement and shoved the last two potato wedges in his mouth, brushed his hands together and stood.

Harper and Tyson stood in back near the closet-sized bathroom, watching as the older couple expertly folded back the table, slid the benches sideways, and popped a mattress out of the narrow couch. The sheet on it smelled musty, but thankfully nothing like Wendy. Two pillows were pulled out of a cupboard, and a thin tan blanket and puffy homemade quilt.

"You sure you wouldn't like to stay up for games?" Wendy asked hopefully.

Harper would rather have clawed out her eyeballs than engage with this woman any more. That wide smile, simpering kindness, and the unscratchable itch inside Harper's shoulder blades made every second miserable. She hoped she was wrong. But if not, might as well get the show started. If Wendy, and possibly

Fred, were paranormal beings with ill intentions, they would choose a moment when Harper and Tyson were most vulnerable to make their move.

"Games sound wonderful," Tyson said. Harper elbowed his ribs discreetly. Tyson grunted and rubbed his side. "But we're spent after everything that happened today." He put his arm around Harper, who allowed it for appearances' sake. If he tried to kiss her again, though, she would slap him so hard he would lose sense of direction.

"Feel free to make use of the facilities we have. Push the lever by the base of the toilet with your foot to flush. There are fresh washcloths on the sink if you need a cleaning. Fred and I will go sit outside and enjoy the evening air for a bit."

The muggy, damp evening air, with a thunderstorm threatening. Harper's eyes narrowed at the broad backs of the retreating couple. The RV door slammed shut, and she was alone with Tyson for the first time in hours. Harper released a long breath.

"I call the bathroom first."

Tyson sat on the bed, bouncing and wincing. "Be my guest."

Harper took her time freshening up, but kept one ear open for any sounds from outside. The rare car driving by, the wind rushing past the sides of the RV. A quiet roll of thunder in the distance. She turned the water off and set the used washcloth down, then turned the handle of the door. It creaked open.

"Thank goodness," Tyson said, standing outside the door.

"Ah!" Harper yelled. Her heart beat surged in her chest. "Why are you creeping around the bathroom door?"

"I'm not creeping! I was trying to see Wendy and Fred outside. Did you notice if they took a flashlight or anything with them? It's dark and lightening started a bit ago."

"Don't tell me you're worried about them." Harper squeezed past Tyson's bulk filling the narrow corridor.

"They could just be people."

Harper scoffed. "I don't believe that for an instant."

"Is it really so hard to believe that truly nice people exist?"

"Nice people with chunky peanut butter and gag-worthy body odor who feel comfortable picking up strangers on the side of the road?"

Tyson's expression didn't change. "Yes."

"I'll believe it when I see it. If we wake up in the morning without incident, you can say 'I told you so.'" Harper left the dim light above the stove on as she walked to the end of the RV where the hide-a-bed was set up. The bathroom door closed behind her.

She lay on the mattress. Every position she tried emphasized the bones in her body. Shoulders and hips both pressed painfully into the barely-cushioned surface. It tempted Harper Harper to bring out her wings and cushion herself from the miserable excuse for a bed, but she risked getting caught. If Tyson was right, and Wendy and Fred were normal people, coming back into the RV to a raven-woman sleeping in their spare bed might give them heart attacks, or worse, they would dial 6-1-1 and have the Stiffs swarming the area within a few minutes.

Harper listened to the sound of running water and the rumble of thunder. The RV creaked and rocked as a large semi-truck drove by.

Voices murmured behind her head.

Harper sat up and twisted toward the window behind her. She held one of the thin blinds down and peered into the pitch darkness. A ghostly wisp of green flashed across her view and disappeared. Harper scooted closer to the window, but she didn't see the green wisp again.

The bathroom door opened, and Tyson stepped out, a shadowy, but familiar figure as he approached the bed. Harper's heart rate increased again, and she frowned. This was Tyson, not some ghoul in the night. He hadn't scared her this time. Then why did her breath shorten when she looked at him, hair tousled and standing on end from where he had run wet fingers through it?

Tyson eyed her but didn't say anything as he removed his shoes, then climbed over to the other side of the bed and lay on top of the covers. He stared at the ceiling.

He cleared his throat. "I can sleep on the floor if you want."

"There isn't room. Besides, Wendy will think we're still fighting."

"It happens, you know. Couples fight."

"On their honeymoon?"

Tyson laughed. "All right, you have me there." He looked at her as she peeked out the window again. "You see something?"

"I'm not sure," Harper admitted. She backed away from the still-dark window and burrowed under the scratchy blanket. Her heart slowed.

Tyson shifted and pulled the quilt over himself, staying above the scratchy blanket.

Personal preference or chivalry? Either way, Harper's heart responded with an uptick in beats. She took deep breaths, willing it to calm down. There was no reason to be nervous around Tyson. He knew what she was capable of, and he respected her.

Rain pattered on the roof above. Harper expected Wendy and Fred to return any moment, but the RV door remained shut. She couldn't hear voices anymore, either.

"Tyson?" she whispered.

Tyson faced her, expression obscured by the pitch darkness. "What?"

"What are you thinking about?" Harper swallowed, moistening her dry mouth.

Tyson sighed. "I was thinking how things were at the camp. Losing Fletcher and the camp leaders in such a short time..." He paused, then coughed. "It's a lot to deal with."

"You're worried about the residents?"

"I am."

Harper thought about that. "But Violet wasn't a good leader. She wasn't protecting residents. She actively sent them to be tortured, encouraging them to give up everything for some stupid laws."

"You only knew her a short time, Harper. Don't judge her so harshly." His voice sounded rough.

Harper flexed her hands under the blanket and faced him. "What about your friend Reya?"

"What about her?" He moved, seeming uncomfortable. Did it matter what had happened to his childhood playmate? Harper hadn't known the fox-shifter, but she knew the girl was important to Tyson. Reya was, in fact, one of the reasons he had become a paranormal counselor.

"You never told me what you found out."

"There wasn't time." He paused. "The records in the apothecary indicated that she died." His clipped voice hid his true emotions.

"Died? Of natural causes?" Harper couldn't believe that, not for a minute.

"No," Tyson admitted. "Lethal injection."

Harper sat up in the bed. "And you still defend her? Violet? How can you?"

"Because grief makes people do weird things." Tyson faced Harper, who shook her head furiously.

"You aren't going to explain away that witch's behavior with grief. Who was she grieving when she killed Reya? Are you going to excuse that away with your psychology degree? You don't have any proof she or James wasn't involved, and everything points to them being there. Violet wasn't innocent. You don't have to mourn her." Harper clenched the blankets.

When Tyson finally spoke, his voice held a dismissive tone. "None of us are innocent."

Harper heard the words, felt them pointed at her. She wanted to say something to rid herself of the feeling of his disappointment in her. She hadn't pulled the trigger, but she had aimed the gun, so to speak. Violet and James were dead because of her.

Harper lay with her back to Tyson, fighting back the swell of emotion blocking her throat. Tyson adjusted the covers, staying on top of the bottom blanket. Warmth radiated from his back, a small comfort against the pain and guilt of what had happened the past few days. Fletcher had ended his life after his wings were surgically removed.

The orb had taken something from her, and Harper didn't know what. She didn't want to think about the empty patches in her mind that felt sterile and empty. She wanted to shut her eyes and dream of finding her parents, of reuniting with them in a safe and secret place where they could live out their lives in their raven forms without fear of persecution or restriction.

Despite her resolve to stay awake until Wendy and Fred came in and went to bed, Harper's eyelids grew heavier and heavier until they finally sealed. She slept in fits and bursts. Gravelly voices muttered. A door clicked open, then shut even more quietly.

A snuffling sound wormed its way into Harper's awareness. An acrid stench wafted through the room. She moaned and turned onto her back, pulling the covers higher, only they wouldn't move. Something held them trapped. She tugged harder. A cackling filled the RV. Harper paused and breathed in. The smell overwhelmed her, making her eyes water, her senses tingle.

A heavy object landed on her chest, crushing the wind out of her. Harper opened her eyes but could see nothing. There was something pressing against her eyes, a blindfold of sorts. She thrashed and screamed against a fabric gag in her mouth. A set of hands with an impossibly tight grip pinned her hands to her sides.

A shout next to her—Tyson. He struggled the same she did, a gag muffling his shouts for help.

The weight on top of her shifted, and Harper bucked. The object— or being—flew off with a thud. Harper rolled off the bed and landed on her shoulder, striking a ledge on the uneven RV floor. Her hands scrabbled at the blindfold and tugged it partway up.

In the nearly pitch dark of the RV, a lumpish, squat figure crouched a few feet away from her. A slight gleam off its teeth and eyes telling Harper betrayed its position. It snarled and leapt for her. Harper ducked and rolled under the hide-a-bed, scraping the top of one shoulder. A sharp pain radiated from her skull and she realized the creature had grabbed her hair. She screamed through the gag as the creature pulled at her from under the bed.

Tyson's cries were growing quieter as Harper reached back and pulled against the creature's grip. Another creature sat on top of Tyson's chest, bouncing and chuckling with dark glee, leaning close to Tyson's face and sniffing loudly.

Tyson would suffocate if Harper didn't act. She let her wings out, feeling them thrust through her back near her shoulder blades. One hit the wall with a sharp pain, the other folded against the cupboards on the opposite side.

The tug on her hair released. Harper stood, folding in her wings. She grasped the gag to remove it and sing a Song that would send these creatures to an early grave, but the creature sprang up from the floor and rammed into her head, sharp claws scrabbling for purchase on her face.

Harper grabbed its hands and fell into a kneeling position. She felt around for something to hit the creature with and touched the rough fabric of Tyson's backpack on the floor. She slipped her hand through the gap in the zippers at the top and grasped the curved bone handle of the *ulu* knife. It hummed strangely beneath her fingers. She jabbed it backward, striking flesh and making the creature shriek in pain. It fell from her shoulders and she stood, panting.

"Tyson!" she screamed. He had managed to get his blindfold off and wrestled hand-to-hand with the dark form still sitting on his chest. Harper started toward him with the knife, but the injured creature jumped onto the bed in front of her, howling in rage.

Harper tossed the *ulu* knife at Tyson over the creatures' heads. The moment his hands touched the knife, it burst into a bright multi-colored light. The creatures dove for cover under the bed. Tyson stood. Bleeding from a dozen scratches on his face and arms, he held the knife in front of him and shouted in a tongue that Harper had heard before, but didn't understand.

The creatures squealed like pigs. Harper crouched down and the one nearest to her, bleeding from a gash on the side of its face, hissed.

She looked at Tyson. "I don't think they like your knife."

"You think?" Tyson laughed breathlessly.

An irritated chittering came from under the bed, and two pairs of yellow eyes glared out at Harper. Now that she had light, Harper could see the mottled, lumpy grey skin, like toads' skin, and the thin, gangly arms and legs supporting portly bodies.

Goblins.

CHAPTER THREE

BECCA

A MUFFLED VOICE BROKE through Becca's consciousness, and she jerked awake with a hiss of pain as her head rattled against a cold metal floor. Quinn peered into her eyes, a deep furrow in his forehead. He shook her shoulders.

"Becca!"

Becca licked her lips and tried to respond, but only managed a drunken slur. Had she been drugged? She moved her hands to sit up, but the motion proved impossible. She strained at the cuffs digging into her wrists. She looked at Quinn in panic, the words coming from her mouth senseless babble. Mid-sentence, her tongue untwisted and she could speak again.

"—don't understand!"

His hand cupped beneath her chin, then slid away as he sat back on his heels. He let out a sigh. "You had me scared for a minute there."

Becca's mind reeled. She tried to recall what had happened before she got here.

Actually...where was here? It looked like the back of a utility vehicle. Steel walls and tiny, dark back windows on double doors. She pulled experimentally against the handcuffs and winced as the motion rubbed against the bandages on her injured arm.

"Here, I got you." Quinn gently wrapped his hands around her arms and picked her up. His touch relaxed her nerves and her heart rate slowed.

"How come you're not cuffed?" Becca asked, gathering her legs beneath her and standing. She swayed as the truck turned a corner, and she leaned into Quinn's broad chest. It wasn't a bad place to be. She breathed in, and his dusty scent tickled her nose.

Quinn wrapped an arm around her shoulders, keeping her in place. A metal band around his wrist pressed through her shirt. "I broke mine. The chain, at least. I'm surprised they weren't reinforced somehow. Or I'm stronger than they thought." His voice rumbled against Becca's ear. She grinned to herself, but the grin slid from her face when she considered their situation.

"Did you see what happened to Tyson and Harper?"

"Aberration enforcers hit me with the tasers. I remember one of them punching Tyson before I blacked out, but unless they're being transported in another car, it's just us."

The truck passed over a bump and Becca shrieked as the force threw her toward the side of the truck. Quinn lunged for her, one arm looping around her back and the other catching the wall before they struck it. His brown eyes stared into hers.

Becca tilted her head back to look at the metal wall mere inches from her skull. "That would have hurt."

"We should sit down." Quinn dropped onto a metal bench built into the back of the utility vehicle. Becca squeezed in beside him. She flexed her fingers, still caught in the handcuffs behind her back. She started to ask Quinn to break her handcuffs, but before she could get the words out, the van slowed, halted, and the engine turned off.

The front door latches released. Footsteps sounded on pavement, and the doors swung wide. The sudden daylight flared in Becca 's eyes. The man at the door had a bushy, sand-colored mustache and pale green eyes. He seemed coiled, ready to spring if Quinn or Becca chose to attack, but when he spoke his voice was steady.

"Rest stop. One at a time. Ladies first."

Becca glanced at Quinn, noticing he held his hands behind him as if he were still cuffed. She nodded and he nodded back. Blood rushed to her ears as she carefully hopped from the van onto the pavement. A gas station stood before her, baking in the late afternoon sun. Her escort walked directly behind her, hiding the handcuffs from the view of patrons in the gas station. Legal hire or not, he obviously wasn't eager to expose his purpose to the public. He smiled at everyone they passed, then stopped at the door of the ladies' restroom.

"I'll be waiting for you out here. Any funny business and your friend gets it." He lifted the edge of his leather jacket and showed her the butt of a gun sticking out of a holster there.

Could a gun kill Quinn? A bullet in the right place could, most likely.

Becca shoved her hands out to him. "Hard to do anything essential with these on."

The man reluctantly took out a key ring and unlocked the cuffs. He jammed them in his pocket. "Get on with it," he growled and gestured at the door.

Becca pushed on the heavy door and went through. She leaned against the bathroom sink, staring into the mirror, cringing at her reflection.

Never mind that. How could she get out of here? The only windows were near the top of the wall, and narrow enough that she couldn't slither through. Too bad she couldn't shift into snake form after all. She snorted at herself. As if that would ever happen. She turned on the water and splashed her face before turning the water off again. Might as well use the bathroom while she was here.

When she had finished, she still had no idea how she could get out. Hopefully, Quinn would come through. She would be ready to run.

She cautiously pushed open the door. The man immediately spotted her from where he stood, handing a cashier his card for the chips on the counter. Becca didn't think twice; she bolted down the nearest isle, dodging an older man and squeezing past a pack of teenagers to break through the doorway. A bell chimed behind her as she left amid the close shouts of the man from Aberration Management.

"Quinn!" she shrieked, pumping her arms and legs. Black wings flared over the top of the nondescript white van and Quinn leapt out and up. A gunshot cracked and Becca crouched behind a truck parked on the other side of the gas pump. Had they hit Quinn? She popped her head over the truck bed. The man who had stayed to watch Quinn pointed a gun at her. Did it hold real bullets? Would they really kill those they had been sent to collect? Staring down that barrel, Becca froze. Her head swam and her vision flickered. A flash of reddish-blue light, like a thermal scan, flared in her vision, and everything muted.

An arm grabbed her waist and dragged her down.

"What are you doing?" Quinn whispered in her ear.

Becca shook her head and her vision doubled, then normalized. "Escaping," she whispered back.

"I don't think so." The man who had taken Becca inside cocked his gun, standing between them and the gas station. They turned to find the other man between them and the road beyond, his gun pointed at them.

"How bulletproof are you?" Becca muttered.

"I'd rather not test it out." Quinn drew his wings into his back and they slowly receded from around Becca's shoulder. She resisted the urge to stroke the feathers as they shrank and disappeared. She closed her eyes against the threatening tears. They had failed. And it was unlikely they would get another chance like this one.

One of the men grabbed Becca's upper arm, hauling her up. She protested loudly, hoping to draw attention from some on-looker now that Quinn looked more human. They might take pity, call the police. The man's hand slipped for a moment, and Becca lashed out, catching his shin, but he adjusted his grip, this time grabbing her bandaged forearm.

Fire lanced through her. She screamed in pain. Her mind flashed with green, yellow, and black. Her whole world dilated and narrowed, alternating perspectives until a roiling sickness rose in her stomach.

A muted shout rang out. Becca turned toward it. A bee stung her shoulder.

No, a knife pierced her.

And then the sun sank slowly, fog creeping into her vision and turning everything blurry.

A jolt brought her out of the fog and she awoke groggily. It took longer than last time to get rid of the drowning feeling. Her arm ached fiercely, throbbing. She should take the bandage off and check for infection, but she resisted. She glanced down to her shoulder to check for damage only to see a tiny hole in her shirt, like that made by a syringe or similar. Not a knife, then. Her head ached and her stomach clenched in hunger. The acrid smell in the van made both worse.

Once again, Quinn was already awake. He sat cross-legged and calm beside her, watching her wake up. Had he been darted? What had happened at the gas station with her vision?

"They didn't cuff you again?"

"I don't think they have anything strong enough to hold me. But they threatened me enough with your life that they knew I wouldn't be going anywhere."

"Think you could get me out of these things?" Becca rolled over and offered her hands, which were connected at her back.

Quinn blinked. "Oh yeah. Sorry." He grasped the base of the cuffs where the chain attached, then tightened his grip and grunted. Becca bit her lip as the force of his hands pressed her skin into the hard metal. The metal gave out with a snap and her hands flew apart. She brought her arms forward, shaking them out and rubbing the sore skin.

"Thanks for the bracelets," she joked, holding one up.

Quinn's mouth quirked upward. She smiled and tilted her head for a kiss. Quinn obliged, offering her a swift peck before he looked around the car.

"I'm sorry the escape didn't work out." Becca shook her wrists, trying to get used to the weight of the broken cuffs on them.

"I woke about an hour before you. We've been driving the entire time. Do you know where Aberration Management headquarters is located?" Quinn tilted his head.

Becca gripped the edge of the seat beneath her. She pursed her lips thoughtfully as she searched her memory. "Aberration Management is one of the more secluded factions. They keep their locations more secretive than the Naturalization camps, mostly because they have a bunch of illegal practices they're keeping under wraps—testing, military training, stuff that the general public gets squeamish about. So no one knows where the facilities are unless they work there or, like us, they're taken."

"So that's a no." He shifted in the tight seat, glancing at her. "What I can't figure is why they took you. They came for Harper, right?"

"Yeah. Tyson said that Violet called them in to collect her. They had some sort of supernatural reading device. Harper and that orb were behind me. They could have gotten a false reading." Becca shrugged and stared at her hands. Her gaze traveled to the filthy bandage on her arm. The edge of the wrapping hung limply open. Beneath, she could see a glimmer of green.

She frowned. Wounds should not be green. Green meant severe infection.

But the bright green jewel tone on her arm *shone*. Gangrene wasn't shiny.

Quinn made a sound of agreement and settled back against the wall behind him, folding his arms and closing his eyes. Thinking or sleeping? Becca fingered the edge of the bandage, eyes flicking from Quinn to her arm. She didn't want to alarm him, but she needed to know if her wound required more medical attention than the bandages and antiseptic cream she'd been trying on it. She tugged a bit of the bandaging off and pulled back the gauze.

Some clear, tacky fluid seeped from the wound, but nothing like blood or puss. The skin around it looked healthy. As she unwrapped a section of the bandage above her wrist, the entire patch of skin gleamed back at her, green and scaled.

Becca's breathing hitched. She reached across with a trembling hand and gently touched the smooth scales. It was like touching the cool, slithery body of a snake.

Transformed. What had that mummy done to her?

Becca covered the arm with the gauze and bandage, the wrapping looser now that it had lost some of its stick. She swallowed the bile rising in the back of her throat and tilted her head back, breathing through her nose so she wouldn't be sick.

She laid her other hand on top of the bandaging. Another, larger hand covered her own. Becca looked to Quinn. His eyes were still shut, and no other part of him had moved, but his hand stroked across the top of hers. Becca's insides warmed like a steam vent in the depths of the ocean. She leaned her head on Quinn's shoulder. At least they were still together. She should definitely tell Quinn about her arm.

Something thudded on the roof and the vehicle rocked on its suspension. It jerked to a halt, throwing Becca sideways and out of her seat. Quinn stood, his partially extended wings keeping him anchored on his feet. He trembled as if holding the half-transformation taxed him. He reached a hand out and caught Becca by the wrist, swinging her around and against him. Shouting and feet running on pavement outside were muffled through the vehicle's armored exterior.The vehicle rocked again, this time more violently. It creaked and nearly tipped, then slammed down on its wheels. Becca couldn't help it; she screamed. The vehicle stopped moving, and rapid fire sounded outside. *A machine gun?* Becca broke out in a sweat.

Footsteps on the roof. A scream, blood-curdling and drawn out. And then, oddly enough, a harsh trilling melody. It sounded like the grating of tires on pavement, a guttural scraping that dug into the depths of her eardrums and rattled around in her head.

Becca curled her toes against the sound. Quinn said something about getting out of there, then he grunted and rammed into the vehicle's doors feet-first.

Becca jerked away from the banging, holding her hands against her ears, but the grating song-sound still lingered.

A hissing sound escaped her lips, which were now coated in a hard, strange substance. She stumbled into the side of the van and struck her wounded arm. Fire flared on her skin and she sucked inward. The edge of the bandage slid off to reveal not skin, but scales.

The shiny green scales crawled up Becca's skin in a diamond pattern from past her wrist to where her elbow began. The pale, human underside of her arm remained for a moment longer, but as she watched, the scales spread outward, multiplying. Transforming.

"What'sss thissss?" Her words come out with hisses, an extra-long tongue flicking out of her mouth and sending an avalanche of information into her brain. It overwhelmed her human senses. Images flickered in her mind like scenes from a strobe-lit dance party. Her human vision blurred until all she could see was the bright flare of yellow light as the van doors burst open.

"Quinn!" Becca cried out, stretching her arms out in front. "My eyesss!" The visions flickered again as her tongue went out. The red and yellow splotches surrounded with cool blues and greens reminded her of an infrared sensor. Becca's ears felt stuffed, all sound distant like when her ears popped at different elevations. A vibration moved through her body, centralizing in her jaw. She turned as a mass of red and orange stumbled toward her. She slithered out of the way, toward the back of the van.

She *slithered*. Her legs were no longer part of her. Instead, they had melded into a single form below her torso. She bobbed up and down in panic. Her altered world spread before her, vibrations shaking her body. Strange colors plagued her vision every time her forked tongue flickered without prompting. Two orangish blobs landed on the ground, the iridescent shapes of wings outstretched on each of them, just like the figure to her right.

One of them raised its arm, holding a long blue-colored tube. A red hole opened where its mouth should have been, and it raised the tube.

Becca heard a slight pop and a sharp sting blossomed against her shoulder. A needle had pierced her skin. She reached with a scaled hand and grabbed the fletched end of the object. She couldn't see the feathers, but as her tongue flicked out the image became clearer. A dart. Like a poison dart.

Her torso wavered and her head dipped, sending her crashing to the ground. The poison moved sluggishly through her veins, so she lay there, body convulsing, mouth open and drooling onto the pavement. Her mind and body took on a creeping heaviness, starting with the fused form of her legs and moving to her torso and arms. Finally, her face succumbed to the buzzing weight of paralysis.

A figure bent toward her. Becca closed her eyes against the converging and diverging kaleidoscope of infrared colors. The last thing she heard, with a residual tingling in her jaw, was the sound of Quinn screaming her name.

CHAPTER FOUR

QUINN

BECCA'S LONG BLONDE HAIR splayed on the dark pavement as she twitched with fading convulsions.

"Oh hell. Hell. No, no, no... Oh hell, Becca." Quinn couldn't stop saying the useless words as he knelt down next to her on the ground.

He reached a trembling hand out to touch her, then withdrew it in a fist and stood. "What did you do to her?" he bellowed, wings flaring out to either side. He faced off the two men, men he thought were like him until they attacked Becca.

Becca, who had turned into a serpent.

Quinn beat his powerful wings and puffed out his chest, flexing the muscles in his arms. In the back of his mind, he realized that animals in the wild did this when defending a mate or territory, but the primal aspect of his animal self had control. He saw two rival raven-shifters threatening to take her from him. They had harmed her. He would harm them.

He leapt into the air and pumped his wings, then dropped toward the men, legs extended. One man leapt out of the way, but the other waited calmly. When Quinn's foot came within range, the man grabbed it and twisted, spinning Quinn into the ground. He landed heavily, panting, and stood again, surging forward with his hands ready to strike, to strangle.

"Stop this madness," the calm man said. He held up a single hand in Quinn's face. "We do not intend to harm you."

"Not me," Quinn growled. He struggled to form words, to fight past the instincts in his mind that said he needed to defend Becca and drive these strangers, these *competitors*, away.

"You know this *namigiak*?" the serious-faced man rubbed his crooked nose. His companion stood by him, brushing off the strange vest he wore and sweeping his untied hair over his shoulder. The man with the bent nose spoke to his partner in a fluid language. The words tickled the back of Quinn's mind with their familiarity.

"I don't know what you just called her, but that's Becca. And yes, I know her." Quinn rubbed his mouth and turned to look at her. A sinuous tail blended into her torso, and as he watched, the emerald scales faded to a dull grey, then to the pale, soft color of Becca's skin. Quinn glanced away when he realized her jeans had been pulled off during her transformation. Her longer shirt covered her, but he would still respect her privacy.

The crooked-nosed man moved toward the van and Becca. Quinn's hackles rose and he stepped forward, but the other man grabbed his shoulder.

"We will not harm her. Watch."

The crooked-nosed man rummaged around and came back with a blanket, which he carelessly threw at Becca. It landed across Becca's shoulders, mostly, skewed and crumpled.

Quinn growled and the man released his shoulder, allowing him to go to Becca and straighten the blanket. His fingers brushed the cold clamminess of her skin. What had that dart done to her?

"Will she wake up soon?" Quinn asked. Both men looked at him.

The man with the bent nose shook his head. "Not for many hours. She will sleep. We will be away long before she wakes."

"I'm not leaving her." Quinn's face hardened. He clenched his fists, and flared his wings. The man with the crooked nose raised his own wings, meeting Quinn's posturing with some of his own. His partner barked a foreign word and the man froze, but he didn't back down or submit to Quinn.

"Where is your sister?" one of the men asked.

"Harper? We were rescuing her from the camp when we were taken."

"They mistook the *namigiak* for one of our people?" the man with the broken nose said. "Bah, useless."

"Our people?" Quinn echoed. He looked at them, then at himself. Same skin tone, same black wings, and that language... he remembered it from his childhood. "Did you know my father and my mother?"

A curt nod from both.

"We do not have time for this," the man with the crooked nose growled.

"Tarkik is correct." The other man glanced to the sky. "Soon we will be noticed. You must come with us."

Quinn glanced back at Becca. The men followed his gaze, and the man with the crooked nose—the one called Tarkik—snorted.

"That *namigiak* is a danger to us all, Silla. We should leave her here and find the sister." He glared with undisguised malice at Becca.

"She's not dangerous! She isn't like that," Quinn insisted. But he paused as he recalled the flash of green scales and the fangs springing out of her mouth. How had a simple cut from a mummified corpse caused this?

"Did you know she could take this form?" Silla asked, his voice level and calm.

Quinn shook his head.

Tarkik snorted. "She isn't important. It is his sister we should concern ourselves with."

Quinn gritted his teeth. "Harper is long gone. If the authorities haven't caught up with her, she could be anywhere in Oregon."

Silla's wings shrank down. "Your captors traveled quickly, then. Would she follow you?"

"Yes. But she doesn't know where we're headed. She might go into hiding." Quinn shivered thinking of Harper out there, alone again, with the authorities hunting for her harder than ever. Especially once they heard that the Aberration Management team meant to detain her had failed. Would Tyson have gone with her?

No. Probably not.

"Put up your wings," Silla said softly. "We are about to have company on the road."

Quinn didn't ask any more questions, but withdrew his wings. Tarkik did the same and turned to face the road. No blood marked their backs. How did they manage to protect their skin from the transformation? Had a witch spelled their skin too?

"We can return for your sister," Tarkik said over his shoulder. "It is essential we get you to the village."

A van drove past slowly, eyeing the wreckage of the truck, the bodies. The driver rolled down his window.

"You folks all right?" he asked.

Instead of responding, Tarkik whistled. Quinn's bones vibrated. His mind perked up, hearing the new tune. He tried to follow its complex rhythms, but listening left him breathless, his mind reeling.

The effect it had on the driver of the van was more profound. The man turned to face the front of his car and rolled up his window without another word. Quinn watched as the van drove off, a sensation like awe building inside of him.

"How did you do that?"

Silla merely glanced in his direction. "You have much to learn of our people. The Song is useful for many things. Death, illness, destruction, but also the finer arts of persuasion, forgetting, and camouflage." He lifted his chin. "Come. We must be away from here before the authorities are drawn in."

Quinn stepped back toward Becca's unconscious form. "I won't leave her here. It isn't right. She's alone, and she's never transformed before. She'll be scared."

"The snake isn't our problem," Tarkik growled. "It is our enemy. We cannot bring her to the village."

Quinn crossed his arms. "Then I'm not going either."

Tarkik clenched his fist. "Our journey will not be for nothing. You are needed in your village. Do you feel no loyalty to your people?"

Quinn raised his eyebrows. "*My* people? I grew up orphaned in the farthest reaches of the foster care system. *Becca*," Quinn emphasized her name, "cares about me far more than you do, and I also owe her my life. Where were you all those years? Why not save us when we were younger?"

"We were not sure you existed until recently!" Tarkik spat.

Silla watched the exchange in silence.

Quinn shifted uneasily. "You've given me no reason to follow you. If I stay, I might find Harper."

"Your grandfather seeks you," Silla said quietly. "Would you know him?"

Quinn's jaw dropped open. He rubbed it with a hand to hide the shock. He'd never considered he might have family other than his parents still living. "My grandfather?"

Silla nodded. "We do not know the fate of your parents, but your father's father is yet alive, as are his sisters and brothers and their children. There is much we have to teach you about being a true Tulukaruq."

"Our people dwindle," Tarkik interjected. "The men are nearly gone now, and our women do not bear children easily. A child of Raven is born once per year. With our wilderness disappearing and the hunts for our kind increasing each year, we are losing more people than we can replace. We need strong men and women to rebuild our tribe."

No wonder they had risked leaving their village. Quinn swallowed. He and Harper had talked about this for years—finding a secluded village in the far north to settle and be free from persecution. He also needed to know what had happened to their parents. These men could hold the answer.

Except Harper wasn't here. And Silla and Tarkik looked at Becca as if she were a monster.

Quinn thought for a long moment while Silla and Tarkik gazed steadily at him. Finally, he spoke. "I'll come. But I have two conditions."

Silla's eyebrow raised, but neither native man spoke.

"First, we will return to find Harper or we will send someone else to seek her out. I won't abandon her to be hunted by the government here. Second, Becca stays with me." He straightened, fixing his face with a stony expression.

"The *namigiak* will bring sorrow to our people," Tarkik said. "She will destroy us. We cannot bring her."

"Then I'm not coming with you. I don't care if she's cursed. And you can hold me responsible for her actions."

Tarkik began to protest again, but Silla silenced him with a wave of his hand. Silla's eyes fixed on Quinn's. "You understand that as an outsider, she will be punished more harshly than a tribe member? And by claiming her as your charge, you may also take on any punishment she incurs while among us?"

Quinn licked parched lips and shifted his stance. "I do."

"We cannot guarantee our chief will not sentence her immediately to death when we arrive in the village. She would be safer here," Silla warned.

"Do you have any ideas for how we can find Harper?" Quinn asked, ignoring the lump in his throat and the glare from Tarkik.

Silla studied him. "You know where she is?"

Quinn rubbed his fingers together at his sides. His shoulders drooped. "No. We were captured by Aberration Management and didn't see what happened afterward."

"We can assume she escaped, or we can assume she has been caught and taken to a higher security facility. We did not see another vehicle traveling with this one." Silla jutted his chin toward the overturned van. "Either way, your sister will need to be retrieved at another time. We are required to return within a designated time frame. If we do not, others may be sent out. We won't risk them. We will return to the village and our chief. He will decide when we come back to find your sister."

Tarkik grunted and stalked to the van. He shifted, bringing out his wings, and lifted the van until it crashed to the ground, right-side-up.

"What is he doing?" Quinn asked.

"We cannot wait for darkness to fly. We need alternative means of transportation. The van will do for now." Silla approached the nearest unconscious member of the Aberration Management team and rummaged through his pockets.

"You're leaving the men here?" Quinn swallowed at the flat look in Silla's eyes. He hadn't figured out if the men were even alive, but clearly, Silla didn't care.

Silla tossed something tiny and metallic at Quinn, who fumbled, but caught it pressed against his shirt. A key. Becca still wore the 'bracelets' from the handcuffs.

"They would pay us no courtesy. We will not waste time and resources and risk being seized by the state to save them. If you insist on it, you are a fool. Another vehicle will pass by here, and someone will check on them. They are not dead yet."

Yet. Quinn swallowed past a mouth tasting of cotton.

The van rumbled to life, and Tarkik yelled in his native tongue.

Silla turned to go, then hesitated. "Your actions may have severe consequences. You need to understand this."

"I understand." The words sounded hollow coming from his mouth. He retrieved Becca's jeans and knelt beside her, removing the metal bands from her wrists. He wrapped the blanket more tightly around her for modesty's sake, then picked up the jeans and lifted her. She weighed more than he anticipated, but that wasn't too surprising. He had less of his supernatural strength while in human form.

"Put her in the back." Silla jutted his chin out, holding the dented van door open.

"She'll roll around and get hurt. I'll sit with her." Quinn adjusted his grip, keeping his eyes trained on Silla's. Not challenging, but holding firm.

Quinn could tell the man didn't like it, but he didn't argue as Quinn climbed into the van, ducking to avoid hitting his head, and sat cross-legged on the floor with Becca tucked in his arms.

The van door slammed and bounced back open. Silla slammed it again, with a force that rocked the van, this time sealing Quinn and Becca inside.

Quinn breathed until the trembling in his hands quieted. In the filtered light from the privacy-screened windows, he glanced at Becca's peaceful face. Would the serpent emerge again, here in the van? And would the Becca as he knew ever wake up?

He hoped he could keep her alive long enough to find out.

CHAPTER FIVE

TYSON

"HOW DO YOU KNOW they're goblins?" Tyson climbed off the bed, still holding the *ulu* knife with shimmering ribbons of colored light coming off it. The goblins screeched and scooted to the back wall, cowering and covering their eyes with spindly fingers. Their chubby bodies trembled, and they kept whimpering.

Harper looked a bit pale, but it could have been the light coming off the knife. "Can you put that thing somewhere else? It's blinding."

Tyson put it behind him. As soon as the light dimmed, the goblins surged forward with angry clicking noises.

"Don't put it away!" Harper screamed.

Tyson whipped the knife around, slicing easily into the fabric of the hide-a-bed couch fabric next to him. The goblins scampered back, chittering and groaning, hiding their faces in the corner.

"I take it they don't like light."

"Light, fire, salt, and apparently smooth peanut butter and cold beverages."

Tyson barked a laugh at Harper's dry humor. His hand felt sweaty on the handle of the knife, so he switched hands and wiped away the moisture. The goblin's eyes followed the knife.

Harper backed away from the goblins under the bed and stumbled through the dark RV. Did she expect Tyson to just hold the goblins here while she...?

The lights flickered on, and the goblins hissed, crowding closer under the shadow of the bed.

"Do you really think this is Wendy and Fred? Or did these guys attack them outside first?" Tyson asked, gesturing with the knife. Harper's wings rustled as she knelt back down next to him, pinned tightly against her back. She pointed at the goblin on the left.

"That one has hair. I'd wager it's Wendy."

Tyson squinted. When the goblin turned its ugly, squat face toward him, the scraggly strands of filthy brown hair that sprouted from the top of its head like a sad, droopy plant flopped over its eyes.

"I don't know, Harper. Are goblins shapeshifters? I thought they stayed in one form, and lived in caves."

"Caves, sure, but also laundromats, gas stations, alleyways, greasy cafes, bars. If it's a grimy, lowly place that should probably be shut down, you'll find goblins nearby. They're usually more of a pack, so I'm surprised to find these two wandering around by themselves." She eyed the two goblins, who had fallen still.

"You know a lot about goblins."

"There was a pack in one of the neighborhoods I lived in once," Harper said. She bit her lip and chewed it a minute, her eyes drifting as if she remembered something. Judging by the look on her face, it wasn't pleasant.

"If you need to talk about it—"

The words snapped Harper out of her reverie, and she scowled at him. "I don't need therapy, Tyson. We need to decide what we're doing with these *things* and figure out where we're going. Because no offense, but 'head north' isn't doing it for me right now." She pressed off the floor and stood. She kept her wings out despite the cramped space, folded against her back like a soft shell.

Tyson looked back at the goblins. He looked at his knife. The colors were duller in the bright light of the RV, but still drifted off the blade in tiny multi-hued streams. He stared at the goblins again. "Harper, they can understand us, right?"

"Mhm," Harper responded. Rustling sounds filled the RV as she rummaged through cupboards.

"Any idea what they intended to do to us?"

"They sit on your chest and paralyze you while they slowly drain your soul." Harper's manner-of-fact voice was punctuated by the slamming of two cupboard doors. She walked over and dropped something next to him. "Usually takes a month or so to finish it, longer with just the two of them. I wouldn't be surprised if this is their gig. How they survive. They drive up and down the state, taking in hitchhikers and snacking on them. It's a pretty smart for goblins."

Tyson eyed the objects next to her. Plastic zip ties. "Hope those aren't for me."

Harper's scowl showed she didn't appreciate the joke. She jutted her chin at the goblins. "I figure we have two choices. Kick them out and steal the RV, or tie them up and bring them with us. Either way, we have a vehicle."

Tyson glanced back under the bed. The goblins were eerily quiet, no more chittering, no more shrieks or hisses. Just huddled under the bed like bedraggled alley cats. "Do you know how to drive an RV?"

"Never have before. But how hard can it be?"

Something in her tone made Tyson raise an eyebrow at her. "Did you ever learn to drive?"

"Officially?"

Tyson rolled his eyes. "Any chance we could convince them to return to human form?"

"In goblin form they can't come into the light. Their skin is extremely sensitive. Better to keep them under the bed."

The goblins looked like they were trembling. The larger, rounder goblin with no hair clutched at the other goblin's hand. They managed to look pitiful.

"They know the area," Tyson offered. "They could be useful." His back ached. He sat up and stretched it. He put the knife behind his back without thinking, but the goblins didn't move. Huh. Really must be scared of light. Which was good since the knife had stopped letting off streams of light. It looked like it had before with the carved bone handle and gleaming blade. He had nowhere to put it, so he held it loosely in one hand, feeling awkward.

Harper leaned against the countertop slightly behind where Tyson sat on the floor. "Where are we even going? Do you know? Have you had any more visions?"

Tyson shook his head.

"Maybe we should find someone who knows more about this stuff. A seer, or a soothsayer or something. They might know about your powers, and we could get a more clear direction."

"I know of one." A muffled voice came from beneath the bed. Tyson jerked his head down to look into the shadows, and saw

Fred in human form, smashed in the narrow space between the murphy bed and the floor.

Tyson blinked. Harper's wings rattled against her back in a warning manner, and she crouched low in a defensive position. "If you're smart, you'll stay under there," she growled.

"Do you want a soothsayer or not? Let me and my wife return to human form. We'll drive the RV, take you where you want to go. This one's real, I promise."

Tyson considered the man lying under the bed. "It sounds pretty reasonable, Harper. As long as at least one of us stays awake, right?"

Harper's hair brushed her cheeks as she shook her head. "No way. Two of them could overpower us." She looked at Fred, whose cheeks were flushed. He grimaced, apparently feeling the tight squeeze. "You can come out, but the other one stays. We'll keep the lights on in here, and no funny business or my friend takes that knife to your *wife*." Harper's lip curled at the word, as if she couldn't imagine goblins honoring a marriage contract.

Tyson cringed at the threat. Harper swayed, looking unsteady on her feet. The grief of Fletcher's death, followed quickly by use of strong magic and being on the run were taking their toll.

"You sleep first," Tyson said, standing up and moving out of the way as Fred inched his way out from beneath the bed.

"Like hell. You'll sympathize with him and get us in deep shit."

"I won't. Look, I'll keep the knife out the entire time. I won't talk to him unless I have to. But you have to sleep."

"Are you saying I can't handle staying awake?" Her eyes narrowed.

Tyson put his hands up. "I'm saying that you're tired. Let me take the first shift. I'll wake you in a few hours."

"Two. Exactly two," Harper snarled.

Fred stood up, brushing off his rumpled clothes. A wave of the sickly-sweet goblin stench rolled off of him. "Ah, that's better!" He grinned, his too-straight, too white teeth gleaming in the fluorescent lighting.

Tyson gestured toward the front of the RV. "If you have a map, I want to see where you're taking us."

Fred shuffled down the narrow corridor of the RV. Harper grabbed the goblin-man's arm, and despite her short stature, managed to get right up in his face.

"If you try anything that could get me or my friend here killed, anything at all, I will fly you straight up as high as I can and…" She made a fist and released it in a dropping motion.

Fred nodded frantically and Harper released him. She glared at his back as he headed for the driver's seat, then glanced at Tyson.

"What? You look like you just saw me kick a puppy."

Tyson swallowed what he wanted to say. Despite what Wendy and Fred had tried to do, they were sentient creatures with thoughts and feelings, and maybe they could work together toward a common goal. Instead, he shrugged. "What were the zip ties for?"

Harper examined her fingernails. "Just in case." She leaned down and picked them up off the floor. Wendy the goblin hissed when she came into view, and Harper bared her teeth back.

Tyson watched the exchange. It was far from an ideal situation, but so far no one had died. If the goblins cooperated, Harper and Tyson could get what they needed and be on their way, no harm done.

Behind him, Harper snatched pillows and the blanket off the bed and laid them out on the floor in the kitchen area. Tyson hurried past her 'nest' as she punched a pillow, and approached the front of the RV, where Fred muttered at the steering wheel.

"Can you get her moving again?" Tyson asked, taking the passenger seat.

Fred's forehead creases smoothed. He grinned. "She wasn't ever broken. I took her out of gear and slid her to the shoulder so you'd think she was a goner."

"Very tricky," Tyson said.

Fred's grin widened.

Tyson wasn't sure he should be encouraging nefarious acts, but getting Fred in a good mood would go a long way. "So, where to?"

"The soothsayer we know, she lives on the edge of this wood, and about twenty miles east. An hour's drive and we're there. I'll warn you though, she ain't cheap." He chuckled so deep in his throat it was almost like a gag.

"What does she charge?"

Fred looked at him, mouth quirking upward to one side. "Not money."

Tyson nearly swore. He should have expected it. Magical beings rarely dealt on human terms. He'd had a semester of classes on this while getting his paranormal psychology degree. Paranormals dealt in blood and bone and hair and the things that were most important to you. Fairytales spoke often of the deals fairies and witches made that went south for the heroes. They were textbook examples, literally now, of how not to deal with otherworldly beings. Most of those types of deals were illegal, but that didn't stop some from practicing.

"Is she licensed?" The words tumbled out of Tyson's mouth before he could stop them.

"Why, are you?" Fred cackled, beating the steering wheel with a fist.

"Never mind," Tyson mumbled. "Where's the map?"

Fred pointed to his head, tapping against his skull. "In here."

"You said you had one I could see!"

Fred gestured at the wide RV window and the road beyond. "You can see where we're headed clear enough."

Tyson shifted uneasily in his seat. From the back of the RV came a hissing sound, and Harper hissed right back. When Tyson glanced over his shoulder, he saw Harper crouched in her nest, facing off with Wendy the goblin. Harper turned around and curled back up in her makeshift bed on the floor, throwing an arm over her face to combat the bright overhead light that kept the goblin trapped beneath her.

"You aren't married," Fred stated.

Tyson jerked his head back around. "How could you tell?"

"There's a certain glow missing. But you like her."

"What?"

A deep-throated chuckle came from Fred again. He shook his head and rubbed at his greying beard. "You got it bad, kid. You think goblins don't know love? We live on love. We drain its essence from our victim's souls every night as they fall asleep. We feast on it. And we mate for life, unlike most humans." He scowled.

Tyson blinked. *Fascinating.*

Fred sighed and shook his head. "Anyway. It's there." He jabbed a finger into Tyson's chest, taking his eyes off the road for a moment to look at Tyson. "A delicious, barely acknowledged spark."

Tyson's hand went to his chest automatically, as if he could feel the warmth of a literal candle flame through his skin. He turned around in his chair to glance back at Harper again. She'd fallen asleep, mouth open as she breathed deeply, chest rising and falling. She looked small without her wings, but Tyson would never forget how it looked to see her soar through the sky.

And as he looked, he caught his heart skipping in its rhythm, accelerating until heat flushed his cheeks.

Fred made a smacking sound and Tyson turned and caught him licking his lips. He focused his eyes forward and tried not to think about Harper, just in case the goblin driving the crazy bus got it in his mind to pull over and drain the love out of Tyson completely.

Despite his resolve to stay on guard, Tyson caught himself drifting off. He adjusted his grip on the *ulu* knife, then placed it in his lap, one hand on top to keep it from being stolen. His head nodded onto his chest. His fingers touched the naked blade of the knife, thrusting him into a vision.

He stood over the steaming entrails of a dead polar bear, hand gripping the ulu knife dripping with blood. Tyson's breath fogged as exhaled and knelt down, examining the entrails. It wasn't him, but it was him. He'd never slain a polar bear, but part of him was familiar with what to do. He thanked the bear and sliced chunks of meat away. Several other men joined in, talking in a language Tyson didn't understand, only he did here.

"What message does the bear have for us?"

Tyson glanced down at the pile of steaming entrails. The bloody lines made pictures appear in his mind that somehow made sense. Go north. Go north and find the snake. Go north. Go north and meet the gods.

CHAPTER SIX

BECCA

BECCA SUFFOCATED IN A pale pink fog. It clung to the folds of her mind, weighing down her attempts to rise into consciousness. The throbbing, pulsing pain in her head broke through the mist obscuring her mind and brought her back to the surface of the conscious world.

Her eyelids fluttered open. She glimpsed a face above her, and felt arms cradling her.

The pain turned to more of an itch, burning furiously. Becca reached to scratch it, but her hands wouldn't separate. Her eyes widened. Quinn's grip tightened on her and she stopped struggling, looking into his brown eyes.

"Why—" Her voice croaked, and she stopped to clear it. "Why am I tied up?" She looked down. "And where are my pants?"

"Do you remember anything?" Quinn's low voice rumbled through her side pressed against his chest.

"I turned into a snake." Her chin felt wet as she spoke. She rubbed it against her shoulder, embarrassed Quinn had watched her drool in her sleep.

"That hasn't happened before, has it?" He handed her a pair of neatly folded jeans, and she relaxed slightly. But when she offered her tied hands, he hesitated, and doubt crept in again. Did he trust her?

"They want you to stay tied."

They. Becca didn't care to know who right now. She wanted to get dressed and get back to normal. Would she ever feel normal again?

"Put it back on if you have to. Otherwise, you'll have to dress me."

Quinn obliged, untying the rope and throwing it across the van. "I'm sorry I let them do that to you. We don't have to..."

Becca wriggled under the blanket, tugging the jeans back on, then came out from under it, combing through her hair with her fingers. She paused, looking at Quinn, who avoided looking at her. How could he see her in the same way after seeing her like...like *that*? She squeezed her eyes shut.

"How do you feel now?"

Becca opened her eyes. His concerned expression hadn't changed, at least not to the one of horror she had imagined.

"Hungry," she said at last. Quinn breathed sharply, and Becca laughed. "Human-hungry. I want a sandwich or something. Do you feel this hungry after shifting?"

His face broke into a relieved smile. "Sometimes. Depends on how much I fly."

Becca glanced at her hands. "What happened after I shifted? I was...scared. I don't remember much." She remembered too much. The weird reddish-blue heat vision, the disorienting sounds that had been nothing like human voices, the molding of her legs as they pressed together and became a serpent's tail. It was both amazing and terrifying. How many hours had she spent as a child imagining what it would be like to turn into a wolf, or a bear, or a bird? How many birthdays had she wished that she could be a were-anything?

Now it had happened. She could turn into a snake. But could she control it?

She turned her arm over. The itching had faded, and a crinkly, off-white casing of dead skin surrounded it. She brushed at it, and the dead skin fell away, revealing her entire forearm covered in a swath of green scales.

She had shed. Like a snake. A choked laugh escaped her lips.

"Becca?" Quinn's tone, like that of a concerned parent, brought her out of her anxiety and back to the present. She blinked and smiled at him.

"I'm all right." She *would* be all right. Especially once she got some food. Then she could think clearly. "Is there anything to eat?"

Quinn reached to a plastic sack beside him. He rustled around in it, pulling out a sandwich wrapped in plastic. "They stopped at a gas station a while back." He unwrapped the hoagie and handed it to her.

Becca eyed it and looked at him. "You already ate?"

"Yes." His eyes held too much guilt for him to be telling the truth.

Becca chewed in silence, eating just half of the sandwich. She held the rest out to Quinn.

Quinn shook his head. "No, I think you need it more than I do."

"Take it." She waved the sandwich in front of him, lettuce dropping into her lap.

He gazed stone-faced at her, lips pursing.

"If you don't take it, I'll put it on the floor. Wouldn't want good food to go to waste, now." She lowered the sandwich.

Quinn grabbed it out of her hand. "You're terrible. I was trying to be a good boyfriend."

Becca smiled. "You are a good boyfriend. And now I'm being a good girlfriend by making sure you don't starve just to feed me." She batted her eyelashes and Quinn laughed. He obliged her, taking out a bite and letting out a small moan.

"See!" she crowed triumphantly. "You were hungry."

"I never said I wasn't hungry."

"No, but you did lie to me." Even though he had been trying to provide for her, she couldn't handle lying. "Just be honest next time, okay?"

Quinn swallowed and nodded. He finished the sandwich in silence.

"So, who's driving?" Becca tilted her head toward the front of the van.

"They are..." Quinn shifted as if uncomfortable. "They seem to be like me. Raven born."

Becca touched his arm. "That's wonderful though, isn't it? It's what you've been searching for. Do they know your parents?"

"They did." Quinn looked at her hand on his arm. "But they don't know what happened to them. They say my grandfather still lives." He took a breath. "I think I want to meet him."

"But?" Becca turned her head, trying to catch Quinn's eyes, but he wouldn't look at her.

Quinn sighed. He put his hand on hers, rubbing warmth into her chilled fingers. "But I'm afraid of what it might cost. I don't think they'll let us be together. They even...He swallowed visibly. "They suggested that the chief of the village might have you killed."

Becca's heart skipped a beat. She licked her lips and unfolded her legs, stretching them out before her. She stared at the floor of the van.

Someone wanted to kill her.

The thought left a funny sensation beneath her ribcage, an uncomfortable prickling. She tried to shrug it off. "Huh. Well, that's inconvenient."

Quinn laughed, shaking his head. "You're unbelievable." His mirth disappeared, and his fingers stopped their stroking across her skin. He finally met her gaze. "But that's why we're dropping you off at the next stop and calling you a Ryde. You can take it back to your house. No one knows you've Turned. You can live a normal life."

Becca snorted. "Yeah right. With who my father is? One of his instruments will tune into my signature. Or they'll start blood testing soon. The tech is being developed, you know. It's only a matter of time. Home is the last place I should go." She shuddered at the sudden image of her father putting her in one of the labs he had started as a way to discover more about paranormals. No way she could talk to him. She'd wanted to get away from him as a human.

"But your father sent the mummy. He'll know what species it is. Maybe there's a way to get the venom out of your system and change you back." He sounded so earnest, so hopeful. How could she make him understand she would never wanted to go back to her father? And she wouldn't leave Quinn to face his tribe alone?

Unless he wanted it.

"You want me to go?" she asked.

Quinn hesitated, just for an instant. "I want you to be safe."

"You can't guarantee that, no matter what I choose or where I go." Becca adjusted her seat on the hard van floor, feeling every bump the vehicle drove over. "I want to come with you. I'm not ready to leave you. And I hate to think of you facing all of this alone. Meeting family members you've never met, that isn't easy. I want to be here for you."

"But—"

Becca stuck a finger in the air. "Let me finish. I'll go to this village with you, and if they threaten to take me on the long walk, if you know what I mean, I'll offer to leave. Surely they'll let me leave, no harm no foul."

"You know I trust you, Becca. But it's this snake thing...I'm not sure you'll be able to control it."

Becca swallowed against the rock-hard lump forming in her throat. "I don't have anywhere or anyone else to go to, Quinn. If I leave you, I'm alone." She tucked her bound fists between her kneeling legs and tried to stop trembling, but she couldn't. "If I lose control and transform and you're gone and there's no one else to help me, no one to stop me, I'm afraid of what I might do."

The silence in the van was deafening. Becca stared at the van floor, swaying as the vehicle turned a corner.

"You're the only one who can help me through this."

Quinn closed the gap between them, drawing her into his chest, putting his face in her hair. "I didn't think of that," he said after a moment. "I assumed you'd be safer, and other people would be safer, if I went without you. At least if we're together, I can make sure no one hurts you, and that you don't hurt anyone else."

Odd, to be comforted by words Becca knew meant she could transform into an uncontrollable were-snake at any moment, and Quinn might have to protect other people from her. She burrowed in closer to him all the same, grateful at least that Quinn's perspective of her hadn't changed as much as she feared.

The van rolled to a jerking halt, and Becca heard the front doors open. She sat up out of Quinn's arms and brushed her hair back from her face reflexively. The back doors of the utility vehicle swung wide, and two figures with dark skin and matching scowls stared at her. She took in their wide stances, the relaxed way they held themselves as if nothing she did could affect them. Staturing.

Becca stood, unable to straighten fully due to the height of the van. She refused Quinn's offer to help her, instead walking slowly to the opening on her own, maintaining eye contact with the men at all times.

"She should be blindfolded. And bound," one of the men said.

"No, Silla. Not bound," Quinn insisted.

The men turned their gazes on him. Becca couldn't see much of a resemblance. Besides the obvious matching skin tone and eye color, these men were hardened in a way Quinn wasn't. She rubbed at an itch on her arm, the smooth scales rippling beneath her fingers. She shuddered and tucked her hands in her back pocket. Out of sight, out of mind, right?

"She will board the plane and accept a blindfold. Once we land, she will be bound. These are our terms," the other man, stated.

"Do you think I'm going to memorize the way to your village and tell of my serpent friends?" Becca laughed, but the sound came off hollow and the expressions of the men around her stiffened. She put a hand to your mouth. "You didn't seriously... Look, I got scratched by the fangs of a mummy my dad sent from Egypt. For all I know, I'm the only one like this in the U.S., possibly the world."

"There are more of you. Fewer than there were at one time, but the *namigiak* are still a plague slithering across the earth." The other man, not the one Quinn had addressed as Silla, spat each word out like poison.

Quinn squeezed her shoulder, and it warmed Becca from the inside. She expected him to stand up for her again, to refuse to have her blindfolded and bound.

"We agree to your terms."

Her heart fell. She couldn't stop the protest from escaping her lips. "But—"

Quinn's brown eyes stopped her. He leaned in closer. "You don't have to come with me, Becca. There's still time for us to find another route. One that's safer, more comfortable for you."

She couldn't stand the concern in his eyes. She tightened her jaw and shook her head. She wouldn't be a burden, and she wouldn't leave his side. "It's fine. I'm sorry."

Quinn straightened and nodded at the two men, who turned and walked toward a corrugated metal bunker-like structure. An airplane had been parked outside it, a tiny thing compared to commercial airliners—white with green stripes swooping from the tail across its body to the nose.

A man walked out to greet them. Silla and his partner motioned for Quinn and Becca to stay back and they met the man halfway. Becca crossed her arms and tried not to glower. Their distrust grated on her. Quinn rested his arm on her shoulder.

"Aren't you afraid to be seen as a traitor by association?" Becca asked, an edge of bitterness in her voice.

"They might be my people, but they aren't my life," Quinn said. "You know me better than they do, than they perhaps ever will. I'm not about to ruin our relationship for their sake."

She smiled at him, putting her hand over his. Then she looked back over the paved landscape and noticed another man approaching. "Who's that?"

"Co-pilot?" Quinn suggested.

The man stood tall, dressed in cargo pants and a grey shirt with buttons open to reveal a patch of hair on his chest. He had a face like a middle-eastern Calvin Klein model, chiseled jaw, dark thick brown hair, and evidence of a beard growing in. He held a canvas rucksack over one shoulder.

"He's not a pilot. A passenger?" Becca whispered to Quinn.

The man looked between the two groups—the native men talking with a sandy blonde-haired man with a nice tan, presumably the pilot, and Becca standing with Quinn, both of whom wearing rumpled clothes and a tad worse for wear. He surprised Becca by changing his course for them, squinting into the sun.

"You flying with Jared today?" the newcomer asked.

"I suppose we are," Becca said. She glanced at the other party of three. Their voices rose and the gestures grew more agitated and sharp. Apparently, Quinn's people weren't keen on this other man joining them on their flight.

"The name is Avaan." The man held out his hand to Quinn, who clasped it so hard their palms struck with a slap. Quinn seemed to squeeze too tight. Becca winced at his show of bravado, but it made her feel bubbly inside at the same time.

Avaan's smile broadened and Quinn released the grasp. And then Avaan's eyes turned back to Becca. He held his hand out. She gave it a brief shake, and when they stopped, she forgot to let go. Forgot everything but his velvet, caramel stare...

Quinn cleared his throat, and Becca shook her head, coming out of her stupor. She dropped Avaan's hand.

"We might not be traveling together after all. Tarkik seems furious." Quinn looked at the other group, where one of the men stood facing off with the pilot, who had his hands up defensively.

Silla and the other man, Tarkik, approached the small group.

"We have been informed that our travel plans collide in an unfortunate manner." Silla addressed Avaan, not offering a hand in greeting, but his voice stayed smooth and calm. "Could we convince you to travel tomorrow?"

"We are headed in the same direction, are we not? Bound for the great Arctic Gates?"

Tarkik stepped forward, his broad shoulders pushing Silla aside. "What business do you have in the Alaskan wilderness?"

Avaan shrugged. "Photography. Travel photography. I'm on assignment and cannot delay, even by a day, if I'm to meet my deadlines. But the plane has enough seats for us all." He glanced at Becca out of the corner of his eyes. Becca tried to ignore the tugging sensation in her stomach. She frowned. Her heart rate climbed, pounding, as if telling her to run from this man. But that was ridiculous.

Silla and Tarkik exchanged looks. Quinn anticipated they would use the Song to convince Avaan to change his plans, but then Silla spoke. "We will not disrespect our relationship with Jared by arguing further." Silla nodded at Avaan. "We will travel with you."

Jared, the pilot, clapped his hands and rubbed them together. "Glad that's settled. Let me do some last-minute checks and we'll get you folks on board."

Last minute checks took an hour and a half, while the five passengers stood and avoided eye contact with each other. Becca wanted to ask Avaan more questions about his work as a photographer, but Quinn kept his arm locked around her and Silla and Tarkik put themselves between Avaan and their wards.

After the painful wait, they finally boarded. The plane was narrower than most commercial planes. Four seats were lined up on each side, for eight seats total. The white leather looked expensive, and when Becca sat down, she realized her seat swiveled so she could face Quinn who sat behind her.

She could tell it took effort for Quinn to smile back at her through the tension that followed Silla and Tarkik onto the plane. The two men settled in the same row in front of Becca, filling it. There was no mention of a blindfold. Apparently Silla and Tarkik felt it more important to maintain a semblance of normalcy in front of Avaan, despite their lack of luggage.

Avaan took a seat in the row across from Becca, setting his rucksack beneath his table. He smiled at her and at Quinn. "Seems a shame to waste an unexpected opportunity to meet someone new. Do you mind?"

Becca's eyes darted to Quinn, whose face remained impassive until he raised an eyebrow at her. Her decision?

She smiled at Avaan. "Of course not. I was curious about your..."

Avaan leaned forward, adjusting his back, and a short flute fell out of his shirt, dangling from a leather cord. The painted wood gleamed blue, and Becca's eyes followed the path of its swing, mesmerized.

Avaan noticed her attention and glanced down. He tucked the flute quickly away beneath his shirt as the plane taxied. He flashed a brilliant white smile at her.

Becca blinked. "That instrument. I've never seen one like it. It's beautiful."

"It's an old family relic. I like to keep their memory close, you know?"

The answer was benign enough, but Becca's heart raced in her chest, her pulse climbing. She breathed deeply, encouraging her nerves to settle. Something about the flute made her feel as if she shared an airplane with a tiger instead of a beautiful man with a friendly smile.

CHAPTER SEVEN

TYSON

A FIERCE, FIRM TAPPING on Tyson's shoulder woke him. He sucked in the bit of drool at the edge of his mouth and looked up into Harper's cross face. Tyson didn't attempt to apologize, or even greet her. Instead, he stood and slid past her, walking through the RV to the makeshift bed.

Wendy made agitated sounds from beneath the fold-out murphy bed across from him, but she didn't make an appearance. Tyson curled up in the blankets still warm from Harper's body. His bones felt chilled, as if they had experienced more than just a dream through the frozen tundra.

Go north. Go north and find the snake. Go north. Go north and meet the gods.

He meant to puzzle over the phrase, to work at it and dissect every part until he understood what implications it held for his own journey. Because he knew it held some importance, if he could stay awake long enough to figure it out...

"You snore." A sharp elbow dug into Tyson's side. He groaned and rolled over. Harper poked him again. "Come on, we're here."

Tyson opened one eye, looking into Harper's face. He peeled the other open and sat up, rubbing both. A tiny growl came from under the bed, and without looking, Harper swung one leg forward and struck the goblin beneath, eliciting a squeal.

"You don't have to be so mean," Tyson said.

"Says the man who nearly had all of the feeling sucked out of his soul," Harper retorted.

"Fred mentioned that. It's kind of neat, in a way. Did you know they mate for life?"

"Are you flirting with me?" A smile flickered across her face, then turned into a grimace. He'd said something to irritate her. Or maybe she just really hated goblins.

Tyson scrambled off the bed and brushed his clothes. "We're at the soothsayer's? What does it look like?"

Harper leaned across the bed and pulled open one of the brown and orange gingham curtains. "See for yourself."

Tyson had expected a broken down cottage in the woods. Or a tent at a carnival. Anything other than the busy auto shop outside the window. "Here?" He frowned.

"That's what the man says." Harper gestured toward Fred. "Get your backpack and knife. I don't imagine our ride will be waiting for us when we get done."

Tyson shouldered his backpack and made a point to nod and thank Fred as he exited the RV after Harper. He thought he heard Harper snort, but Fred waved cheerily and wished them luck before the screen door slammed shut behind them. The engine roared and the RV signaled and merged back onto the road. So much for their ride.

Tyson squinted, putting a hand up to shield his eyes from the sun. A man in overalls appeared from the shaded garage, rubbing his hands on a filthy blue rag.

"How can I help you two?" the man drawled, sniffing and wiping his nose, adding another grease smear to his face.

"You know Charlemagne?"

The man spit, squinting at them. Realization dawned, brightening his entire face. He slapped the rag on his thigh and barked out a laugh. "You mean Charlie! Yeah, come on."

Tyson and Harper exchanged looks. A soothsayer named Charlie didn't bode well to Tyson. What could a redneck auto mechanic tell him about interpreting ancient visions?

The man in overalls took them winding through the shop. "The name's Beuford. You can call me Bo. I hope you know what you're getting into. Charlie, well, she's something else."

The shop smelled like motor oil and dust. They stopped a brown-painted metal door that said "f— ice" with the other letters scratched off. Bo knocked.

The door opened a crack and a woman stuck her head out. She had a nest of hair sticking out every direction from her messy bun and a bandana attempting to tame it or cover it up. Grease smears and who knew what else decorated her coveralls, arms, and face.

"Hey Bo! What'd ya bring me?" She looked at Harper and grimaced, then saw Tyson at the back of the bunch and snaked a hand forward, grabbing the front of his shirt. She reeled him in, making sniffing noises. Her eyes widened.

"Um, excuse me. Hi." Tyson pushed against her hand, trying to get her off of him. He cleared his throat. "Are you Charlemagne?"

"Ha!" The woman laughed. "Call me Charlie." She stepped back and snapped her fingers. The office behind her glowed orange with swirls of pink inside, and the pulsing beat of electronic dance music wafted from beyond the door. The woman's smile shone, and Tyson blinked at the glare from her teeth.

In a moment, the coveralls disappeared, and she wore a black shirt with neon green writing, the sleeve slipping off her shoulder to reveal the strap of a purple leotard, and a neon pink skirt flared out from her waist. She looked like an 80s dancer, with her hair sprung out from its bun into a curled pouf, and she suddenly wore rouge and eye shadow in place of the grease smudges.

"I'll be working on the crossover we got in today, Charlie."

"Have at it, Bo." She grinned at Tyson. "It's not every day we get someone like you in here. Step into my office." She jerked her head toward the door. "Your friend can wait outside while we chat." And then she *winked*.

Tyson glanced to Harper, who had her hand over her mouth like she stifled a laugh.

"If this is a soothsayer, I'm a rockstar," Tyson grumbled.

Harper shrugged. "She does have magic. You have to at least give her that."

Tyson huffed and squared his shoulders before slipping into the neon-lit office. Gone were the stacks of paper he had glimpsed through the glass window, now shaded with a set of blinds. Charlie sat on a desk, her head moving in time to the beat.

"What is all this?" Tyson asked, shouting over the growing music volume. "Some kind of joke?"

"Never a joke, darling. We soothsayers and dreamwalkers channel our nearest generation ancestor who last held the power. Mine happens to be from the happenest era ever, don't you think?" She tossed her hair.

"Not sure I can take any of this seriously," Tyson admitted.

"At some point, you're going to have to. In order to come into your abilities fully, you'll need to go through what your ancestor went through to get their abilities."

He winced. "Does it involve dancing?"

"Maybe," Charlie didn't seem offended by his lack of enthusiasm for her craft. She looked him up and down, then turned to her shelves where a line of naked little dolls with multicolored hair stood glassy-eyed. Trolls. Tyson remembered those. As Charlie muttered under her breath, the trolls' eyes glowed in a color to match their hair, one by one. Charlie snatched a Rubix cube off the end of the shelf and turned it four times, fingers almost blurring. The surface glowed white, reflecting in the soothsayer's eyes.

"Your grandfather on your father's side guides you."

The glow faded from the cube and the troll's eyes simultaneously.

"That's it? I could have told you that," Tyson said, shifting his gaze from Charlie to the trolls and back again. *Without the creepy trolls.*

Charlie clapped her hands. "Oh! You're having visions already. That's good. Do you have a focal point?"

Tyson gave her a puzzled look. He adjusted the backpack strap slung over his shoulder.

"An object of familial importance that your ancestor could have owned," Charlie explained.

"Like a knife?"

Charlie made a scrunched up face, looking at the disco ball in the ceiling, then paused. "Well, I suppose. It's not as brilliant as I hoped, but it could be a knife, yes."

"My grandmother gave it to me. When I touch it, sometimes I get visions." *Other times light shoots out of it to defend me against goblins.* He left that part off, though he figured of all people Charlie would understand.

She pointed straight up at the glowing, floating ball. "The disco ball. Seriously. My aunt gave it to me right before she died. Who knew she was a soothsayer! Some called her a for-tune-teller, but that's sort of a derogatory term, you know? We're not to be confused with the scam artists that show up at fairs and carnivals and only predict drama and happy endings." She rolled her eyes and clicked her tongue between her teeth. "Anyway, what brings you to my shop?"

Tyson wished he could get away from the strobing, pulsing lights. They were giving him a headache. He rubbed his temples and shut his eyes for a moment, and tried to think of why he was here. Harper wanted him to get more specifics from his visions. He opened his eyes. "Can you help me, uh, fine-tune my visions? They're hard to understand."

Charlie let out a bell-like laugh. "That's part of it, sweetheart. You have to learn to interpret them yourself. It will get easier after you complete the rites of passage."

"Rites of passage?"

"Yeah. Journey to your homeland, find your mentor. They'll prepare you for the rites of passage. Every soothsayer, or dreamwalker in your case, goes through them."

"Then there's nothing you can do?" His shoulders slumped. His homeland was in Alaska, where his grandparents had come from, and they'd already been headed there. But Alaska was a huge place. How could he tell where to go to find this mentor?

"I can take a reading, but I'll warn you, it's tricky looking into the aether for other seers like yourself. Our abilities can mix and do some pretty strange things. But seeing as you're a fledgling, I doubt there would be much interference." Charlie reached up to the twirling globe and unhooked it from the ceiling.

Tyson remembered what Fred the goblin had said about cost. He shifted, coughing to clear his throat. Charlie paused and looked at him expectantly. "So, er, what would that cost, exactly?" Tyson winced. It sounded rude, but he couldn't agree to this unless he knew upfront what he would have to pay.

Charlie waved one hand, almost dropping the disco ball. "Oh pshh. For a fellow dreamwalker, I'll consider it an investment in the future. You can pay me back if I ever need a reading." She laughed clear and high, and Tyson cracked a nervous smile.

"Still want to know?" Charlie asked.

Tyson nodded.

Charlie held it in relaxed, bent arms, staring into it like a crystal ball.

Tyson stepped back like it was a bomb, his mouth suddenly gone dry. The globe's metallic surface bled to white, and his mind flashed back to seeing the Beryllium orb in the basement of the lodge at Camp Silver Lake, Harper's hands glued to it, her eyes lit up with an otherworldly light. She'd been out of his reach entirely.

He unclenched his hands, flexing them, breathing in through his nose and trying to convince himself that this would be different. Charlie controlled this orb, not the other way around.

"Gates," Charlie intoned, an invisible wind lifting her curled locks slightly. Her eyes remained fixed on the transformed disco ball. "Gates. Arctic. Dreamwalker. Tribe. Gods."

She breathed in, shutting her eyes, and the disco ball dimmed. She shook herself all over like a dog after swimming, and smiled at Tyson.

"Did you get all of that?"

"Gates, gates, arctic, dreamwalker, tribe, gods." Tyson ticked the words off on his fingers.

"Very good. I'm impressed. I can't always remember what I say."

"Is that all you saw? Just the words?"

"Oh no. There are images too. Just a moment." A stack of blank canvases hid beneath the long desk at the back of the room. Charlie dragged one out and concentrated on it, her eyes flashing psychedelic tones. The trolls behind her did the same, their beady little eyes pulsing out an unheard rhythm. And, as if she'd painted it, a scene appeared on the canvas.

Tyson's mouth dropped open as Charlie blinked and offered him the painting. He took it gingerly, as if the paint were still drying, but the surface felt more like it had been printed. "This is amazing!"

"Thank you. I have some natural talent for painting, but these days it's so much quicker to scan and print." She laughed at her little joke, picking up the disco ball from the desk she'd sat it on and tiptoeing to hang it back up. It didn't light up this time, to Tyson's relief. He wanted to focus on the painting.

It displayed a mountain scene. Two huge mountain ranges on either side of a valley with a river running through the center. *Gates. Gates. Arctic.* Why had Charlie said "gates" twice? Perhaps because there were two mountains on either side of the other, like a gate? Tiny figures stood in the valley on either side of the river.

On the left side, a figure stood dressed in native garb, its face covered by a mask with a terrifying expression. Tyson shivered. On the opposite side stood a crowd, most of whom didn't have detailed enough faces to make out, but several in the front did, and the more shocking thing was that two of them had jet black wings extended. An old man with long, greying hair, a young man standing next to him. And next to the winged men stood a blonde woman with green skin.

Tribe. Tyson swallowed the lump in his throat and adjusted his grip on the painting. Aside from the green skin, it could be Becca. Had they escaped Aberration Management and found Harper's tribe somehow?

"See anyone you know?"

"Maybe," Tyson croaked. He scanned the rest of the painting. A bright white splash of paint glowed near the bottom right-hand corner, but no figures that could represent the gods Charlie had mentioned.

"Know where you're headed?"

"I think so." He handed the painting back to her.

Charlie took it, looking somewhat dejected. "I don't suppose you have a place for this in your backpack." She chuckled to herself, then propped it up on a nearby desk and snapped her fingers. The lighting went from a warm glow to the stale ambience of flickering fluorescents. Piles of mismanaged papers cascaded across the desks, burying the trolls and Rubix cube. The disco-crystal ball hid under the guise of a broken ceiling fan.

Charlie thumbed her pockets and grinned at Tyson. "Transformation is a fun thing, my friend. You should look forward to discovering your forms."

I like this form well enough, I think, Tyson thought as Charlie opened the door. He stepped out into the banging, clanging noise of the shop, letting reality wash back over him. Charlie slapped him on the back.

"You come back when your adventure is over, eh? I like to hear how the whole story plays out."

"Of course." The words fell automatically from Tyson's lips. He licked them and blinked at the perplexed look on Harper's face. She glanced from him to Charlie and back again, crossing her arms over her chest.

"Finished already?" Harper asked.

Already? They'd been in there for what felt like an hour. "I think so," Tyson said.

"He's a good one, Harper King. Don't underestimate him." Charlie raised an eyebrow and adjusted the filthy bandana on her head.

"S-sure," Harper stuttered, as if she wasn't sure how to respond. Tyson smiled. He waved as Charlie passed him to get back to work, and he could have sworn she winked at him.

Bo escorted them out of the auto shop and into the bright morning sunlight. He wished them luck and jogged back into the shop, leaving them standing on the side of the road together. Tyson squinted, looking up and down the highway.

"So, thumbs out?" he asked reluctantly.

A horn honked, drowning out Harper's response. There were no cars on the road. Tyson looked behind them to see a blue Jeep roaring out from behind the shop. It pulled to a stop beside them, and Charlie slapped the side.

"I heard you needed a ride. Ain't nothing more reliable than this buggy." She jumped out, tossing Tyson the keys. He caught them, blinking rapidly. He swallowed past the lump in his throat.

"You sure about this?" he called out.

Charlie waved and gave him a thumbs up, already headed back toward the shop. "Just bring it back in one piece, if you can manage," she hollered.

Harper's jaw had dropped. Tyson had never seen her so shocked, and it made him laugh.

"So, I got us a ride," he said, feeling a bit smug.

Harper punched his shoulder. "Don't let it go to your head."

They climbed inside. Tyson slung his backpack into the back seat, and started the Jeep, gripping the wheel.

Alaska, here I come.

Tyson immediately reached for the radio dial. Harper groaned, but didn't stop him. He turned to his favorite station—news and country music. The jaunty tune of the previous song faded and a voice crackled to life as Tyson signaled to enter the highway.

"*That was Ann Garner and 'She's Crazy.' Thanks for the request, Allison from Prosser. Speaking of crazy, have you seen any psychopathic paranormal murderers, lately?*"

Harper sat bolt upright. "Turn it up."

Tyson adjusted the dial.

"*That's right, folks. We've got a report that two unstable individuals escaped from a Naturalization camp here in Oregon. Authorities are concerned about the damage these two can do, so they have given us descriptions of the perpetrators and ask that if anyone has more information, to please call in now.*

"*They are a man and a woman traveling together. The man is Caucasian, has brown hair, brown eyes, and stands about average height. His abilities are unknown. The woman appears to be of Native Indian origin and has short black hair, brown eyes, and is about 5'1". She is a dangerous type of shifter— a raven, with unprecedented abilities.*"

Tyson and Harper stared at each other. A horn honked, and Tyson swerved back into his lane, heart pounding in his chest.

Someone had reported the incident at Camp Silver Lake, and now, they were wanted.

CHAPTER EIGHT

HARPER

"*THESE TWO HAVE BEEN marked as extremely dangerous. Do not approach or attempt to restrain on your own. Dial 6-1-1 upon sighting or if you have any information.*"

The radio host finished the broadcast and cut to a commercial. It took Tyson a moment before he turned the volume down. A stunned silence filled the cab of the Jeep.

Tyson glanced at her with so much frequency, Harper expected he would have whiplash later. She didn't have the energy to tell him to stop, and to his credit he didn't ask her what was wrong or try to fill the silence. They were being hunted. Every human, and some law-abiding paranormals, would be on the lookout for them. Crossing state lines hadn't helped them.

Who could have told?

"It was Lilith, wasn't it?" Tyson said after a long moment. "The deaths had to be reported or someone would have come looking. Smart move on Lilith's part to set up a scapegoat. Everyone saw us fly away during the fight that broke out. It's too good. And she pays you so you won't suspect when she reports it. She doesn't care if you take the fall."

Harper nodded numbly. The credit card seemed to burn in her back pocket. Lilith planned all of this out. She got Harper to make Violet and James vulnerable so the witch could kill them in cold blood, then made sure no one would suspect her. It was brilliant. And Harper had been too blinded by her own fury to question it.

She flexed her fingers, staring at the half-moon crescents in her palm from where her fingernails had dug into the skin.

She was a wanted fugitive. Wanted not just for being inhuman, but because they thought she had killed two people. Had she? Were the deaths of Violet and James Petrov her fault?

Tyson must have sensed her mood because he turned the music back up on the radio and drove without saying anything else.

It gave Harper too much time to think. Her thoughts replayed the events of the previous morning—the Beryllium orb, their escape from the camp—and she kept tripping over the hole in her mind. She worried at it, prodding it from different angles, wondering what she could have forgotten that would leave such a big, empty hole in her subconscious.

She tried throwing different memories and ideas around to see if something would spark, but... nothing. It made her want to curl up in a corner and cry, but there were no corners to cry in while road-tripping in a Jeep with a camp counselor who listened to country music.

Tyson took them to a drive thru somewhere in Washington. Harper had missed the signs for the city, which wasn't like her.

"Harper? Did you hear me?" Tyson asked, concern laced so thickly in his voice Harper immediately wanted to jump out of the car to get away from the sound of sympathy. She rubbed her face instead, sighing and crumpling up the half-eaten burger in the paper in her lap.

"What did you say again?"

"I asked if you wanted to hear what I learned from Charlie. You haven't asked."

He would have expected her to demand a blow-by-blow account of what happened in that "soothsayers" office. Harper had meant to, but she'd forgotten when the radio broadcast came on.

"All right."

Tyson gave her a puzzled look, but after an hour of driving in silence, he seemed eager to talk. He launched into the story, something about psychedelic trolls and a magic painting, but one part caught Harper's attention.

She sat up, blinking at Tyson. "She said 'tribe?'"

"Yes, she did."

"And they had wings."

"*Some* of them did," Tyson emphasized. "One of them might have been... "

The last word blanked out the moment it reached Harper's ears. She shook her head, trying to get rid of the sudden sensation that she'd gotten water in her ears.

"Say that again," Harper insisted.

"What? Some of them did?" Tyson's brow furrowed.

Harper shook her head. "No, the last bit."

"I think one of them was... " His voice garbled at the end.

Harper frowned. It had happened again. Excitement bubbled inside of her. This had to have something to do with the hole in her mind. It *had* to. She bounced in her seat impatiently, wondering how to go about discovering what or who the Beryllium orb had taken from her when she didn't know anything about it.

Harper wiggled her tongue around in her mouth as her mind churned, looking for words, and then she made a clicking sound. "Who was captured with Becca, Tyson?"

Tyson said a word, or a name, something that made his mouth open and stretch around sounds Harper couldn't hear.

"Are you okay?" Tyson asked, his forehead creasing now.

Harper sat back in her seat and watched the road go by, aware of Tyson's stare. He knew something or someone that Harper was supposed to know. Something she had known, until the Beryllium orb took it from her.

"Are we going to them?" She asked finally. "Becca and... did the soothsayer give us directions?"

Tyson turned his focus back on the road. Harper leaned back and put her feet on the dashboard. Tyson shot her a disapproving look, but didn't lecture her. He cleared his throat. "I have a location. And the words she mentioned seemed to be a series of interactions or events. Find the mountains in the Arctic, the dreamwalker, the tribe, and the gods."

"I'm not keen on meeting any gods."

Tyson barked a laugh. Harper raised an eyebrow at him. "What?"

"You know, all that trouble over you at camp, them sending Aberration Management after you, they suspected that you are a demi-god."

Harper laughed. She couldn't help it. "I'm not immortal. I don't have any special abilities. I can turn into a bird."

Tyson lifted a finger from the wheel. "What about your song?"

Harper opened her mouth in an 'O' then shut it. She shrugged. "It's just something I can do. I'm not related to any gods."

Tyson studied her and dropped the subject. More driving. More silence filled with crooning country stars and their guitars. Harper found herself watching Tyson at one point, his look of concentration as he watched the road, tapping to the rhythm of the music on the steering wheel. She took in his dirty, torn t-shirt and the fact that he was still missing shoes. Harper busted out laughing.

"What?" A quirky grin popped onto Tyson's face, combined with a perplexed, raised-eyebrow look. "What is it?"

"Your shoes!"

"Well, yeah. I figured we didn't have time to stop." He shrugged and smiled a bit sheepishly.

"Pull off at the next exit. You can't go to Alaska barefoot." Harper couldn't stop laughing.

"Okay, it is funny. I'll give you that. I just got focused, you know?" He signaled at the next exit and together they found a department store. Tyson had to stay in the car until Harper returned with footwear—a sturdy pair of hiking boots and socks. Then he joined her to help gather the rest of what they would need. Snacks for the road and the trail. A new set of clothes for both of them. A backpack for Harper.

Tyson grabbed a winter coat and Harper laughed at him, but he shoved it in the cart anyway.

"You need one too," he pointed out. "It's not warm in Alaska, even in the summer."

"I don't get cold." Harper smirked, crossing her arms.

"I assume that's a native thing," Tyson remarked, surveying the items in their cart. "Water."

"Right." They circled the store again, also picking up other hygiene essentials that wouldn't overwhelm their backpacks. When their turn came at the checkout, Harper took the shiny plastic card out of her pocket, and Tyson froze. She glanced at him.

"I checked the balance when I got the boots." Harper said quietly. She passed him the receipt, watching his eyes widen when he saw the number. Almost $3,000 remained on the card.

Blood money, as Tyson had called it.

The cashier rang them up and Harper silently swiped the card, sweating under Tyson's gaze. *I didn't ask for the money.* Harper told herself. *It would be stupid to waste it.*

"I'll pay for our food," Tyson said as they walked out of the store with their purchases.

"You don't need to."

"You'll want something left when you meet up with ... You never know. I want to split the costs. I have plenty. Bachelor living in Oregon. I didn't really have girlfriends." He grinned, but it seemed flat.

"As in, no girlfriends to blow your money on?" Harper teased.

"Exactly."

"Was that by choice or..."

"Hey now." Tyson tossed bags in the trunk. He stopped after a moment, frowning at the pile of plastic sacks.

"What's that look for?" Harper asked.

"In a few hours, we'll hit the U.S.-Canada border." He turned to her. "You don't have a human ID on you. And mine might be flagged, now that the murder has been reported."

"Can we go around? Not go through Canada?" Harper swallowed. She had ditched her ID when she left the foster system a few years ago. If they looked her up, they would find her recent residence in Camp Silver Lake and know exactly what she was. They wouldn't make it through.

"Fly over?" Tyson asked.

"They have guns, don't they? Big ones. I'm not sure I can carry you plus all this high enough out of range." She gestured at the trunk.

Tyson sighed and rubbed his face. He had a layer of stubble coming in on his cheeks and chin. They hadn't gotten anything for him to shave with, and she suddenly wondered what he would look like with a beard. She screwed up her face trying to imagine it.

Tyson noticed and laughed. "What's that expression for?"

"Nothing." Harper said, looking away quickly. A beard would look good on him, she decided, as long as he grew his hair out a bit too. Not that it mattered to her.

"We have another problem." Tyson dragged a map out of one of the bags. "Driving would take us roughly five more days. By then…"

"It could be too late," Harper finished. She rubbed her hand through her hair, looking around the parking lot at people passing.

Tyson snapped his fingers, making her jump. "We need to find a witch."

"And you couldn't have thought of that when you were getting cozy with the soothsayer?" Harper grumbled.

Tyson gave her a look and continued. "Charlie wasn't a witch. She couldn't open a portal. At least not to our realm." He stopped and turned to the trunk of the car again, rummaging through several bags. He pulled out a package, looking triumphant. It was the burner phone they'd bought.

"When did you put that in there?" Harper made a face.

"I thought you saw. I just didn't want to get stranded in Alaska without a way to call for help."

"Help that would think we're murderers," Harper shot back.

Tyson held up a finger. "It also comes with a data package. We can look up registered witches in the area."

"That's a huge risk. A registered witch isn't going to help renegades."

"They're not all snitches. A lot of them won't question why you need to get somewhere. They just fill out the paperwork for a portal and send you after you pay them."

Harper reached to grab the phone out of Tyson's hand. He held it out of reach, a split second grin crossing his face at her frustration. She growled.

"What if I knew how to find an unregistered witch?" Harper asked, somewhat hesitantly. She twisted her fingers around each other.

Tyson shook his head emphatically. "Now way. They deal in illegal methods of payment. Your firstborn child, that sort of thing."

"But no paperwork."

"Not worth it." Tyson wrestled with the plastic packaging on the phone, finally pulling out the pocket knife they'd bought for when an ancient magical knife wouldn't do.

Harper tapped her foot, wondering how to convince him to not go the legal route. Sure, it could be dangerous working with witches that had no regulation, but leaving a paper trail was the last thing they wanted to do. And what if the witch recognized their faces or names and called the Stiffs? Harper watched Tyson struggle for a moment before he managed to get through the tough plastic. She sighed.

"Okay. We find a registered witch. But we use false names, and we need to change up our appearance a bit. We look like…"

"People who escaped a government camp, were attacked by goblins, and had an existential experience with a soothsayer?"

"Yeah, that." Harper picked up a bag and double-checked to make sure it had her clothes in it, then pointed to a store next to the department store. "I'm going in there to change. A shower would be better, but I don't see us getting one of those any time soon. Wipe down with what they have in the bathroom and don't draw too much attention to yourself."

"I'll wait with the car until you're back." Tyson slipped the phone out of its casing and into his hand, pulling out the instructions with it. He closed the trunk door.

Harper jogged off. There was no one in the bathroom, and she had a quick and easy wipe down and change. It felt good to be fresher. She'd bought a comb, and with it she was able to get her hair to lay flat. She still had that pinched look, though it was less noticeable after eating so well at camp for a few days. The food was the one thing she'd miss. Well, and Kamri and Ian. And Fletcher.

She shook off the rising tide of grief. No time for that. She made it back to the car and found Tyson where she'd left him. He'd successfully gotten the phone up and running, and was scrolling through lists of registered witches who were in business.

"Can they get us across the border?" Harper asked.

Tyson nearly jumped out of his skin. "Geesh, make some noise, will you? And no, they can't. Not legally. And portals have a significant, and personal, signature. No registered witch would risk her license. We can have her put us down in a wooded area near the border, and we'll come up with a plan from there."

"That only saves us about a day of driving," Harper argued. She threw her hands up. "This isn't worth the time."

Tyson barely glanced at her, nose in the phone. She nudged his shoulder. "Go get dressed and let me have a look at that thing." Tyson raised his eyebrows, and Harper sighed. "I promise I won't sacrifice your firstborn child to get us into Alaska."

He handed the phone over and jogged across the parking lot.

Harper navigated to ParaWeb. It took some finagling, since the last port she had used had vanished. She dug through the forums until she spotted a username she recognized: Night-walker327.

Nightwalker327 was a vamp. At least, she claimed to be a vamp, and claimed to be a she, but all of that could be fake when you dealt with anyone in ParaWeb. It was the paranormal equivalent of the Dark Web, only, well, darker. And better hidden. If humans heard about it, they were taken out. The rumors were that the creator of the ParaWeb had a team of technology-trained psychics who monitored the logins. If they thought you were a threat to the system, you got shut down.

Harper had heard about the ParaWeb after she left foster care and ended up on the streets. The people she met through ParaWeb, like Nightwalker327, had given her leads on her parents.

Harper clicked on the name and sent a DM. The response came within moments, as she figured it would. Nightwalker327 was plugged in all day long.

I don't deal with anonymous. The message read.

This is Harven078, Harper replied. She didn't have an official account on this forum, and wasn't keen on setting one up.

Did you find him?

Him. Not them. Harper nearly typed back, *Did I find who?*, but she didn't want to sound imbecilic. And Nightwalker327 would figure Harper might not be who she said she was if she asked a question like that. For now, she tucked the information away in her mind. Him had to be this person the Beryllium orb had stolen from her, but she couldn't dwell on it now.

It's complicated. I need your help with something else.

Always willing to help. I know you'll return the favor someday.

The implication of payment pending sent a chill down Harper's spine. She shivered and glanced up at the building. Tyson wasn't in view yet. Her thumbs flashed across the keys.

I need a portal to Alaska. Transporting two people. An unregistered witch or anything you have. I'm in Kennewick, Washington, but headed north.

A longer pause before the response came. *How prepared are you?*

I can handle anything. False bravado, and Harper knew it. There were plenty of things she couldn't handle. But Tyson had his magic knife and she had her song, if she could manage to sing it again. Surely they could make it through whatever obstacles Nightwalker327 mentioned.

There's a tunnel on the other side of the city. Fenced off, overgrown, abandoned-looking. Don't let it fool you. There's a portal inside, highly unstable. It will take you anywhere you think about when you step inside. Enter one at a time, and whatever you do, don't think about how hungry you are.

Harper laughed out loud, then covered her mouth and looked to see if anyone had heard. The next message came immediately and had a set of coordinates, which Harper memorized quickly. And then another message.

It's guarded.

Harper didn't have time to ask by what. She saw Tyson crossing the parking lot toward her. Tyson might be exhibiting powers, but he still couldn't be trusted with something of this magnitude. Sure, he seemed to be slowly changing his opinions about Naturalization, but it had only been a few days. She didn't need him to have a moral crisis about what went on in the ParaWeb.

Thanks, Harper typed before clearing the history and shutting the whole thing down.

"I found us a portal. No illegal payment required."

"How?" He was smart to be suspicious.

Harper smiled. "An old friend." At least, Nightwalker327 was unlikely to do anything that would get Harper straight up killed. She had a reputation as a guide, and she took it seriously. Harper headed for the passenger seat of the Jeep. "I've got the address. Come on. We can be in Alaska by sundown."

Tyson didn't object, to her surprise, but buckled in next to her and started the engine. Harper pulled up a map on her phone and scrolled with her fingers, looking for the coordinates that Nightwalker327 had sent over. They led to the middle of a field beside a running trail.

Tyson grumbled as he unpacked everything and shoved the items into the two backpacks. He had to carry his winter coat, but otherwise everything managed to fit.

"What about the Jeep?" he asked, staring at the keys in his hand.

"Can't you tell her where it is? Through, I don't know, astral projection or something?"

"Uh, no. Or at least, I'm not sure if I can do that."

Harper shrugged—she wouldn't lose any sleep over it—and watched Tyson from the trailhead.

After some thought, he pocketed the keys. "In case this portal doesn't work out, you know. And I realized I can look up her shop on my phone and call her at some point."

"Okay, then. So, five minutes in, we should see a rectangular, fenced enclosure," she said, tucking the phone in her back pocket. She handed Tyson a granola bar.

"I'm not that hungry," he said.

"Eat it anyway," Harper replied, taking a bite of her own. It seemed like a normal day. Birds chirped. A river rushed nearby. The breeze rustled branches and the long grass on either side of the trail. They could have been a couple out for a short hike on the paved trail.

Harper turned a bend and suddenly, there it was. No attempt had been made to hide it from view. Anyone could see the fence surrounding a concrete ramp leading to a tunnel underground. A gate guarded the front with a decently sized chain and lock on it. Inside, the tunnel walls were covered with colorful graffiti—bright yellows and reds and blues and purples, words Harper couldn't quite make out no matter how much she squinted, which made her suspect they were well-disguised runes. Inside the fence, the entrance of the tunnel was grown over with tall weeds.

Whatever this place had once been, it now had the eerie feeling of having been abandoned, which made Harper's skin itch.

"What now?" Tyson had the sense to whisper his question, at least.

"I'm not sure," Harper murmured. She reached forward to touch the lock. Her finger went straight through it, and she smiled. So there was magic at play here, after all. She pulled open the gate, Tyson's protest cut off by the quiet squeak of the gate's hinges. Nothing stood between them and the tunnel now except those weeds.

Harper stepped inside. "Close the gate."

Tyson obliged, the hinges squeaking again. As soon as it closed, the sounds of the hiking trail were cut off. The silence was stifling. The air felt thick and warm.

Harper reached back and touched Tyson's chest, stopping him in place. She breathed slowly, eyeing the dark entrance to the tunnel. "The portal is through there. It will take us anywhere we think of when we enter it."

"We can't just think 'Alaska.' We could end up on different sides."

Harper took the phone out again. She opened to a browser page, a photo of two mountain ranges in Alaska that stood side-by-side with a valley in between.

Tyson read the caption below the photo out loud. "Gates of the Arctic. Huh. Arctic gates. Go figure. Think that's what Charlie meant?"

Harper nodded. For some reason, speaking felt... dangerous here. Like the tunnel sucked the intentions out of the words, making them hollow and meaningless. She didn't want to speak unless she had to.

"Okay. We can picture that. Anything else?"

Harper held a finger to her lips and put the phone away. She pointed at the tunnel. "I was told it's guarded," she said in a low voice.

"Whispering won't keep us from hearing you," a male voice echoed out of the tunnel, and a group of five emerged from the entrance, stepping through the weeds. The plants were a holographic image, like the one Harper had seen James Petrov make in his class.

They were faced with four males and a female. One male stood at the head, his long hair pulled back into a manbun revealing the shaved sides of his head, which were tatted. His thick arms crossed over his leather-clad chest, and he smirked at the rest of his crew, jutting his chin toward Harper and Tyson.

"Look what wandered in. Do you think they have passports?"

The others laughed. Harper scanned them, taking in the piercings, dyed and half-shaved heads, tattoos that wiggled across their bodies... She blinked. She could have sworn she saw that one on the bald guy's bicep move. He grinned at her and flexed.

"Passports?" Tyson's voice in her ear made her jump.

"Hey, I said no whispering!" the guy in leather shouted.

Tyson jumped back.

The leather-clad guy chuckled. "You clearly aren't prepared to be here. Walk back through the gate without asking any questions, and you'll forget you ever saw this place. Literally."

Using the portal wasn't optional. They had to get to Alaska, and fast. Her hands clenched into fists. The buds of her wings slipped through the skin on her back, tingling where they poked through. She saw Tyson's warning glance from the corner of her eye but ignored it.

Tyson raised his hands, stepping forward. The gang stiffened, and the girl's hand glowed green. She had magic. Harper suspected they all did. Her eyes darted around. They were in a cage, essentially, with the fence on all sides, including above them. She couldn't fly them out if things turned bad. It would have to be a fight.

"Beck has a way of taking care of trespassers like you." The guy in leather motioned and the girl with the glowing hand stepped forward, a broad grin on her face. She swirled her hand around, sending a spiraling mini tornado into the air. It leapt off her hand and enlarged.

Harper leaned back in spite of herself. Tyson put a hand out in front of her, as if that would do anything to protect her. Or was he trying to stop her from attacking them?

"Stop," a cold, commanding voice came echoing out of the tunnel. When the woman emerged, her face gleamed with so much metal she could hardly be recognized as human. Her hair hung past her shoulders in knotted electric-blue dreadlocks.

The man scowled. "I told you we could handle this. You don't need to reveal yourself over these cyphers."

The blue-haired woman held up a phone, the screen flickering with the purple and black static background of the ParaWeb. "Their faces are all over the place, Yonks. They're being called heroes." She walked forward until her nose nearly met Tyson's. She stood the same height as him, slightly taller with her thick boots. "Standing up to the man. Taking out the traitors. Nice going. Besides," she turned her head back to the gang, who stood shifting their stances, "I know this one."

Her finger jabbed Tyson in the chest and her dark lips widened in a malicious grin. "Remember me from summer camp, Miller?"

CHAPTER NINE

QUINN

QUINN PROMISED HIMSELF HE wouldn't be the jealous boyfriend as he watched Becca laughing for the third time at something Avaan had said. The man had an insufferable charm, and he gazed at Becca with glittering eyes that reminded Quinn of a serpent.

He stopped his train of thought. He couldn't keep associating serpents with negative things. Becca was a snake now, in a way, and he could always trust her, couldn't he?

Quinn stared out the window, one hand rubbing the 'V' engraved on the metal disc he had found at his childhood home. Should he show it to Silla and Tarkik? Would they know what the symbol meant and why it haunted him? He watched as they rose above the cloudline. He could almost feel the bite of the air at this altitude, the way his lungs surged with vigor as he breathed it in. He could feel the rustling of his feathers in the breeze...

"You wish to be out there. I know that look, that longing. Come." Tarkik kept the pitch of his voice low. Becca glanced at the man, but didn't say anything, returning her focus to Avaan.

"Are you kidding?" Quinn protested. "We can't just jump out. We'll depressurize the cabin."

"There's a chamber we can use in the back."

"What about..." Quinn's eyes darted to Becca, who cocked her head at him.

Tarkik followed his gaze. "You are a fool."

"I will watch." Silla spoke from across the plane, sitting stiffly in the upright seat, arms crossed over his chest.

Quinn touched Becca's hand. "I'm going out. I'll be back soon."

Becca hesitated a moment before her entire face lit up with understanding. She nodded enthusiastically. "Have fun."

Quinn followed Tarkik to the back of the plane. The chamber Tarkik referred to was basically a closet, airlocked away from the rest of the plane. Quinn never would have expected to find such a thing on a plane so small. Quinn quickly peeled off his shirt. Tarkik handed him a helmet, then put one on himself.

"It contains a headset. So we can talk."

Quinn fiddled until he figured out how the headgear went on. It felt nice and tight on his head, and a chin strap underneath insured it wouldn't fly off when he spiraled.

Tarkik punched a keypad, and a hatch opened beneath them.

Quinn plummeted toward the ground at a terrifying rate. If he opened his wings now, he'd snap them off. Through stinging, wind-burned eyes he saw Tarkik release his wings gradually, a display of control unlike any Quinn had seen. He tried to mimic the motion. His wings snapped back with the force of the air and jerked his shoulder blades, making him cry out, but he stretched them out fully and swooped through the air, the ache fading and forgotten in the exhilaration of flight.

Glorious. Every time he flew, Quinn knew he'd made the right choice to leave Camp Silver Lake. He could only hope Harper had managed the same.

Tarkik wheeled through the sky and slowed his flapping to fly next to Quinn. The headset crackled, his voice coming through. "You look much like your father when he was younger."

Quinn cocked his head sideways. "You knew him? Were you friends?"

Tarkik barked a laugh. His ponytail kept his hair out of his face, which Quinn envied. "No, Miksa and I did not get along. He took risks, leaving the village, befriending other people beyond the safety of our borders. We fought about it often."

Quinn could believe that. "There is such a thing as being too safe. You lock yourselves up and get stifled, and may lose opportunities for improving the quality of life." The small plane sped ahead, easily twice as fast as Quinn could fly at a manageable pace. His brow furrowed and he flapped his wings harder, pushing against the wind.

"Do we need to worry about getting left behind?" A chill filled him. Could this have been their plan all along? Would Silla execute Becca on the plane, or arrange an accident for her and the extra passenger? Could his people be capable of that kind of violence?

"They will circle around if we get too far out. I've told the pilot we stepped out." Tarkik's laugh buzzed through the speaker in Quinn's ear. "You are wise, but foolish still. This serpent daughter will be our ruin. She will not be able to contain her other form in our midst."

Quinn squinted upward into the sun, where the plane flew ahead of them higher in the sky. "There are other innocents to consider. I won't abandon Becca to figure out her new abilities on her own. That's how shifters get killed."

"She will be killed if she threatens any one of us," Tarkik warned.

"Is this why my father left? Because of your oppressive need to protect your people at the cost of others?"

"Isn't that what you are doing with the serpent-woman? We all protect those in our best interest. How is this one woman worth more to you than your entire tribe?"

"Becca isn't a danger to anyone." Quinn swallowed. As a new shifter, Becca seemed unaware of her abilities, like a werewolf. That made her dangerous until she learned to gain control. "She will figure it out."

"I will not offer our people as a sacrifice to her learning."

Quinn flared his wings, stopping mid-air. He flapped to hold himself aloft, crossing his arms over his chest. "Silla said your chief would decide. Is that good enough for you?"

The other man studied Quinn for a long moment, then turned and flew away, dipping and climbing. Soft static filled the speaker in Quinn's ear, tempting him to take it off, but he didn't want to lose it. He noticed the small plane banking as it turned back toward him; Tarkik must have called the pilot.

Quinn stayed back, enjoying the flight much less now. Below them, the sparse cities and towns thinned out to patches of forest and finally the famous wilderness of Alaska. Quinn breathed in the freshest, coldest air he had ever encountered, his lungs expanding. A satisfying burn moved through his muscles as they worked to hold him. He lived for moments like this.

A metallic thud jerked Quinn from his reverie. The plane shivered in the distance, and he flapped his wings, gaining altitude and speed until he caught the plane. The hatch he had dropped through with Tarkik hung open, and the native man flew right behind him, flapping hard.

Quinn grabbed the edges of the platform and drew his wings into his back as he heaved himself up. The barest lip existed for him to climb onto, and only his supernatural strength made it possible for him to reach the metal bar on the wall above his head and pull himself straight into the plane. He reached a hand down to Tarkik, who grunted as he took the offer of help.

Quinn threw off the helmet and tossed it to the side as Tarkik prodded the keypad on the wall. The plane tilted violently. Quinn's shoulder struck the opposite wall of the closet-like chamber, then tumbled through the open door. He righted himself, eyes scanning for the cause of the disturbance.

A serpent tail nearly filled the length of the plane, glittering and green and thrashing as the top of the serpent—the torso and face that belonged to Becca—hissed and scratched and spat a sizzling liquid at the door to the cockpit.

"Becca!" Quinn called out, stepping over the end of the wildly twitching tail to reach her. Avaan cowered beneath a table, peering out at Quinn and clutching the small wooden flute that dangled from beneath his shirt.

Silla lay unconscious on the floor, two fledged darts rolling on the floor of the plane out of his reach.

"Move!" Tarkik bellowed.

Quinn surged ahead, wracking his brain for something, anything he could do to remind Becca of her humanity before Tarkik darted her again. Quinn dodged her massive tail and grabbed her around the middle, pulling her away from the door.

Becca shrieked and hissed, her fingernails scratching Quinn's arms as he pulled on her.

"Becca, it's me! It's Quinn!" He gasped desperately as she pried his arms off her with an immense show of strength. Her slitted yellow eyes showed no recognition, and green scales spread across her fair skin, covering both arms and part of her neck.

A sharp, talon-like fingernail sliced into Quinn's forearm and he cried out in pain, reflexively releasing Becca, who coiled her tail beneath her and reared, hissing. The metal door behind her had pockmarks in it, as if her venom were acidic enough to eat through metal. He swallowed and stepped backward, holding Becca's gaze. Nothing human remained there. No recognition.

Becca had truly turned into a monster.

"Down!" Tarkik barked. Quinn dropped without a second thought and Becca struck the air where he had been standing. She hit the floor behind him instead, hissing and writhing until the struggle left her and she lay still.

Panting, Quinn pushed the heavy serpent tail off of his legs and crawled toward Becca's head. The end of a feathered dart stuck out of her chest, barely visible beneath her. Quinn touched her hair softly, and gradually, the tail disappeared.

Quinn grabbed one of the thin blankets off a nearby unoccupied chair and threw it across Becca's body. Tarkik approached to retrieve the dart, yanking it unceremoniously from Becca's shoulder and tucking it inside a wooden tube in his pocket.

The plane had stopped its violent rocking, and a crackle came over the intercom.

"Everyone all right? What was that thing?"

Tarkik crossed to an intercom speaker and pressed a button underneath. "The serpent is taken care of."

"Thank God. We're nearing Bettles. Do you want me to drop you off there or take you in?"

"Take us in. No need to introduce this monstrosity to the trading post. We'll deal with it." Tarkik released the button and turned on Quinn, fists clenched and white. "Still believe she isn't dangerous?"

Quinn rested a hand on Becca's head. "She doesn't know what she's doing."

"That doesn't lessen the threat. In fact, it worsens the threat. You've put innocent lives at risk."

"What choice did I have?" Quinn argued. "If I left her back there, she would have threatened just as many lives, if not more. At least here I can keep an eye on her."

Tarkik pointed. "Once we reach the village, she will be contained. Fortunately, the human government has no say in our justice proceedings, and once the chief agrees to the execution, I will see it carried out."

Somewhere behind Quinn, Avaan let out a small gasp. Quinn tightened his grip on Becca and glared at Tarkik, his heart thudding in his chest. Tarkik passed him without another word and knelt beside Silla, who rolled over and attempted to sit up.

Quinn wondered if he'd made a horrible mistake. He could have told them no, could have avoided bringing Becca into this mess if he hadn't been so bent on finding out what happened to his parents. He contemplated, for a brief, insane moment, jumping out of the airlock with Becca, but he wasn't confident he could fly with her long enough to get them safely to anywhere civilized. And how would they avoid getting caught then, if they survived?

He would appeal to the chief. As a child of one of the village members, former or otherwise, surely the chief would listen to him. Maybe Quinn could convince them to preserve Becca's life.

The plane dipped, starting its descent. Quinn stood and carried Becca to an empty seat away from everyone else, holding the blanket to keep it wrapped around her body, and buckled her in. Her head lolled, but she seemed otherwise secure. Quinn retrieved her jeans and sat across from her. No one said a word.

The plane bumped and alarming grating sounds filled the air.

Quinn caught sight of a parachute opening from the back, dragging them to a halt. Avaan rushed by Quinn, darting glances at Becca with wide eyes. At least the stranger couldn't report them or call the Supernatural Task Force from the middle of true Alaskan wilderness. If he had a phone, it wouldn't get a signal out here. That thought made Quinn's mouth quirk up in the slightest smile, but it straightened out when it occurred to him that the Stiffs weren't needed out there, not with the justice system Tarkik implied.

Silla and Tarkik cast their shadows across Quinn and Becca, gazing at them with drawn expressions.

"Dress her and meet us outside," Silla finally said.

They turned together and exited the plane.

A few minutes later, Quinn stepped off the ramp carrying Becca in his arms. Silla came forward with rope to bind her wrists and a piece of cloth to blindfold her. Quinn fought every instinct to run as he watched them truss Becca. A sick weight settled in the bottom of his stomach, banishing the edge of hunger in his stomach.

"It's cold. She needs a coat," Quinn said as Silla walked away. The man didn't respond, and Quinn regretted leaving the blanket on the plane.

Avaan stood a ways off, hesitating for some reason. Quinn couldn't be certain the man had heard the conversation, but Avaan walked forward, shrugging off his coat and putting it over Becca. The two men exchanged looks, not friendly, but Quinn was grateful for the gesture for Becca's sake. As Avaan turned away, Tarkik held up a dart, examining it in the harsh daylight.

Quinn's breathing hitched.

"You are on our land, now." Tarkik twirled his dart. "A man with a camera is considered a pest in these parts. A pest that must be eradicated, lest it unbalance our ecosystem. I'm sure you understand."

Avaan smiled hesitantly, but the expression didn't reach his eyes. "I'll snap a few panoramic shots and be out of your hair in a few days. What else do you expect me to do?"

Tarkik grinned darkly and tucked the dart away, then stepped forward. Silla barked an order and thrust his hand into Tarkik's chest. Tarkik glowered.

"Bring him too," Silla said. "His word may turn the chief's mind in our favor. Then you may carry out the consequence for trespassing on our sacred land."

"Trespassing?" Avaan sputtered. "This is free land, public land! You can't do anything to me."

Silla leaned in. "Oh, believe me, we can do much. And no one will think twice about what happened to you when we tell the press that we found the unfortunate traveler at the bottom of the mountain. He must have slipped." Silla pressed Avaan's chest and the man stumbled back a few steps, sending a rock tumbling over the side of the mountaintop. It would be a long fall.

Quinn considered whether he should get involved. Could he set Becca down and catch the man before he fell to his death? Or should he respect the right of these men to defend their village? He adjusted his grip, muscles tensing.

Avaan swallowed. "Will you kill us?" He nodded his head toward Becca. "The snake woman and me?"

"We will protect our people at all costs. Fortunately for you, our chief will make the ultimate decision." Tarkik jerked at the straps on a pack he seemed to have conjured from nowhere.

Had it been on the plane? Quinn couldn't remember. He knelt on the ground and struggled with Becca's limp limbs to get the coat properly in place. Avaan watched, but did not offer to help this time. When he'd finished zipping Becca into the coat, Quinn hoisted her into his arms. The tension in the air had dissipated for now, but if Avaan did anything unpredictable, Quinn could see that changing.

"Where are we headed?"

Silla pointed. Quinn peered over the edge. He couldn't hike the entire way with Becca clutched in his arms. He'd fall, and most likely hurt her.

Silla and Tarkik released their wings in sync.

Avaan seemed amazed. He grinned at Quinn. "You can do the same, eh? I thought you and the other man had found another room to speak in privately, but I suppose the sky is your room when you can fly!" He laughed.

Quinn rolled his eyes. He'd left his shirt back on the plane, a fact he noted with some discomfort. He could retrieve it now, except the airplane's engine rumbled to life, and it rolled off the mountaintop, launching into the air. The pilot waved through the window of the cockpit as he circled the five individuals on the mountain, then flew off into the deep blue sky.

"We will coast down the mountainside, land, and hike to the village," Silla explained.

Quinn let his wings slowly unfurl from his back, practicing the control he'd learned from watching Tarkik fall from the plane.

Avaan chuckled nervously. "For those of us who don't have wings, what is the plan exactly?"

"I will carry you," Silla said.

Avaan looked to Tarkik, who shrugged. "You can trust he won't drop you, the honorable bastard."

Quinn held back from laughing at the expression on Avaan's face. He walked to the edge of the mountain, looked into the expansive valley, and took a deep, shuddering breath. From this height he felt as if he could draw a deeper breath than before, like his lungs were uninhibited. Harper would have loved this.

Quinn pushed away the thought of his sister, who he had left behind in the turmoil at Camp Silver Lake. After settling this matter, he and Becca could return together and find Harper and Tyson.

He squared his shoulders, backed up carefully on the uneven ground, then took a running start, flapping his wings and leaping into the air. His wings caught the updraft and he glided, flapping every so often to keep himself aloft. Tarkik took off, shadowing behind Quinn, and Silla followed, his takeoff marked by a frightened yelp from Avaan.

Cold air rushed past Quinn's face, making his eyes water. Rock and grass and a river passed below, his shadow marking the landscape. Despite what loomed in front of him, Quinn couldn't contain the pure joy he felt at flight, and a smile spread across his face. He belonged here, unhindered by law or fear.

The ground arrived faster than he expected, with the extra weight from Becca in his arms. He coasted farther than he usually would, trying to slow himself down before he broke his legs on the ground below. Flapping, he dropped the remaining distance to the ground, jarring his bones but otherwise safe. Becca flopped against him, still unconscious.

Quinn's muscles burned from carrying her. He adjusted his grip and kept his wings out, using them as balances to counteract the additional weight Becca put at his front. He couldn't ask Silla or Tarkik to carry her and Avaan's hands were tied.

Not that Quinn would trust that man with Becca's life; not in a million years. Avaan had landed with Silla some distance behind and kept glancing at Quinn and Becca, as if trying to get a better look at her. Quinn tightened his hands, pulling Becca into him and marching determinedly forward.

"How far to the village?" he asked as Silla walked up.

"We will rest on the other side of the second river." Silla pointed to a gleaming ribbon in the distance. "We will reach Hrafnar before the sun reaches its peak."

Quinn wondered if they should have kept flying. If Harper had been here instead of Becca, they would have. But the two human additions to their party made flight a much less desirable travel option.

"Have you contacted the bear tribe?" Silla asked Tarkik.

Tarkik grunted in response.

"Wait, bear tribe? How many species live here?"

Silla blinked. "Bears, wolves, cougars, foxes; other avian types, such as eagles and hawks. The predators of this land all have a human-shifter counterpart, although many are dwindling in number."

"How is this possible?" Avaan asked. Quinn glanced at him. Did the man live under a rock? Most, if not all, people knew about the existence of paranormals. Avaan caught his look. "That the land is untouched by your government, I mean."

"We have an agreement with the government. It is fragmenting, and no longer honored as it should be. This land was meant as a refuge for those willing to agree to avoid human contact at all costs, to remain in the purest parts of the wild. In recent years we've had poachers visit these lands. We treat them as the trespassers they are, though we have discovered some were sent by the government. They are not satisfied with the land they have and they want to steal ours. It's the same story, retold with new peoples."

"Will you leave, then?"

"No." Silla barked the word. "We will fight. We will grow our numbers. We will protect our lands."

Tarkik hiked ahead of them and Silla kept pace with Quinn. It was hard to tell whether Silla worried Quinn would run, wanted to protect him from Becca if she woke up, or offered companionship.

"That's why you want us. My sister and I," Quinn said. He looked sideways at Silla. "Do any others know about this refuge?"

"Some do. The ones that remember do."

Quinn shifted Becca's weight. He contemplated throwing her over his shoulder, then decided that would be undignified. "The ones that remember what?"

"That the tales are not just stories to be told in an igloo during a snowstorm, but many contain the truth of Raven and the creation of the world."

All Quinn could see besides an empty, grassy valley were the mountains rising on either side. Quinn stumbled on thick tufts of grass growing sporadically from the ground, and since he couldn't see his feet, he was grateful more than once that his wings helped him balance. His boots sank into the marshy surface.

At least they were more practical than tennis shoes would have been. Quinn was suddenly glad for Becca's unconsciousness. Her lightweight running shoes wouldn't have lasted ten minutes walking through the patches of bog he kept running into.

The rain began two hours into the hike. Tarkik and Silla didn't seem to mind, but Quinn hated being damp and worst of all, he had to draw in his feathers, which left him more prone to tripping. Becca's deadweight wore on his arms, shoulders, and back. Just because he could carry her didn't mean he found it easy.

"How long until this dart stuff wears off?" Quinn asked Silla.

Tarkik let out a harsh laugh from ahead. "You are wishing you let us kill her in the first place."

Quinn was too tired to rise to the jab and defend Becca. Having her safe in his arms gave him enough assurance for now. Quinn focused on Silla, who studied Becca's face.

"It will be soon."

Silence filled the empty space in the valley. The chill of the air crept into Quinn's bones and his arms trembled. Ahead, Tarkik paused and rummaged through his pack, then pulled out a folded skin of some kind, approaching Quinn with it.

"Put her down," he said.

Quinn eyed the ground, then found a suitable patch of grass and carefully laid Becca on it. She stirred, mumbling, then settled back into unconsciousness.

Tarkik thrust the skin at Quinn, who took it and unwrapped a vest like Tarkik and Silla wore. Reinforced slits opened the back where his wings would come out. He unfastened the bone toggles on the front, fingers brushing the unfamiliar velvety material.

Quinn pushed his arms through the vest and refastened the front. Instantly, his chest warmed. His arms didn't mind the cold as much with his torso covered.

Silla pulled some packages from his pack. "We typically hunt fresh food while at home, but tonight this will suffice," he explained, peeling back a thin layer of plastic film from the paper bowl and handing it to Quinn. Some sort of dehydrated chicken with rice. Tarkik had started a fire inside a ring of rocks, rain sizzling as it struck the flames. A small pot rested on some rocks in the fire, filled with melting snow. Summer in the Alaskan mountains was colder than Quinn expected it to be, and seeing snow still surprised him, not to mention evening had passed and the sun hadn't fallen completely. The brightness unsettled him.

The water boiled. Quinn took his turn pouring some over the food. He dug in with a set of bone cutlery provided from the packs. Becca moaned again, tossing her head, and Quinn crossed the rocks to sit next to her, blowing on a bite of the food so it didn't burn his tongue.

On a whim, he reached across Becca's face and moved a bit of hair behind her ears. His fingers lingered on her cool skin, letting the small spot on her cheek steal his warmth. She felt colder than he'd like. He set his food down and maneuvered himself behind her, bringing her against his chest, then resumed eating.

Silla passed the fire, holding another steaming bowl.

"Now we're feeding it?" Tarkik snarled, tossing his empty food package into the fire. The thick paper bowl caught fire readily, turning black and collapsing in on itself.

Quinn gestured to Avaan. "Did he get any?"

Silla looked at the bearded man, fire gleaming off his face as he sat stiff and upright, bound hands in his lap. "He refused it when I offered. He said he is fasting for deliverance from captivity."

Strange. Quinn took the second bowl from Silla. "Thank you."

Silla's dark eyes gleamed. "We will keep her alive, but only until her fate is decided."

Tarkik stomped off, headed for a line of trees in the near distance. Quinn watched him sit on a rock at the edge of the wooded area.

Silla sat closer to the fire, but angled toward Quinn. Quinn took it as an open invitation to speak.

"Have you seen her kind before?"

Avaan seemed to perk up, but he didn't move.

"Once," Silla replied. His hands rested on his knees. "They are rare here. It is difficult for a serpent to survive in such harsh conditions, and so we are protected. The were-serpent I encountered in my youth found the village, and the terror and death it caused among our people was devastating. Six young were killed, two elders wounded. We do not reproduce easily and this loss nearly ruined us."

All three men looked to Becca, who stirred again. Quinn's eyes landed on her arm, obscured by the sleeves of her coat. How far had the scales spread after her last transformation? And how long until they covered her completely? Would he lose her for good then?

Quinn scooted closer, wrapping an arm around her.

Becca blinked, stirring.

"It's freezing." She murmured, snuggling in closer to Quinn. The other two men looked away. What did Silla think of their closeness? Tarkik no doubt thought it an abomination.

"I'm glad you're awake," Quinn said. "Are you hungry?"

She nodded, teeth chattering. "I transformed again, didn't I?"

"You don't remember?"

She shook her head. "I remember some of it. It's like my memory glitches when I try to think about it. Is everyone all right?" The last part came out in a hush.

"A few bumps." Quinn avoided looking at his forearm, where the angry red streaks from her nails marked his skin. He shifted his arm out of sight. "Nothing to be concerned with."

Her face froze frighteningly still. She swallowed and glanced down. "I'm a monster, aren't I?"

Quinn pushed past the memory of the thrashing tail, the yellow serpent gaze, the fangs. "It's not Frankenstein bad." He hoped she would smile.

"Frankenstein was the doctor, you know." She choked on the words, and Quinn pulled her closer, drawing in a long breath with his nose against her hair, relishing the fact that she still smelled like Becca.

Quinn held out the bowl of food, which had cooled to luke-warm. Becca took it, spooning food into her mouth silently for a time.

"Were you scared the first time you..." She trailed off. "You had your parents then, to explain things to you."

Quinn crossed and uncrossed his arms. "Yeah, for a bit."

"Give me some time. I'm sure I can figure it out."

What if she didn't have time? Quinn stayed silent. He looked to Silla, who sat staring into the fire, and Avaan, who looked to be meditating with his eyes closed.

"I like the getup." Becca tugged on the edge of his vest, a smile playing at the edge of her lips. "You've gone native, as they say."

Quinn gave a half-hearted laugh. "Yeah, I have. It's warm. It has a place for my wings, look." He took his arm off her shoulder and leaned forward so she could see for herself. Her fingers traced the slits and he shivered at her touch.

"Nifty. You're not cold?"

"It's summer here."

Becca went silent, finishing her food. Quinn took her empty bowl and put it in the fire. He handed the utensil to Silla.

"Thank you."

Silla blinked, then nodded. When Quinn turned around, Becca had the sleeve of the coat pulled up, and she gazed at the place where her wound had been before. Emerald scales glittered to her elbow. When she noticed Quinn's stare, she tugged the coat down and clasped her hands. Her smile said nothing was wrong, but her eyes said more.

Quinn sat beside her and drew her close. With that scaled arm hidden, he could pretend nothing had changed. He leaned his head on hers.

"I thought you might hate me," Becca said quietly.

Quinn hesitated. "Can I be honest?"

"Yes." A new tone trembled in her voice.

"I'm not sure how I feel about it all yet. I don't know what you are, or if there's a way to control it. But I know I care about you." Quinn turned his head and breathed in her scent again. It wasn't flowery or even pleasant after several days of traveling and no showers, but it was her. That thought made his head rush.

Becca shifted in his arms and looked into his eyes. Quinn faced her. They were a breath away from kissing when Tarkik's footsteps sounded on the path. Quinn pulled back, swallowing. He locked his gaze with Becca's, hoping she saw the assurance there. His feelings for her hadn't changed. He just needed time to get used to how things were now.

And figure out a way to save her life.

Quinn watched the two men stomp out the fire. The sun had gone down, but twilight remained. Quinn felt his exhaustion. It must be late, even though the sun didn't agree.

"Things are different now, aren't they? Whether we want them to be or not." Becca watched Tarkik sit down beside Silla. "Your people will never approve of us."

"If it came to that, I'd choose you." The lie slid off his tongue, and Quinn swallowed, regretting the words as soon as he spoke them. *Just be honest next time, okay?* Becca's words from earlier came to mind, when they shared a sandwich in the van. He shook his head, clearing his throat. "Listen, I don't know what's going to happen—"

"You don't have to make any promises," Becca said, putting her hand on his arm, then let it slide away, her heat lingering on his skin.

It only made Quinn feel worse.

CHAPTER TEN

BECCA

ONE OTHER SET OF eyes remained open after the fire died down. They belonged to Avaan. Becca blinked away from the hypnotic stare, disturbed by Avaan's attention. Every time she looked at him he gazed back, and he never broke first. Her eyes watered.

From the smoke.

Becca had spent so much time resting from those darts, she couldn't possibly fall asleep now. Plus, her upper arm and shoulder itched, and she feared scratching it and feeling more dead skin peel off.

She adjusted her positioning on the ground, leaning back against Quinn who slept upright on a large boulder. Even Tarkik and Silla were asleep, apparently at ease enough not to have a guard. Their hearing was probably keen enough they would wake and halt any escape attempt, especially considering the open land and the still-bright sky. Strange, that. A blueish purple tinge blanketed a sky dotted with stars.

She turned her head and again met that silky, milk chocolate gaze. She licked her dry lips. She felt... odd. A magnetic pull lurched in her stomach. It crawled up her spine and into her head and made her yearn to be next to the man with olive skin cast in the purple hue of the eternal twilight.

Becca cleared her throat and drew her knees in, wrapping her arms around them. She worked against the too-large coat sleeves, trying to get them out of the way so she could clasp her hands.

"Are you warm enough?" His rich, lilting accent carried through the air and straight into her ears. His attention made her face heat, and she found herself ducking her head and fidgeting with the offending coat sleeves. She stared at them a moment.

"Oh, this is yours, isn't it?" Her hand flew to the zipper. "I'm sorry, you must be freezing. You can have it back."

His eyes glittered. "I'll not have you die of exposure on my watch. It is a gift."

Becca rubbed at the heat rising yet again in her cheeks, then blew on her hands to cover her embarrassment. "It's very generous of you. But I think there's not much that can be done about my eventual fate. I'm a serpent that's landed in a nest of eagles. Or near enough." She rocked a bit, her back striking the boulder behind her.

Quinn stirred, grunting, his long hair blowing in a breeze across his face. An owl hooted in the distance.

"You may be surprised at what comes to your aid in the last moment. Nothing is done until it is done." Avaan turned his shoulders to face her more squarely.

"I thought you might have split off to take your pictures."

Avaan sighed, clapping his hands in his lap. "They've destroyed my camera. I am captive, as you are, and await judgement from their chief. They expect me to contribute to their cause against you, but I won't." His tone grew fierce and protective. It startled Becca.

She picked up a stick, nudging it into the coals of the fire. A small flame flared up, then died again without something to feed it. "But you don't know me. And if it meant your freedom, maybe you should testify against me."

"It is not my way."

A wind picked up, rushing over the pulsing embers of the fire between them, fanning it back to life briefly with a flurry of sparks. Becca watched it, knowing Avaan's gaze remained locked on her. She knew if she looked now, she would never want to look away, and it frightened her. Did she feel that way about Quinn? What she had with Quinn sometimes felt so subtle, like it didn't exist. Especially now, with members of his tribe here—sworn enemies against the serpent woman she'd become.

Why did she ever touch that stupid mummy?

"Your thoughts are in turmoil."

"And yours aren't?" Becca scoffed. "What's keeping you up, then?" Her voice sounded more aloof than she intended, but it was better. Better not to look into those mesmerizing eyes, better not to give any indication she felt a connection between them.

"I came from my home country straight here. There, it is midday. My body hasn't adjusted yet."

"Fair enough." It was such a mundane conversation, so unlike anything she'd had in weeks, being in hiding and on the run with Quinn, and the events of the past few days. A nice change. "Where are you from?"

"Lebanon. My family has never left. As far as I know, I am the first." He tilted his head and pursed his lips. Becca's heart skipped a beat. Her brain nearly shut down. "Except for an eccentric uncle on my mother's side. But we haven't heard from him since."

Becca's mouth struggled to form words. "It... must be hard... being away from your homeland."

"I had high hopes for this trip. I was promised it would be... rewarding."

Becca laughed. "Some reward. A death sentence."

Avaan held up a finger. "Nothing is done until it is done." His smile widened. "I still hope. For both of us."

Quinn stirred beside Becca, and she glanced at him. Her heart leapt into her throat at the sight of him, his normally serious brow relaxed in sleep. She snuggled into his shoulder, shutting her eyes tight against the temptation to meet Avaan's gaze again. Gradually, the tugging sensation in her body faded, and her breathing slowed.

Quinn shifted again, sitting up further. He faced her and kissed the top of her head softly. Becca sighed. Safe, contented. She didn't have any need for exotic strangers. Quinn would stand by her no matter what. He'd already proven that.

The night passed far too swiftly. Or maybe it was an effect of the never-ending Alaskan summer day. Becca's eyes cracked open as soon as the sun breached the horizon. She rubbed at her crusty eyes and stretched, then realized she needed to pee. Badly.

She wrapped her arms around herself and stumbled across the rocks until she navigated to a spot behind a crag obscuring her from the others' line of sight. Unzipping her jeans with numb fingers, she cursed men and the ease with which they peed in the wilderness. She hadn't thought about asking for toilet paper, but something told her that these Alaskan natives didn't have any.

She shuddered as she zipped back up, praying she didn't have to go number two any time soon.

Emerging from behind the rocks, she found Tarkik staring at her from his seat near the fire pit.

"Morning," Becca said, trying to sound cheerful.

The man grunted and stood, walking away. The other man, Silla, squatted at the fire, stoking it with a long stick.

"My brother is hard-hearted. You will find Chief Aguta a much fairer judge."

Becca fixed her eyes on Silla. "Any tips for winning the ol' chief over?"

Silla blinked. "Do not call him old, perhaps. And do not reveal your relationship with his son."

Becca's mouth dropped open. She shut it quickly, rubbing her hands on her jeans and sitting on a rock across the fire from Silla. She clasped her hands together near her face, leaning on her arms. Her tongue ran along her teeth while she thought.

"Is this some sort of Romeo and Juliet situation?"

"I'm not familiar with those people. Is the story tragic?" Silla asked. Becca eyed him, wondering if he joked, but the serious-faced native man didn't seem to be pulling her leg. His eyes were wide and sincere. He stood and adjusted the steaming pot on the rocks near the fire.

"Their families are feuding. Romeo and Juliet meet at a young age and fall in love, but are unable to be together. They die rather than live their lives apart."

"That's incredibly foolish. And short sighted. They could have found someone else their families approved of."

"That's not the point! People should be allowed to love who they love."

"The natural laws do not agree with you. In this case, it is better to let go of Quinn than to let the whims of your heart taint his reputation among his own people. To give him his best chance of finding a mate here, you must withhold your own feelings." Silla stirred the pot and frowned, then pulled a tiny pouch from his belt and sprinkled brown powder into the pot. A faint whiff of cinnamon wafted toward Becca. Her stomach growled.

Becca folded her arms. "Have you told him this?"

Silla shook his head, then dragged the pot from the fire. How he touched the handle without getting burned, Becca couldn't understand. He grunted. "I have been seeking an opportunity. When you awakened first, I took it as a sign that you would receive the information with more wisdom. He will react better hearing it from you."

"You think that me telling him we can't be together because his family would reject him would be better than you telling him?" Becca scoffed, glancing to where Quinn slept, slumped nearly sideways against the boulder. "It will break his heart." She'd felt this sensation before—a thick weight in her chest, a dull pain near her sternum that spread across her ribs. It throbbed every time she looked at him, taking in his long, beautiful hair falling across his face and those stark, handsome features. Becca swallowed hard, bringing her gaze back to the fire.

Silla spoke softly. "This isn't a tale where love triumphs over all. All those who leave our village—and those who take a mate outside of our people—they are refused entrance ever again. Quinn's parents left our people and would not be allowed to return, but Quinn and his sister are not held responsible for the faults of their parents. We welcome them with open arms."

"Now who's shortsighted?" Becca snorted.

"We do it for the preservation of our people," Silla said in a stern voice. He spooned the steaming food into several paper bowls. "Our numbers dwindle. Soon we will be gone from the earth if measures are not taken to increase the flock."

"Will you marry him off before or after you execute me?" Becca's hands curled into fists. Her eyes burned from the smoke of the fire, making them water.

"You are angry. It is expected." Silla set his hands on his knees. "I would not see you executed, but turned back into the wilderness to find your way. Same with the photographer. Others do not have the same opinion. Our chief will take them all into account. Quinn could defend you without dishonoring himself. Act as though you are no more than friends, and it will go in your favor, I am sure." He handed her a steaming bowl and a bone spoon. Becca grudgingly took both. Her stomach clenched with too much hunger for her to make a rebellious display over breakfast.

It looked, smelled, and tasted like normal oatmeal, except without anything to sweeten it. Though the cinnamon helped, and to her surprise, the dark lumps were cooked blueberries. She hadn't expected to find anything like that out here.

"What time is it?" she asked suddenly, swallowing her last mouthful.

Silla glanced at the sun. "Perhaps 5 a.m."

"It truly doesn't get dark here in the summer, does it?"

"No. We've entered the time of eternal day. It takes time to get used to. Even living here my whole life, I struggle to sleep past dawn when I'm not in my home."

Becca stopped shivering as her body warmed from the oatmeal. Behind her, she heard Quinn get up and, from the sound of his footsteps, he made the same trip to the crag that she had earlier. Avaan also stirred beneath the crinkly metallic blanket. He lay beyond Silla some distance, but Becca could still see his yawn, and when he sat up to stretch her gaze was riveted to the lengthening muscles in his arms and chest.

That hook sensation caught her off guard, wedging itself into a space between her stomach and chest. She rubbed at the spot, swallowing another bite without chewing well. The lump slid down her throat. She gulped hard and it hurt, but she forced the food down, then stared into the half-empty bowl.

Quinn came and crouched next to her, his arm wrapping around her and rubbing her shoulder.

Becca shrugged, but his arm stayed put until she reached up and pulled it off. It dropped, and with it went the warmth and comfort she usually enjoyed from Quinn.

She closed her eyes, not wanting to see his face, knowing he would be confused. They would have to find a moment to talk privately later, though it seemed unlikely given their company.

Quinn thanked Silla and accepted a bowl of oatmeal from him. He kept glancing at Becca, blowing on his first spoonful of the steaming breakfast.

"Good morning," he said at last, putting the bite in his mouth.

"Morning," Becca responded past the lump in her throat. She looked at Silla, who nodded once, solemnly. He approved of her distant behavior, apparently. Becca breathed in deeply to hold the tears at bay and shoved another bite of oatmeal into her mouth. Quinn didn't deserve coldness, but she didn't know how to be his friend without being more, not when the feelings were still there, swirling beneath the agitated surface of her heart.

"*Sebaho*, Rebecca," Avaan said, face split into a charming smile full of glinting white teeth. Becca forced a smile on her face, but couldn't bring herself to correct him on her name. No one had called her Rebecca in, well, ever.

Quinn shifted his weight and leaned toward her, his arm touching hers. Becca tossed her unfinished bowl into the fire, stood, and thrust the spoon at Silla.

"I'm going for a walk."

Silla blinked slowly. "Stay in sight."

"I won't go far." She stalked off, jamming her hands into the coat pockets. She felt hot after sitting next to the fire, but the further she got from the men and the flames, the more she was glad she had an extra layer.

She should have expected Quinn to follow her, but when he did, she hunched over. "Leave me alone." The words tumbled out of her lips of their own accord. She didn't mean them, and she didn't want him to leave her.

"Becca," Quinn murmured, his hand touching her back and sliding across to her shoulder, where he tugged until she turned to face him.

The cold air touched the tear streaks on her cheeks.

"What's wrong?" His expression deepened with concern, his other hand coming up to hold her other shoulder. He drew her into him and Becca allowed it, resting her head on his chest, tears dribbling across her nose and into the vest on his chest. They didn't sink in, instead trembling as a tiny bead of water on the skin's surface before rolling off to the ground.

"Silla said…" She hiccupped. "He said if we're together in front of the chief, you will be exiled, basically. Like your parents."

He exhaled into her hair. "My parents were exiled?"

Becca nodded against his chest. "He said they left the village, which isn't allowed. Neither is being mated to someone outside the village."

"Now I face the same decisions they did." His hands flexed on her shoulders, massaging them. "I would choose you, you know that."

"No, I don't." Becca pushed away from him, still staying within his arms but putting distance between them so she could look into his face. "And you don't know that either. You keep saying it, but you can't know it before you've even met them. You've searched for your family your whole life. Would you leave them so easily for what I've become?"

Her eyes searched his and when he didn't answer immediately, she continued. "At least until after you meet the chief, and he delivers his verdict for me, I think we should take a break from...us." She gestured between her chest and his, breathing into the tightness clenching through her body.

Quinn squeezed her shoulders. "I don't want to do this."

"Neither do I. But it's our best chance."

"I want to help you." His voice shook.

Becca's smile faltered, but she held it all the same. "You still can. As my friend."

He shook his head. "When all this is over..."

Becca stepped back further, forcing his hands to drop. "We can see where things stand then." And then, because that felt too much like a knife falling between them, she smiled again, more genuinely this time. "I'm glad you're here."

She watched his throat move as he swallowed. He stared at her, his brown eyes drinking her in, as if memorizing how she looked in that moment. Her chest swelled with the pain of it, but she held her expression frozen until he breathed out.

"I wish you weren't."

His words stopped her heart. She cocked her head.

Quinn licked his lips and shifted his stance. "I mean, I wish you weren't in danger. And that things could be whatever we wanted them to be."

"But you agree this is necessary." Her legs, her hands, even her face trembled.

"Yes. Until I understand what this is all about. But if they even hint like they're going to kill you, I'm flying us both out of there. I don't want any part of a tribe that kills people out of prejudice."

Becca moved forward numbly and folded herself into his arms, which wrapped around her without hesitation. She inhaled the scent of him, slightly different with the skin vest on. Her heart pounded and her head felt dizzy with the desire to kiss him.

A desire she ignored, for now.

The group crossed the river and entered the woods. Silla distributed dried meat and fruit among them. Through the trees, Becca caught glimpses of darting brown critters, and birds sang readily. They walked in silence. She snuck a glance at Quinn. If she'd been in his position, she would be asking a dozen questions to find out what awaited her at the village, but Quinn wasn't a big asker. He observed. Becca had a feeling that if she asked the questions... well, they might do more than just bind her hands.

The thought made her stumble and an arm reached out from behind and caught her around her waist. As soon as she was steady, Quinn let go.

"Thank you," Becca said, swallowing past the lump in her throat. It felt wrong to not give him a peck on the lips or cheek, but it was for good reasons. At least she tried to convince herself of that. Quinn deserved a chance to decide if this village, and these people, were the place he belonged. She had been in his life a short time compared to how long he'd searched to find a place in the world where he could be himself and thrive.

Quinn glanced away, squinting in the afternoon sunlight.

Silla stepped up in front of Becca holding a dark blue cloth. Tarkik did the same with Avaan. "We are required to blindfold you at this point."

Becca held out her hands willingly. Would willing compliance be a consideration in her trial? The cloth slipped around her head, obscuring her view of Quinn. She was stuck with the image of his pitying expression and the feeling of Silla's rough hands tugging her along.

He was a good guide, quietly warning of rocks to step over and the like, but she still stumbled in the darkness of the blindfold. She found a rhythm to being led, and appreciated more than ever that it was Silla guiding her and not Tarkik, who no doubt would have walked her into a sprained ankle or worse if he could get away with it. She would have preferred Quinn to either of them, but he didn't offer to lead her, and she didn't ask. It would look better for him if she entered the village as a prisoner, even if that thought did make her heart pound, and an itching sensation traveled up her scale-coated arm.

She focused on the senses she had left. Birdsong on the wind, trees rustling, and a deep throbbing sound.

"Is that drums?" Avaan's voice piped up, surprising Becca. It sounded different when she couldn't see his face, but her memory summoned an image easily enough.

"Tarkik went ahead last night and told them of our coming today. The drums are celebratory, to welcome back a son and brother," Silla explained.

Quinn.

The sounds of the village grow louder. Feet stomped and smaller feet ran. A fire crackled loudly, the wood popping as it was consumed. Becca could smell meat cooking, but not like the chicken or beef from home. It was somehow richer as it mixed with the smoke, most likely caribou, or whatever they ate out here.

There was laughter and conversation in the angular sounds of the Inuit tongue, none of which she understood. More female voices than male, she noted, though perhaps the men were quiet, or gathered elsewhere. She wished she could see the dwellings and what they were made of. Were they teepees, like many of the Native American tribes of the southwest United States? Or log-made or stone buildings? Her imagination went wild as she was guided deeper into the village. The laughter quieted as she passed, and conversation turned to whispers. Was it for her or Quinn? They did make up an odd-looking party, she supposed. Two prisoners of different nationalities and a newcomer of their own kind.

Becca's heart rate climbed again. What if the villagers rejected her and decided not to let her live? Would they burn her over their fire? Shoot her with an arrow? Fly her into the sky on those ebony wings and let her plummet to the valley floor? Her thermal sense sharpened, the colors shifting through the slight gap in the bottom of the blindfold near her nose.

The snake was awakening.

Becca's body tensed and the itching spread to her chest and abdomen. She inhaled deeply and slowly, focusing on staying human, maintaining control. Going rogue now would certainly get her killed. She had to stay calm. She recited the words to her favorite song in her head, and then every other song she could think of. It seemed to help.

She ran her tongue against her teeth, taking comfort in the normal rounded tip and her human-shaped teeth. The itching subsided.

They halted. Words were exchanged, and Becca recognized the sound of a door opening. Silla pulled on her bound hands and led her forward. The temperature dropped slightly, and even with the blindfold on Becca could tell it was darker. The outside sounds muffled. They had entered a dank room.

Silla's words broke the "You'll remain here, bound, until after the feast. Tomorrow, our chief will see you."

"Can the blindfold be removed?" Becca asked.

There was a long pause, and then she felt fingers at the back of her head. The cloth dropped away. To her surprise, Avaan was across the room. Becca arched her neck, rolling tension out of her neck as she glanced at the ceiling. It wasn't far above her head—perhaps a foot or two. And the arched support beams were made of thinner logs stripped of bark, with stretched skins sewn together expertly and overlapping each other to make a roof. The dirt floor comprised a circular area that several grown men could lie down comfortably in.

Silla led her to a thick support beam across from Avaan and took out another length of rope. He made her step through her arms, which put them behind her, and he deftly wrapped the second rope around the binding on her hands before fixing it to the joint made of logs. It was long enough she could sit, and also long enough she could reach a dark, circular pit to her left, presumably the 'bathroom,' but not long enough she could reach the doorway they had entered through. Or Avaan. He had his own pit, she noticed, and a curtain hung across that half of the room, blocking the pots from view of each other. She shuddered.

She was not looking forward to the inevitable moment when she would be forced to use the dirt toilet.

Silla gestured toward a wide bowl and a flat plate in the center of the room. There was liquid in the bowl. Becca could tell because the surface rippled. The plate held a dark, round bread or cake and a pile of steaming food.

"There is food for both of you, and you each have a pot to use as a facility," Silla said. "If you cannot reach it, call out and someone will assist you. I do not need to remind you, but I will—any attempt at escape is a death sentence. Our chief is a fair judge and I do not think you are in any real danger of losing your life tomorrow, so do not do anything foolish. Another meal will be brought in the morning."

"Will Quinn be allowed to see me?" Becca blushed as soon as she spoke the words.

Silla's eyes glittered, and he seemed disappointed. "Not without an escort. He is very important to the village, and we will not risk him."

Risk him escaping? Or being killed? Becca wanted to ask, but she bit her lip instead. Silla removed Avaan's blindfold and left the hut, disappearing down the short entrance tunnel. A stream of light entered as he lifted the front flap that served as a door, and Becca heard him speak briefly to someone standing outside. A guard?

She sighed and sat, careful not to lean against the wall. She couldn't be sure how sturdy it was. Would it hold her weight? She didn't test it. The food smelled good now that she had rested for a moment. She could still hear some conversation outside the hut, but it sounded farther away now. The hut was surprisingly well-insulated, and the coat made her sweat. She wished she had asked Silla to take it off.

"Please, eat your fill." Avaan's voice filled the hut.

Becca looked up, hair hanging in clumped strands around her face. Sweat and dirt no doubt coated her skin. Attractive. "You already skipped a meal."

"I am fasting."

"For deliverance. Right." Becca's voice sounded bitter, but she didn't try to soften it. Anyone who believed they would get out of here alive was delusional. Even if the chief let them go, someone like Tarkik would dispose of them soon enough. Or a bear. Whichever came first.

"It is difficult to have hope, but think of it as a unique experience to tell the grandchildren," Avaan said. "Whatever gets you through. Just do not despair."

"Have you been in prison before? Because you sound awfully familiar with things."

Avaan shifted his seat, stretching his legs out in front of him and leaning his head on the pole behind him. "I have been contained once or twice. My country is not as peaceful as yours. We've had many wars within our own lands, amongst our own people."

"How long will they keep us here, do you think?"

"A day, as they said." Avaan sounded so sure, Becca almost believed him.

"Do you wish you hadn't come?" She pushed herself to her knees and made her way across the dirt floor like that, hands still bound behind her. Her stomach clenched, and she didn't think the food would taste any better cold. She might as well eat now.

"Do you?" Avaan asked.

Becca shook her head. She eyed the plate below her, realizing there was nothing to hold back her hair. She grimaced. This would be messy. Self-conscious, she leaned forward, ripping off a piece of the bread with her teeth. It was soft enough to bite through, though chewy in texture, and she had to grind her teeth to get a piece in her mouth.

She chewed and swallowed, then moved to the meat. Tossing her head to one side and coming at the plate from an angle, she was able to lick and bite at the stew. The meat was stringy, the stew barely salted, but it filled her stomach. She wiped her mouth on her shoulder when she finished, pleased that she'd eaten as neatly as she had. A long drink from the bowl finished her meal, and she sat back on her heels a moment, glancing at Avaan.

He hadn't spoken a word while she ate. To his credit he hadn't stared or made things more awkward than they needed to be, but now his eyes rested on her—a steady, calm gaze that unsettled Becca more than her current surroundings. She thought about retreating to her wall, but why should she? She crossed her legs and sat near the food and water, staring back at him.

"I have a confession," Avaan announced. He scooted away from the wall, his hands bound similarly to Becca's, but he didn't come the full way, stopping about two feet short of reaching the center of the hut. "I am not here as a photographer. Not mainly, at least."

She should have seen this coming. He was too handsome not to be hiding something. She tried to appear disinterested. "Oh?" She glanced away from him, to one of the walls, observing the tight seams between animal skins.

Avaan sighed. "I was a photographer in Lebanon. I traveled to Syria seeking a certain piece of information, and while there I came across a Tarot reader. You are familiar with Tarot?"

"The cards? Somewhat." Becca had researched it, of course. Anything with a hint of paranormal found its way into her mind eventually. She'd found Tarot interesting, amusing, even, but never gave it much thought beyond that. It hadn't been magical enough to hold her attention, just luck of the draw and subjective interpretation.

"This reader drew cards for me. I would meet someone, a woman, in a place I had never been, and she would bring me great fortune or great ruin. I did not believe much in the Tarot until that day."

"Because you met a woman in a place you have never been? That reading is so vague it might as well be a newspaper horoscope."

"Ah, but there were more cards. I pulled a moon and also a serpent."

Becca recoiled, then recovered. Just a card. It didn't have to mean anything. But she still found the words falling out of her mouth. "And what do those cards mean?"

"Things are not what they seem. Caution required. Success almost guaranteed."

This time, Becca laughed. A horoscope indeed. " I hope you didn't pay her. What would success be to you?"

"Right now? Escape! But at the time, I hoped this journey would find me a partner. The serpent is a card representing feminine power and allure. The moon could have meant the exposure of someone I'm meant to be close to. Or someone I should stay away from."

"How can you know which to follow, then? Seems like a pretty useless fortune telling." Becca's chest tightened. Her gaze drifted toward the smile she saw in the crook of his mouth. Despite that, she somehow knew he was sincere. Was he really professing to believe that Becca was some sort of soulmate for him based on a single Tarot card reading?

"I'm feeling rather fortunate so far." He released a full smile so charming it might have been predatory, teeth gleaming in the darkness. Becca scooted back, putting more distance between them as she leaned back against a pole.

A deep throbbing vibrated the earth beneath Becca. The walls quivered. The sound was drums, Becca realized, the relentless and rhythmic pounding of drums. Whoops and hollers come from outside. Becca wondered what it must look like. Did they have Quinn in ceremonial garb? Anyone else might look ridiculous, but knowing Quinn, he would pull off the tribal headdress look and manage to look dignified, no matter how large it was. Becca let herself imagine it, almost forgetting Avaan and the strange conversation they'd had.

But then he spoke. "I am something of a performer myself. Do you mind if I play a tune?"

"Might as well." Becca shrugged. Better than more of that awkward conversation.

Somehow, Avaan's hands came free from his binds. He tugged at a cord beneath his shirt and dragged out a thin pipe. The surface was cobalt blue and had various holes in it, like a flute, only this one was certainly handmade.

Before she could ask how he'd undone his bindings, Avaan had placed his fingers and put the instrument to his lips.

Instead of the high, reedy sound Becca expected, the tone of the pipe was both airy and rich, with substance to it like she'd never noticed in a flute-like instrument. She sat up straighter, staring at Avaan's fingers as they moved deftly across the holes. His eyes remained locked on Becca's as he weaved his notes around the beats of the drums outside.

Her eyelids grew heavy, and her head wove in time with the music. A hum started deep in her throat, matching the unfamiliar tune. Her mind relaxed, and then emptied.

Avaan said something.

"What?" Becca mumbled, eyes half-lidded.

"You serve the music. You will listen to me now. "

"Yes," Becca intoned.

"You must call me *amir*. Do you understand?"

"Yes, *amir*." A screaming voice inside of Becca's head faded into a muted grey nothingness. The music threaded its way around her.

Her arms were the first to change, scales climbing from wrists to shoulders, spreading across her neck. Avaan smiled, and Becca smiled too. When her master was happy, she was happy too.

CHAPTER ELEVEN

QUINN

FINGERS TRAILED THROUGH QUINN'S feathers. Preening, they called it, which of course he knew but he'd never experienced it like this. Usually he picked through his own feathers, straightening them, rearranging some, plucking out annoying bits of fluff.

The women who attended him now stroked luxuriously through his wings with expert hands, pausing to massage knots out of his tense shoulders where the wings connected with his shoulder blades. He was in bliss, pure bliss. Another woman rubbed grease through his hair and brushed it to a fine sheen. Despite his having not had a bath, he looked and smelled far better than he had in days. Yet mentally, he was miserable.

Harper should be there with him. Becca should be there with him. Instead, Harper was who-knew-where on the run, accused of murder, and Becca was imprisoned in a shack with that prissy journalist, awaiting word of her fate.

"Your shoulders are so tight. You must relax," the young woman working his shoulders said, her voice trailing over his shoulder and into his ear. She was pretty. Thin, with long dark hair like his, dressed in one of the caribou skin vests that allowed slits for her wings. Here, everyone kept their wings out when it was practical, tucking them against their backs. The sound of rustling feathers filled the flat-topped tent they sat in.

"How do you keep from bleeding when your wings are brought out?" He blurted.

The younger women both giggled. The one brushing grease through his hair spoke. "It is a special salve. And eventually, the skin becomes strong enough to resist. Did your parents not use the salve?"

"No. A witch healed it with her magic." His skin twitched, and he shivered remembering the day he'd met Violet Petrov. He was glad that phase of his life was over.

An older woman held up her pot of animal fat and smiled, indicating that she'd like to come closer and rub it into his skin. He nodded approval. His vest had already been removed.

It soothed the ache in his arm from the scratches he'd received fighting the serpent off. They appeared to be healing like any wound, which gave him some relief. He didn't want to know what a mix between his race and the namigiak would look like.

Everything here felt strange, but he wanted to experience this. He wanted to understand the life his people, his parents, had lived and why they had left. He wanted to know if it was the life he should choose.

His chest shone in the lamp light. The older woman stepped back and waved her hands. Two young women brought a head-dress forward. It wasn't like the enormous ones Quinn had seen represented by the tribes in the western United States.

It was made of a ring of tufted white and black fur, about half a foot long. Strings of beads dangled from the leather band. Two black raven feathers dangled on the sides, both decorated with beads as well. Careful hands slid it over Quinn's head until it rested heavily on his brow. The woman clapped her hands.

"Your grandfather will be proud. His own feathers were given to make this for you.

"Will he...will he be there tonight?" Quinn asked.

The old woman laughed. "Of course he will!" She accepted another small clay pot from one of the younger women. This one held a dark substance that she scooped out with two fingers and smeared on Quinn's face.

"What is this celebration about, exactly?" Quinn said, feeling the heavy face paint move on his skin.

"It is our traditional coming-of-age ceremony. You would have gone through it on your fifteenth year. There is dancing, and drumming, and feasting, and sacred agreements made, including the presentation of your future wife."

"What!" Quinn practically yelped and sprang to his feet, his wings flaring out and knocking the two younger women aside. One giggled as his feathers brushed her. He ignored her, facing down the old woman who looked at him calmly. "I can't be married."

"Not married," the woman snorted. "Only engaged, as you might see it. Of course, there will be an exception made and the contract dissolved if you are found to not be compatible, but the process will go much more quickly since you are far beyond the typical age of union among our people. A few months instead of years, perhaps."

"No, absolutely not. I haven't met any of the people here. I haven't even met my own grandfather. I won't be presented for marriage!" He bit his tongue before mentioning Becca. They had agreed to not mention that to avoid putting his people more on guard than they were. But he wouldn't go ahead with this engagement ceremony with his girlfriend sitting in a tent as a prisoner, and if that meant spilling the beans about their real relationship, then he wouldn't hesitate.

The older woman pursed her lips, frowning at him. She leaned near the girls and spoke quietly to one, who shot a glance at Quinn and then dashed off through the tent flap. The other girl knelt and picked up the items Quinn had overturned when he stood.

"I am glad you have brought your feelings to my attention," the woman said gravely. "Having a disruption like this during the ceremony would not have been respectful to the gods. I have requested that your grandfather join us. He will explain things to you, and hear your feelings on the matter."

Oddly enough, the women in the tent both bowed before they left. Why would they have bowed?

Quinn felt ridiculous standing in the center of the tent, wings fully spread and dressed in ceremonial garb. He pulled his feathers tight against his back, but there wasn't much else he could do without ruining the work the women had put into his appearance. They'd let him keep his jeans, after offering a pair of caribou skin pants that Quinn had turned down.

Grease and a thick black and white paint slicked his chest. A furred hat and raven feathers adorned his long, brushed-out hair. He found himself fingering a feather, then remembered what the woman had said about the feathers coming from his grandfather and released it, letting it dangle out of sight.

The tent flap moved, and a man with salt and pepper hair ducked into the room, wearing a vest like Quinn had before and a similar headdress. It was like looking into a mirror in fifty years.

The man beamed at Quinn and slapped a hand on his shoulder. Did everyone dress like this to celebrate a coming of age, or did this man play a special role as Quinn's grandfather?

"Your eyes belong to your mother."

"You're my grandfather." Quinn studied him more closely, but with the anger swirling around his heart over Becca it was hard to feel anything like he had anticipated.

"Yes. I am Panuk Aguta, chief of the Tulukaruq tribe."

"You're the chief? That means my... I..." Quinn clamped his mouth shut before he made a fool of himself. Not just family. Not just his tribe.

Chief Aguta looked at him seriously. "Your mother tired of our way of life. A traveler we intercepted once told her of the world and she pined after it, to the point of not thriving, though we gave her everything. We have sought you and your sister as the final hope for continuing the noble family line leading this tribe."

Quinn clenched his fists and released them slowly, flexing them. "I haven't been here a day, but you've imprisoned my girlfriend and betrothed me to a stranger in the same breath. You're asking me to commit to lead this tribe when they don't know me, and I don't know them? Surely there's someone better suited."

The chief considered him, then walked to a far side of the tent and opened a small wooden box on the floor. He closed it without getting anything out, stood with the box in hand, and walked back to Quinn.

"Tradition has kept our people alive. Without it, we would scatter to the four winds and be hunted for our wings, have them cut off and displayed as trophies in government halls. Would you have that fate for us?"

"No, but I—"

His grandfather held up a hand. "Let me speak. I do not say this lightly. The woman you have brought among us is a deadly danger to us all, but the world beyond even more so. I would rather you stay here than have you leave feeling that we have betrayed you, the way your parents did. We might have a hope of finding your sister, as well, and she will also be given the opportunity to accept the leadership of these people if you, the elder sibling, turn it down. I will understand, no matter your decision, but you must decide by the end of this ceremony. Either you feel the call of this land, of this people, in your bones and blood or you do not. You will know."

"What will you do to Becca? How could I accept the leadership of a people that would have her killed?" Quinn tried to get a sense of these feelings the chief spoke of, but he could not. The anger simmered and his head spun with words he could use to save Becca's life. "She did not ask to become a serpent-woman. She means no harm to anyone."

"And yet she will harm. But because you ask it, we will not exterminate her. She will be given supplies, provisions, and set out to find her way from here. Her survival will be by her own merit."

"And the journalist?"

Chief Aguta frowned. "Is he your friend as well?"

Quinn shrugged. "No. But I'm not sure he deserves to die."

"He might tell others of our existence here in the wilds of Alaska. They might come looking, and we will have to be ready to kill those men. Is it better to end one life now or many later?" Those serious, dark brown eyes watched Quinn, studying his face.

"I don't know," Quinn said at last. He looked into his hands, then dropped them to his sides. "I'm not ready to make decisions like that. Decisions that choose between two people and determine their value based on their usefulness to me."

Chief Aguta nodded. "It is wise that you know yourself. And encouraging. I believe you will know when the time comes what your answer will be."

"You're positive, then, that my parents won't return? Do you know what happened to them?"

Chief Aguta shifted, seeming uncomfortable. "They visited us, many years ago. More than a decade. They encouraged us to join a cause of rebellion that was being fanned into a roaring flame in the lower states. I could not risk losing all of our people in one fell swoop by putting ourselves in the hands of passionate but reckless leaders who did not understand us. I turned them down and turned them away."

"A rebellion? What rebellion?" Quinn hadn't heard of such a thing in all of his searching for his parents. And so far, no widespread, organized movement had come to light in the U.S. since then.

Chief Aguta's eyes hardened. "I do not recall the name. It may have changed. It may have dispersed. I do not bother to track the fate of a violent radical group who does not care for the lives of its members."

"That seems harsh."

"Do not judge things you do not know."

Quinn trembled with the anger that washed through him. He tried to have an open mind, tried to come here with the hope that he could fit, that this could be a place for him to live and avoid the fate that awaited him with naturalization. "That's literally what you were asking me to do just now. Judge whether I can be a good leader. Judge whether we should take an innocent man's life. Don't you see the hypocrisy?"

Chief Aguta rubbed his jaw and tilted his head to one side, considering Quinn. "My ideas and beliefs must seem barbaric to you after a lifetime spent in more modern civilization."

Quinn sighed. "No, just not consistent. It's confusing. And there's so much that's new. I don't want to be engaged to anyone, and I don't want to be in charge of choosing whether a person lives or dies."

"Then you must accept my judgement and leadership as I make those decisions for you. That is what it means to be chief. Trust that I will take the information you have given me seriously, and that your words will contribute to my final choice. As for the betrothal, it can be delayed for now. The ceremony will not be much disrupted. I thought the coming of age ceremony appropriate, since you did not receive one, but we should have considered your feelings as well." He smiled somewhat sadly. Quinn immediately felt guilty, but he didn't say anything.

A woman lifted the tent flap and peered inside. "We are ready to begin. The moon has risen."

Chief Aguta raised his head. "Thank you, Nuniq."

The woman left.

Quinn touched one of the feathers hanging from the band on his head. He'd forgotten they were there.

"We need you here, Quincey King," the chief said. "In this ceremony you will receive your tribe name, the name you will be known by as long as you stay here. And we hope you will stay. If you choose to leave, our tribe will never speak your name again. It will be as if you never came. Choose wisely, for your choice is permanent. There is no room for the undecided here."

Quinn's back stiffened. He nodded curtly. The decisions he faced weighed heavily, a suffocating weight settling deep into his lungs.

"But first," Chief Aguta said, a smile touching the creases in his cheeks, "we dance!"

The drum beats throbbed outside. A deep, throaty singing began. The chief ducked from the tent, and Quinn followed more slowly, standing behind the tent flap, feeling the music sink into his skin and sinew, bringing his blood to life. He closed his eyes. For one night, he would be Tulukaruq. For one night, he would belong to this people.

He stepped through the tent flap and stood before a bonfire that reached to the sky with licking flames and shooting embers. Women danced, wings out and spinning in dark circles backlit by flame. It was a wonder they didn't singe their feathers. Beads glittered on their headbands. White teeth flashed with their smiles. Quinn saw the chief across the circle, gesturing for him to take the empty place at his side.

Quinn obliged, sitting at his left. He spotted Silla, but not Tarkik, and wondered where the serious-faced man was. Had he deliberately chosen to avoid this ceremony? If Quinn stayed, would Tarkik's attitude toward him change?

It didn't matter right now. Quinn watched the singing, spinning dancers. The music was like nothing he had ever heard, though he heard some similarities to beat boxing. Percussive vocal whoops, yells, and beats filled the air. It wasn't perfectly dark. Like the night before, it was as if the world were stuck on twilight.

On a final beat the women froze in their last poses and dispersed. Quinn automatically brought his hands together, clapping in the silence, and all eyes turned on him. Laughter broke out among the tribe, and Quinn stopped, grinning at himself. Apparently they didn't clap to show appreciation here.

Men came forward next, and the drummer started again. Quinn leaned closer to the chief to get a better look at the wide-based drum, big as a man curled up.

A man reached Quinn and gestured, urging him to stand. Quinn stood hesitantly and whoops and hollers followed him to the ring of dancers around the circle. The man clapped Quinn's back and bobbed his head to the beat of the drum. He brought a leg up and slapped it, then brought it down and stomped it. He paused until Quinn mimicked the moves and then the man put his arms out and showed him another move.

Quinn followed his motions, smiling nervously, but as the beats of the drum quickened, his tutor moved away from him and the rhythm took over Quinn's limbs and he found himself moving without caring what others thought of him.

His wings flared and beat wildly, making the fire wave and dance as he spun with the others. He leapt up nearly as high as the fire and landed in a crouch, wings out, staring at Chief Aguta as the man smiled.

And then the music ended.

Quinn breathed hard.

The man from before found him and they shook hands. "I am Tukkuttok."

"I can't promise I'll remember that," Quinn admitted.

Tukkuttok laughed and for a moment, Quinn caught a flash of what it would be like to live here, surrounded by people who were like him, not just in skin tone, but in what they valued, in their wings and love of flight.

He returned to his seat next to the chief and a line of women and men brought platters out. First empty ones, a small dinner-plate size made of polished wood and bone. Then the food arrived. Rich, roasted meats and fish, long white roots, small bowls of bright berries. Quinn indulged in far too much, his stomach tightening against his jeans. He sat back groaning and rubbed his belly.

"The land is rich this year," Chief Aguta said. "I'm glad you get to see it at its best, but you should know that some years are not this plentiful. Some winters we cinch our belts and chew rawhide to take our minds off our hunger. We try not to rely on modern conventions and instead choose to live off the land, but we will not starve." His brown eyes gleamed in the firelight.

"I didn't assume it would be easy."

"No," the chief said. "But it is a simple life compared with the political and social complexities of many other places."

"That must be nice."

"It is." The chief looked to the fire, gazing at his people as they laughed and ate. Quinn followed his gaze, amazed at all the wings he saw. Not everyone kept them out, but most. Tucked against their backs, flaring out as they laugh, flapping in irritation. One thing he expected was missing, however.

"Where are the children?" Quinn didn't hear any laughter.

"Some are sleeping. But there aren't many to begin with. Our women do not easily carry their babies, and fewer of our youth stay than go. We haven't had a coupling this year, I think." The chief's beads on his chest clicked together as he moved.

It made more sense now why the tribe had been so eager to pair Quinn with a mate, but he still couldn't imagine marrying someone he didn't know. Did couples pair for love or just to make children? It was something to ask later.

A woman with silver streaks in her black hair glided forward with a cup on a platter. The chatter of the gathered crowd quieted to absolute silence. Chief Aguta gestured the woman forward and she knelt.

"Quinn, meet your grandmother. Ahnah, our *irnngutaq*."

The woman smiled, deepening the creases in her cheeks. Quinn found himself smiling back at the rosy-cheeked woman. She raised the tray in her hands. Quinn glanced at the chief, questioning.

"This drink is a gift. It is made from caribou milk, and we brew it ourselves for many moons. If Raven chooses, you will receive a vision of your future when you drink it. We hope it will help you make a decision."

"Do I have to drink it?"

"No. It is your choice. But we hope you will choose it."

Bathed in the sea of dark stares, Quinn lifted his hand and took the cup. His grandmother bowed and took the tray away. Quinn lifted the clay cup to his lips and sipped. The drink was sour with a note of caramel. He rubbed his tongue against the roof of his mouth and tried not to make a face. The flavor blossomed in his mouth and the fire blossomed into a detailed image before him, a soaring figure that reminded Quinn of himself.

He was relieved to see that his hair remained long. His face and arms were covered with grime. He hardly recognized the hard expression. He looked ready for war. The image zoomed out, showing him standing at the top of a building that overlooked a city he recognized, a city that burned.

Washington D.C. was on fire.

A song split the air, the words too garbled for Quinn to understand, and the sky above ripped open with a swirling, vortex-like portal. Demons spilled out. Quinn felt a yell attle in his own throat, his fist raised

A flash of white light tore through the image.

Quinn stopped himself before he ran straight into Chief Aguta, who watched him with an unnerving calm. Quinn's eyes were wide, his throat hurt from the scream he'd given. He shook his head and licked his lips.

Quinn's hands shook as he placed the cup back into his grandmother's outstretched hands. The clay felt unnervingly solid, grounding him when everything else—the fire, the vision, his future—felt like it was unraveling.

The sounds of the celebration pressed back into focus: the rhythmic thump of the drums, the murmuring voices, the crackling flames. They felt wrong. As if the world should have been just as shattered and still as he was.

"What...what did I just see?" Quinn's voice rasped. His throat still burned from the scream he hadn't been able to stop.

Chief Aguta regarded him with that same unwavering calm, as though Quinn had just glimpsed something as ordinary as a sunrise. "The vision is a gift, given by Raven. It is what might come to pass."

"Might," Quinn repeated hollowly. He looked down at his hands, splayed and trembling in the firelight. The grime and blood he'd seen on his future self seemed to cling to him even now. "That was Washington D.C. It was burning."

"The future reflects the heart's path," the chief said gravely. "The world you saw is one you may yet shape."

Quinn looked up sharply. "I wouldn't choose that."

The chief's eyes bore into his, heavy with unspoken meaning. "You carry the blood of kings, the blood of this tribe. You will choose, Quinn. Whether you fight it or accept it—that is your choice."

The weight of those words crushed down on him, suffocating. His grandfather's feathers in his headdress brushed his cheeks, reminding him—taunting him—of what he'd become in just one night. He reached up and yanked it from his head, holding it loosely in his hands.

"I need time to think," Quinn muttered, his voice breaking. He turned sharply from the chief, from his people, and stumbled away from the fire.

"Quinn!" the chief called, but Quinn didn't stop. He couldn't.

He pushed past the gathered tribe, wings dragging behind him like a shadow. The noise of the celebration dulled with every step, replaced by the rush of his blood in his ears, the distant howl of the wind. He didn't stop until the fire was just a flicker, the music faint. Alone under the endless twilight sky, Quinn finally stopped and sank to his knees.

His breath fogged in the cold air, too shallow, too fast. His vision blurred, but whether it was tears or smoke or the haunting remnants of his vision, he couldn't tell. D.C., burning. Becca, gone. Himself—unrecognizable.

How had it come to this?

The drums echoed faintly in the distance. Each beat rattled through him, like the ticking of a clock counting down the time he had left to decide.

Quinn's fists dug into the earth as he whispered, "I don't know what to do."

Above him, a raven's call split the quiet, sharp and jarring. Quinn lifted his head just in time to see the dark silhouette swoop low and vanish into the endless sky. Its cry lingered, curling through the air like smoke.

In the gaping silence that followed, Quinn knew one thing for certain: he would not escape this. He would have to decide, and either way he chose, his path might lead to the war he saw.

CHAPTER TWELVE

TYSON

MAL. IT WAS HER smell that made the woman's name leap into Tyson's head. She smelled of sage, an herb witches used often for their healing salves and different spells. Mal's scent was unique, however, in that she combined it with patchouli. Woody and spicy, it made Tyson's head spin, like it had back when he'd first met her. He leaned back, forcing a smile onto his face.

"Mal, of course. How could I forget? You were my first." Harper's nostrils visibly flared, and Tyson realized what it sounded like. He had to backpedal, and fast. "First one I worked on with Tom. You went through Naturalization, if I remember correctly."

Mal laughed, tossing her head back and patting Tyson on the shoulder. "It's all right. I know you had a crush on me. Not that you'd ever admit it, Mr. By-the-Books. Not what you expected to find of a former camp resident? It took me eight months and a bit of help, but I shook off that Reformation agent assigned to me and found me a sponsor and a job. Free as a bird, now, and couldn't be happier. I bet you're disappointed, though."

Harper stiffened. Tyson wondered why her reactions were so obvious. She was normally more closed off. But the bird comment, that one made sense. If Mal had been a bird shifter rather than a witch, she wouldn't have made it through Naturalization with her abilities intact. Harper had to be thinking about Fletcher, and that wouldn't do anything good for this conversation.

Tyson cleared his throat. "Disappointed? No. I've learned a few things since then."

"Well, of course! Or you wouldn't have taken out those government lapdogs in charge of Silver Lake. Petrov, right?" Mal laughed. "It's about time. I've been itching to find myself a rebellion and start taking out those torture camps, but my contract isn't done here."

One of her companions stepped closer. "Mal, you aren't seriously saying you know these two?"

"Just my buddy Tyson here," Mal said, wrapping an arm around Tyson's shoulders and squeezing. "He helped make me who I am today." Her grin was entirely feral, and made Tyson's heart thud.

She'd been a model resident back at Camp Silver Lake. A few piercings, sure, and a tendency to prank the other residents with spells and the like, but all in good fun. Everyone liked her, except Violet and James. And as the Coven Leaders of Camp Silver Lake, they hadn't made it easy for Mal to get her Naturalization approved.

Looking at her now, Tyson realized she had planned this all along. Get Naturalized and get out of the camp as soon as possible. She'd succeeded just six short months after coming to Camp Silver Lake, an almost unheard-of record. Everyone had patted Tom on the back and called it "hope for the future."

"Why didn't we hear about your truancy?" Tyson asked. "The system usually flags Naturalized individuals from our camp when a violation of the terms is made."

The feral grin slid off Mal's face, and the shadows around her eyes deepened. "Don't ask questions you don't want to hear the answers to, little counselor." Her expression lightened a second later. Tyson shivered. Violet could do the same thing, and he'd learned it was an ability most witches had. That terrifying stare seemed to come from the depths of hell. He could inquire further at his peril.

"So," Mal said, "tell me about you. A bit has changed in a year and a half. Running around with a rogue shifter." She jutted her chin out at Harper, whose suspicious expression hadn't changed. "Leaving your job. Something happened to inspire that."

"Well..." Tyson trailed off. She assumed he had something to do with the Petrovs' deaths. But that had been all Harper. It wasn't anything he wanted to be associated with, no matter how 'cool' it made him in anyone's eyes. He glanced at Harper, but she didn't offer him any help, her eyes still locked on Mal.

"It's complicated," Tyson finally said. "Things weren't as they seemed. It wasn't a good fit any more." He swallowed, still gazing at Harper. To his surprise, he didn't feel the pang of regret he expected at the thought of leaving Camp Silver Lake.

Mal chuckled. "'Not a good fit' and you tear the place apart? Wow. Remind me never to hire you."

Tyson ran a hand through his hair, looking away from Harper. "There's more to it, but..." It dawned on him what would make the most sense to say, even if he didn't know what was going on entirely yet. "It turns out I'm not exactly 100% human."

"Sweet justice," Mal said, pumping her fist. She glanced at her crew. "The tormentor has become the tormented. How do you like that?" They whooped together. Two clapped. Tyson felt like he was in another world altogether as Mal clapped his shoulder and squeezed him in a friendly way.

"Welcome to the freak club. I think you'll like it here. Now," she continued without waiting for his response, "why did you want to use our portal?"

"We need to get to Alaska, fast." Harper said. Her arms had relaxed by her sides, but her fingers still flexed, and her gaze kept darting to the rest of the gang members. Always on guard.

"What sort of shifter are you, anyway?" Mal asked, eyeing Harper. "You don't feel like a werewolf."

"R—" Tyson started. Harper cut him off.

"None of your business. Are you going to let us through or not?"

Mal clicked her tongue. "Our instructions are clear. The only ones to use the portal have a passport."

"What does that take to get?" Tyson asked, eager to break the tension building in the air.

"A meeting with our boss. And a whole lotta dough." Mal rubbed her fingers together.

"We might have time for that. When can we see him?"

"*She* might have an opening next Thursday."

Tyson's heart sank. They'd get there faster driving. "Look, is there anything you can do—"

"For an old friend? Sure," Mal patted his cheek, then stepped away from him, rejoining her crew. "But there's a price. For two trips through, one for each of you, you'll have to reveal your paranormal forms."

"Why would you want that?"

Mal shrugged, the off-shoulder shirt she wore dropping further down her arm. "Call it curiosity. Can't hurt, can it?"

Tyson looked at Harper, whose face remained impassive. She dropped the pack she carried onto the ground and tugged off her jacket. Ebony wings sprouted from her back in a flurry of feathers. She had to bend them to keep from striking the edges of the cage-like fence around them.

Even the scowling man who had addressed them, Yonks, looked stunned. Several of the others gasped. Harper did look incredible, with her fierce scowl and those majestic wings. Though Tyson knew she looked even better in flight.

Mal's eyebrows raised, but she otherwise didn't react. She turned to Tyson.

"Your turn."

"I don't have a form to shift into." He spread his arms.

"Get out your knife," Harper urged him, her wings already withdrawn. She shrugged back into her jacket.

Tyson slid his pack off his back and located the outer pocket where he'd hidden the knife. He drew it out, the curved handle fitting easily into his hand now. Nothing happened. It felt warm to the touch, and he wondered if it would be like the goblins, where it would show its ability only if he was threatened.

"Throw a spell at me."

Mal's eyes narrowed, but she raised a hand, gesturing to the four directions with her fingers in a specific configuration, then clapping. A tiger appeared in front of her, orange and black pelt gleaming, larger than any real tiger Tyson had seen in a zoo. It roared, and his knees literally knocked together, but the knife at his side grew hot and blazed with crimson light.

Mal's eyes widened as Tyson raised it, and the tiger lay on the ground, head in paws, reminiscent of a dog. Tyson glanced at Harper, whose eyes had widened. She'd seen him use the knife before, but apparently it hadn't lost its novelty. She looked amazed, almost admiring, and a fluttery sensation started in Tyson's chest.

The tiger purred, bringing him back to the situation at hand. "That's just an illusion, right?" Tyson asked. The heat of the knife pulsed through him and its light remained trained on the tiger.

"In a way. But its teeth would have felt like the real thing." Mal banished the spell with an intricate wave of her hand. "You've held up your end. Follow me."

"I still don't understand what you get out of seeing our forms," Harper said.

"You're a suspicious one. Don't worry, nothing will come of it."

Tyson crouched down to put away the *ulu* knife.

"The boss won't like this." Yonks muttered. The other girl, the one with green hair, murmured in agreement.

"Let me deal with the boss," Mal snapped. "Wait outside if you don't want anything to do with this." The others fell into line behind Tyson and Harper as they passed through the weed hologram and into the dark tunnel. There were no further complaints.

"Without a passport they'll never get through the portal."

"I'll use mine to open it." Mal stopped in the dark center of the tunnel. There was a faint blue light at the far end, and behind them the daylight came filtering through the weed hologram almost as if the plants were real. It was impressively done. Tyson had only seen that quality of hologram done by James, and even his weren't this good. Mal certainly had a gift.

Mal raised her arm and Tyson caught a flash of purple light from the palm of her hand. Harper startled next to him as the silvery portal whirred into existence. Tyson hadn't had much time to think about traveling by portal, but as soon as he saw it he groaned internally. Portal travel. Ugh. His stomach clenched, and he swallowed.

"Remember, this portal is omni-directional. Whatever you think about, you'll be taken to it."

"Whatever you do, don't think about how hungry you are." Harper sounded as if she were quoting someone.

Tyson's stomach flip-flopped a few times. He had to stop thinking about his stomach.

Alaska. He tried to picture the mountain range Harper had shown him on her phone. Not the phone itself. The mountains. He pictured breathing the fresh air, standing in the grass in between the two mountains. He took a step toward the portal at the same time as Harper.

Mal stopped them. "One at a time."

Harper moved ahead of Tyson, passing through the silvery disc of light without hesitation. She vanished and the portal made a slight sucking sound, warping in the center in her wake. Then the surface smoothed.

Gates. Arctic Gates. Mountains in Alaska. There were a lot of mountains in Alaska. He had to get this right. *The Arctic Gates in Alaska.* His breath shuddered through his chest, and he gulped past his fear, ignoring the prickling near his heart.

Mal's hand slipped into his, passing him a piece of paper. Tyson clenched it, looked into her face and nodded.

"Thanks."

"Stay focused." Mal pointed at the portal.

Tyson squared his shoulders, brought the Gates of the Arctic to the forefront of his mind, and stepped through.

There were no knives, this time. No painful prickling, no sensation like he was being blown to a million astral bits and flung to the far reaches of the universe. For the first time, Tyson traveled through a portal and didn't feel sick when he landed on the other side. Something had changed.

He patted his clothes, his chest, and found everything in order, including the folded note in his hand. He looked around for Harper, spotting her a little distance away, farther back from where he stood. The two mountain ranges loomed on either side, like sentinels at a gate.

They had reached the Gates of the Arctic. He hoped. There weren't exactly signs, except it was cold despite the high sun.

Harper shouted a greeting and Tyson raised an arm. She ran toward him. Before she reached him, Tyson unfolded the note.

Lilith says hello.

A chill crept up his spine. Harper arrived, barely out of breath even with the enormous pack on her back, and cocked her head to one side.

"Tyson? What is it?"

He handed her the note. "I think I know who Mal's boss is." And he shivered, realizing the witch might now know where they were.

"I'm never going to escape her, am I?" Harper muttered. "I thought it was over, after... after what happened at the camp." She rubbed her palm furiously, as if there were something on her skin that she was trying to get off. Tyson couldn't see anything, but it unnerved him to see Harper so perturbed.

"Come on. We made it, I think. Let's keep going." Tyson dropped the pack off his shoulders and found the windbreaker he'd packed inside. He tugged it out and pulled it on, immediately cutting the chill by half. He eyed Harper, but she didn't look cold.

She glanced around, eyes squinting into the sun. "That sooth-sayer's painting said the dreamwalker was next, right? So, we should keep our eyes out for him."

"Yeah, I think so. And the second gate, too. Maybe the dreamwalker is through the second gate? I don't know if we're supposed to find him or..." *Or if he's supposed to find us. And who says it's a he?*

There was too much he didn't know for certain. He adjusted the pack on his back, stomach growling a bit. He'd eaten that granola bar when Harper had insisted on it, but he would need to eat more soon. First, he wanted to enter that valley ahead and see if they could spot the second gate. The mountains were about half a mile out, with the narrow entrance at their base. Tyson walked alongside the river that trailed out of the valley, watching the burbling water as it rushed over the rocks.

Harper remained silent. He was getting used to her lack of conversation. She spoke when it mattered. He did wish she'd loosen up and have a regular conversation about something other than magic and hiding and finding those they sought. Something mundane. He glanced at her out of the corner of his eye.

"So, do you have a favorite color?"

His question made her stop walking. She eyed him. "This sounds like a lame attempt to get to know me."

"It is," Tyson admitted. "No psychology tricks, I promise. Just curiosity." He swallowed. Dare he admit that he wanted to be friends? If they were going to keep traveling together, he needed more than the tentative trust built on a mutual need to escape a government camp.

"Purple. Dark purple." Harper finally said. She faced forward without looking at him, but even that small concession made him smile.

"Mine's blue. Or orange. I like both."

"It feels like we're in kindergarten," Harper muttered.

Tyson laughed. "In my experience, kids are the best at making friends."

Distant bird chirps filled the space between them. Tyson worried he'd taken it too far by saying the 'f' word, but it was hard to tell with Harper. She wasn't used to trusting anyone other than Quinn, and it seemed likely that she hadn't had much in the way of friends in her life. She'd gotten along with a few people back at camp—Fletcher, for one, and Kamri and Ian. If the events of the past few days hadn't happened, would Harper have found a reason to stay?

Tyson shook his head. It wasn't worth speculating. After all, if his abilities had started manifesting in obvious ways, he would have lost his job and been shipped off to a camp—most likely in another state to avoid conflict of interest.

And he'd have to face Naturalization, which, as a magic user, would include reporting to someone every minute of every day for the rest of his life to ensure he stayed within the bounds of his Naturalization agreement. Not so bad as having wings cut off, certainly, but miserable enough that he could see why Mal had left the program, and why Fletcher—

Harper cried out, jolting Tyson from his reverie. Standing in front of him, not twenty yards away, was a grizzly bear. It had come out from behind a boulder near the river ahead. It dropped from its hind legs to the ground, and Tyson swore the ground quaked beneath his feet. The bear rushed forward, and Tyson knew he was dead. His mouth went dry, his heart pounded as blood rushed to his ears. He couldn't move.

The bear stopped, its ears twitching, snuffing, turning its head side to side in an agitated manner.

Harper dropped her pack. Her wings rushed out in a flurry of feathers and she flapped them, rising into the air and hollering nonsensical sounds with trills and yips. She beat her wings threateningly.

The bear disregarded her, bearing down on Tyson with a steady gaze. It huffed, almost woofing. Tyson had never heard of a bear barking like a dog, but this one certainly did. It opened and closed its jaws, clacking its teeth together.

Harper swooped over the bear's head. It reached up to swipe at her, but she managed to get out of its range. Tyson tried to remember anything from his science classes. Should he make himself look bigger or play dead? They didn't have any bear spray.

The bear charged again, then doubled back when Harper cawed and threw sand in its eyes. Its massive paw swiped at its eyes to get the dirt out. She flew low again, this time with a rock, and the bear sprang up on hind legs and batted at her. Its heavy paw struck her side, knocking her from the sky. Then it charged.

Harper drew her wings in and quickly flattened to the ground. The bear stopped its charge and sniffed at her curiously. For a second, Tyson thought the strike had killed her.

Play dead.

Tyson dropped to the ground, covering the back of his neck with his hands. His elbows covered his face. He heard the bear growling and making distressed sounds. His own breath fed back into his face, warm and sticky feeling. He tried to slow it down, hoping the pack on his back would be enough to protect him from the bear's jaws.

He kept expecting screams, but he heard nothing. The bear's heavy steps thudded on the ground toward him. He squeezed his eyes shut. The bear's claws pricked his side as it tried to roll him over. Tyson went as limp as he could. Strong jaws clamped on his backpack, worrying it back and forth, then stopped.

Silence.

Had the bear lost interest? Was it leaving? Tyson resisted peeking. And then he felt the teeth again, more delicately this time. And the sound of a zipper on his pack moving. He made a tiny gap between his arm and his head and peered out, catching a glimpse of a naked human thigh.

A man's face dropped down, looking solemnly back at him. He held the *ulu* knife in front of Tyson.

"Is this yours?" he asked in a hoarse, unused voice.

Tyson lifted his head. The man squatted on the ground, completely naked except for a necklace with several carved totem figures, bones, and teeth strung on it. His long grey hair trailed down his back in a ponytail. Tyson blinked several times. His jaw moved, but no sound came out.

"Were you the bear?" he finally stammered.

"I was." The man inclined his head. "Are you the son or grandson of Nukilik?"

Nukilik. His grandfather. Tyson's head moved slightly, confirming.

"Good." The man grabbed Tyson's pack and hauled him up by it in a show of insane, inhuman strength. He slashed the air in front of them with the *ulu* knife and a dark slit appeared. With a single shove, he sent Tyson tumbling, arms windmilling into the void.

Harper's scream was the last thing he heard as darkness closed around him.

CHAPTER THIRTEEN

HARPER

HARPER HURTLED TOWARD TYSON and the bear-man. The bear-man raised the *ulu* knife in the air and slashed downward, splitting the fabric of the universe and opening a dark gash in the air. He pushed Tyson, who fell through the hole in the air, arms pinwheeling.

Harper screamed.

The muscles in her wings and shoulders strained as she pulled up at the last moment. Scratchiness lingered in her throat as she flapped slowly, drifting to the ground numbly.

She blinked at the spot by the river where Tyson had stood. Why hadn't that blasted soothsayer said anything about running into a bear-man and getting thrust into another dimension, or whatever sci-fi mystical thing this was?

Harper's wings flapped a few times, cooling her off. She was panting, she realized, her heart still racing. Sensation and awareness gradually returned to her body as her mind processed what had just happened.

Tyson was gone. Would Harper ever see him again? Could she somehow follow him?

"I didn't think you cared." A dry male voice sounded from behind Harper.

She pivoted, wings ready, hands up, knees bent. A raven stood on a rock. It cawed and ruffled its feathers, staring at her with beady, dark eyes. The rock wasn't big enough to hide a person, and it seemed unlikely the raven would stand there with a human talking so close to it.

Harper narrowed her eyes. "Was that you? The voice, talking to me?"

The raven's beak opened. "It is, and it isn't. This is not my true form, only one that I could appear in that wouldn't terrify you or make you attack."

Harper snorted. The bird didn't startle at the sound, and the way it cocked its head made her realize this was certainly no regular raven.

"Do you have a name, then?" Harper asked, crossing her arms.

"Many names. Most call me Raven."

Harper snorted. "How original."

"It was."

The bird's response made her pause, and Lilith's voice filled her mind. *Have you ever heard the lore of the Raven? A sacred being. Mischievous, creative, trickster.*

And Fletcher. *Are you descended from* the *Raven? Cooler, because he's a god.*

Raven born.

Harper licked her lips. "Are you *the* Raven? Are-are you a god?"

The laughter that came from the bird's throat was a garbled, choked sort of laughter. "You curious mortals. What you don't know can kill you, you know. Let's just leave it at that, shall we?"

Harper threw her hands in the air. "Well, you less mortal beings can do as you please, I guess. Do you at least know what the hell is going on with Tyson?"

The raven's right eye color bled from black to gold and shone from its socket. "He is being tested, as you are about to be."

Harper stepped back. "Well, shit."

"Indeed." The raven nodded gravely. "You could call it deep shit, to coin a mortal phrase. Your journeys will mirror each other. You will emerge triumphant, or you will fail and dissolve into nothingness. And you have until dawn."

"These things never have any middle ground. You should do something about that. I would go for a so-so outcome here." Harper's snark was getting the better of her. Her feathers itched where they met her back, just in that idiotic spot she could never reach. She moved each wing up and down, one at a time and the sensation subsided slightly.

The bird watched her silently, as if waiting for her to say more.

"Okay, so you're saying our journeys will mirror each other. Does that mean if one of us gets injured, the other one gets injured, and if one of us dies, the other dies, and..."

"It does sound like you grasp the idea," the bird said in its dry tone.

"But *why*?" Harper insisted. "Why the hell would I be connected with him in any way? Did someone place a bonding spell on us? How did this happen?"

"The universe has its own kind of magic. I understand as much as you. Consider me a messenger."

"Do I at least get a clue about where to begin? Tyson was thrown into another dimension. Pretty obvious that he's gotta find his way back here. What's my grand task?"

"To find what you've forgotten." His eye bled silver. The orb gleamed at Harper.

"The Beryllium orb."

"You made an unwitting contract with forces darker than you can imagine. They must not be allowed to succeed. Unfortunately, my own bindings prohibit me from returning your memories. It violates millennia-old contracts. But I can point you in the right direction, and you'll find hints from me along the way to keep you on track."

"It seems too simple."

"You don't have all the information you need to make that decision, so I warn you to be wary. Be wary of your pride and your pigheadedness."

"Pigheadedness? Mighty words." Harper walked over to the nearest pack, the one Tyson had dropped. She needed a break from that twitchy bird and its magical eye. She zipped the outside pocket closed, the one that had held the *ulu* knife. She scoured the ground, but found no signs of the knife. The bear-man had taken it into the other dimension.

She ignored the lump in her throat at the thought that she might not see Tyson again and hauled the pack over to where she'd left hers. She observed the contents of both, exchanging a few items, but mostly leaving hers intact. She hated the idea, but she'd have to leave Tyson's here. She couldn't carry both. And she'd have to carry this one in her hands if she flew. Backpacks weren't made for people with wings.

"To begin, you must follow the *inuksuit*. They will lead you where you are meant to go."

"What is an *inuksuit*? And where is it, exactly, that I'm meant to go in this insane wilderness?" Harper huffed.

The raven flew over to a pile of rocks. They were stacked together in the shape of a person. A blocky, crude sort of person, but a person nonetheless. Two stones on the bottom, a wide stone on top of those, and then an assortment of shapes making the head, torso, and arms.

"This is an *inuksuk.*"

"What about when it gets dark?"

"It will not get dark in the Alaskan summer. Sleep when you are tired, eat when you are hungry, and keep following the path. The direction the stones face will tell you where to turn. When the sky goes pink, your journey will have ended."

"And Tyson?"

The bird cocked its head. "If you both succeed, you will find him in the end. Do not worry about that."

"I wasn't worried," Harper snapped. After a moment's thought, she withdrew her wings and shouldered the pack. Seeing these *inuksuit* from the air could be difficult, and she didn't want to miss any.

"Walk north from here, through the mountain gates and into the valley." At that, the raven took off, flapping its wings and soaring into the air. Harper dropped her gaze from the sky and passed the *inuksuk* swiftly without another glance. How often would she find them? Every few miles? Or every hundred feet? She didn't see another one immediately visible, so she angled herself north, toward the mountains standing sentinel ahead.

She passed through them as the sun headed for the horizon. But it never fell. Harper's stomach complained, so she stopped and filled it with jerky and an apple. She didn't want to waste time lighting a fire. The faster she got through this, the better. Brushing off her hands, she surveyed the land for another stone feature before it got too dark to see. Despite what that raven had said, the light was fading.

She spotted what looked like a stack of rocks some distance ahead and hurried to it. It was angled east, so she changed her trajectory. An owl hooted in the distance. Little scuffling noises distracted Harper as she tried to discern what could be making them, but she rarely saw any of the creatures. She expected the twilight to fade and for darkness to force her to stop and build a camp, but the dim blueish grey light never faded from the land. It was like walking in an eternal twilight.

A faint floral scent filled her nostrils as she walked. It was so sweet and unexpected, Harper found herself taking deeper draws of breath. Beneath her feet to either side of the narrow game trail she walked, the path was lined with swaths of tiny blueish flowers on spindly stems. Forget-me-nots. Harper remembered the flower from somewhere, she wasn't sure where. They seemed to grow all around her, carpeting the ground.

And then, out of the strange half-night, a cry sounded. A human cry. Harper surged forward, head looking to either side as she searched for the source.

A rock to her right moved.

Not a rock. Bear. A small one. A cub, lost from its mother? Or maybe its mother was nearby. Harper dropped her pack and unfurled her wings. The bear cub startled, turning to face her with a pale, flat face. No snout. Harper flew into the air and got closer. Not a bear at all. It was a child. She lowered herself to the ground, tucking in her wings.

The child stared at her, mouth agape. Harper couldn't tell the gender, but the child seemed to be aged around six.

Harper held up her hands. "Don't be afraid. I'd like to help. Is one of your parents around?" Based on the blank stare the child gave, he or she probably didn't speak English. She brought up a finger. "Wait a moment."

She went back to her pack and brought in her wings again, replacing the pack on her shoulders. She trotted back to the child, who had ducked behind a nearby bush.

"Come on. Let's find your family." Whether desperate or too trusting, the child crawled out from behind the bush and drew near to Harper. Up close, the child seemed to have more feminine features.

"Do you have a name?" Harper asked, moving forward along the path. That open, innocent face smiled, clueless. Harper pointed to herself. "Harper." She pointed at the little girl.

The chid's face brightened. "Siku!" she exclaimed.

"All right, Siku. We're going to find your family." It shouldn't take that long. Harper could always come back to this place and get back on the path. "Which direction to your family? Mother? Father?"

Siku shrugged her shoulders. Harper frowned and kept her ears and eyes alert for any hint of a tribe nearby. She didn't think this little girl was from her parents' tribe of raven people. At least, the girl hadn't shown any particular recognition when she saw Harper's wings.

A tiny, warm hand slipped into Harper's. She startled, and then realized it was Siku, not some critter trying to crawl up her sleeve. She smiled slightly. Children had never paid her any particular attention, and it felt good to have the trust of this one. Harper couldn't be an abomination if a child trusted her.

They walked for ages. The never-changing light made time stretch. Harper contemplated pulling out the phone from her pack and checking the time, but it was turned off to reserve the battery for a time it might really be needed. Eventually, the sky would brighten again. But how long could she spend searching for this little girl's tribe?

As long as it took, Harper determined. Whatever the raven had said, this was more important. She glanced down. Siku had slowed, moving at a snail's pace. She dropped Harper's hand and yawned. She was exhausted, poor thing.

"Do you want to stop and rest? We can search for your family in the morning." Harper's chest tightened at the thought of delaying her search an entire night.

The little girl didn't respond. Her feet moved at a grudging pace. Her animal skin coat seemed bulkier than before, somehow making her bigger, more like a bear than ever.

Harper continued walking. If Siku started to stumble, they would stop. Harper's own eyes felt dry and heavy.

A dragging sound accompanied Siku's shuffling steps after a time. Harper noticed something dragging at the little girl's side.

Arms. Siku's arms had stretched. Harper's eyes widened. She dropped to one knee and took the little girl by her shoulders, turning her face toward her. The girl's hood had closed tighter around her face, looking like a second skin and showing only the girl's nose and eyes. Harper tried to push the hood back and failed. It was stuck fast. A tiny moan escaped the girl. In front of Harper's eyes, Siku's eyes stretched wide and lit up with a silver light.

Harper got to her feet and stumbled back. "What are you?" she asked, trying to keep the tremor out of her voice.

Siku—or whatever the little girl was now—stepped forward and grew in height an entire foot. The arms stretched again, dragging fully on the ground like long ropes.

The fur grew and sprouted. The evolving creature kept approaching Harper, the sounds it made developing into a cross between a bird-call and a wolf howl. It sounded... mournful. Haunting. Those wide, silver-lit eyes expanded again, widening until they nearly filled the little girl's once-face. The body stretched again, growing until it was taller than Harper, and tiny antler buds appeared on the creature's head.

"Siku?" Harper asked. Had there been a child at all. Had she walked into a trap?

The creature made that wailing animal sound again. A rustling came from behind Harper. She spun to face a line of similar, larger creatures with inhuman, long arms, fur-covered bodies and those terrible eyes like headlights breaking through the twilight.

They closed in faster than Harper could react. She dropped the pack and let her wings expand. The creatures halted in a circle outside the reach of her wingspan. She fell into a crouch, ready to spring up and attempt to take off straight out of the circle. A vertical lift-off was the most difficult, and she'd rarely attempted it and rarely succeeded in getting enough lift.

The smaller creature, the one that had been a little girl minutes before, sounded the eerie wail again and one of the taller creatures came close, bending down and touching its head to the smaller one's head. Little hoots came from them.

"Are these your family?" Harper asked. She didn't know what the creatures were, but by all appearances they weren't harmful. They filled her with a terrible sadness, a longing, a feeling of abandonment.

The eyes in the circle turned on her, including the Siku-creature. Without any words, Harper somehow knew they were asking her a question. If only she could figure out what it was. She felt a tug toward them, something inside of her responding to the unvoiced question.

Stay.

And she found that she wanted to. These beings would accept her, take her in to be part of their pack.

Wings flapped overhead, and the raven landed on top of one of the creatures. It didn't acknowledge that the bird was there, staring at Harper with unblinking silver eyes.

"Urayuli. Creatures made from the lost and unfound children. Harper, they want you to join them."

"I know," Harper murmured. She stood, reaching a hesitant hand to the coat of one. Her wings shrank and a numbing sense of peace came over her. She touched the fur. It was coarser than she expected, but somehow still soothing to her soul.

"The longer you stay here with them, the more you will become like them. You must leave quickly."

"But the little girl. Her family—"

The raven shook his head firmly. "There is no reuniting them now. The Urayuli transformation is permanent."

Harper clenched her fist and let it fall. "Why are they drawn to me, now? I'm not lost."

"Aren't you? A little girl still looking for those that she has lost, those who are lost to her?"

Harper looked up into the looming faces. Even Siku had stretched again, her height nearly the same as the other antlered heads in the circle. She didn't belong here. But then, she didn't belong anywhere.

Harper swallowed. "I need to go now."

The beings didn't move.

"I need to go. Please let me through."

They shifted their tall, furry bodies, but no gap in the circle opened. If she left, it would be of her own accord. They would not stop her, she thought. She grabbed the handle on the top of her pack and walked forward to the wall of bodies. She closed her eyes and pushed through between two of the Urayuli. She had to tuck her wings and force the giant creatures aside, then tugged on her pack as it caught behind her between their bodies. It came free and she nearly fell backward, clutching the pack.

The Urayuli's eyes turned on her, and they stretched out into a ragged line, nearly a dozen of them. More had come from somewhere. They moved toward her, making those haunted, yet somehow enticing calls. They would circle her again. She would change. Her skin prickled as if hair would start growing.

Harper rubbed her arms to be sure. Nothing yet, but she had to get out of here. She flapped her wings, gathering air beneath them, and ran along the uneven ground. She lifted, then didn't quite catch the wind and dropped back to the earth, running and flapping again. She launched herself into the air, holding the pack tight to her chest. Behind her, those silver eyes gazed upward. The bird-wolf calls followed her, lingering in the night air.

Harper stayed low, looking for the familiar path she had left to help Siku. She found another rock formation, different than the one she had left, but close enough to the right area that she came down near it. She had to find her people before dawn.

After her brief flight through the chilly night air, she felt more awake than before, but a heaviness lingered behind her eyes. The Urayuli were close enough that she didn't want to risk stopping for sleep only to wake and find herself made into one of them. She had to keep moving.

The forest sounds were closer now, and louder. She ran along the path through the tall grass, eyes constantly searching for the next *inuksuk*. She passed another before too long, pointing along the same path, now running through a copse of trees. Harper withdrew her wings and kept her pace, dodging branches and jumping over logs and rocks, putting plenty of distance between herself and the Urayuli.

A branch snagged her hair, short-cropped though it was. Harper exclaimed, reaching up to untangle the snag.

It wasn't a branch.

CHAPTER FOURTEEN

TYSON

TYSON BLINKED AGAINST THE blinding brightness of the world he'd landed in. He lifted his head off the ground and shook it, then looked around. The sky was near dark and lit up like Christmas with the famous ribbon of ethereal light.

He climbed onto all fours, shaking his head and staring at his hands. Except they weren't human hands holding him off of the snow-covered ground, but *paws*. Enormous, white bear paws. He lifted them and shook off the snow, revealing black pads and claws.

Tyson shuffled his back legs, too, to confirm it. He raised his nose toward the air and sniffed. It was like a reflex. He caught hint of an owl winging overhead, and a rabbit skittered through the snow behind him. The earth pulsed beneath his paws, teeming with life under the frozen landscape. And there he stood in the midst of it all, breathing chill air but not feeling any of it through his thick white coat.

Someone had turned him into a polar bear.

A sound like a gunshot rang behind him and he bolted, galloping through the snow at a break-neck pace. Power coursed through his limbs, power he didn't know how to control. Adrenaline and instinct had taken over. He barely dodged a snow-covered pine tree, his shoulder glancing off the branches and sending snow cascading to the ground as he came up over a rise and slide, legs sprawling.

The air stilled. A huff in the wind told him he wasn't alone. Tyson cracked his eyes. Even as a polar bear, he could see in color. He'd assumed bears were like dogs and could only see black and white, but the landscape was awash in greens and blues from the shifting lights above, illuminating the brilliant coat of a female polar bear not twenty yards away. Tyson could smell on the air somehow that she was female, and that she, too, wasn't alone.

A tiny bear grunted and another squeaked. The female growled a warning. Tyson slowly backed away, but his return was blocked by the slick hill behind him. The only way out of the situation was around, and this mama bear could charge in an instant.

Her scent changed in an instant. His nose interpreted it in a way his human one never could. Fear. She nosed her two cubs along, glancing back over her shoulder as they conceded their territory to Tyson, who had been preparing for her charge.

He, too, caught another scent on the wind, but his human mind scattered the bear-sense. He needed to rein it in, to focus. The wind shifted through the pines, bringing a myriad of scents, and his bear-self relaxed.

His human mind, on the other hand, did not relax. It was the heart-pounded, heavy breathing, feet racing of those times he'd been the last one up the stairs from the basement with the responsibility of turning off the lights. No matter how irrational, his brain had made as if every imaginable horror breathed down his neck, but of course when he turned around, nothing was there. He lumbered forward in a different direction from the female and her cubs.

He turned around now, eyes scanning the horizon. It was a perfect, peaceful canvas. Perhaps he was just paranoid. What could harm a polar bear, after all? A king of the ice and snow. He padded forward more confidently. He needed to find that other bear-man. He might know how to change Tyson back, how this had happened. He owed Tyson that much, considering the jerk had shoved him through some sort of portal.

Remembering how he'd gotten here made him think about Harper, a welcome distraction from the paranoia that haunted him. He wondered whether she was searching for him or if she'd continued on toward her tribe. He wouldn't blame her for leaving him to his fate. It wasn't like she could follow him here.

A gunshot cracked through the silence and Tyson felt a sting in his shoulder. He growled, head snapping up to find the source of the pain. Another shot broke the stillness, and another. Both went into his belly in different places, and anger surged through his chest. He didn't deserve to die. He hadn't done anything aside from exist.

His pupils dilated and he spotted the two figures on the hill, rifles against their shoulders, headed toward him. He broke out into a sudden run, charging for them. The hunters fired again.

Tyson went down in a spray of snow and blood. The life pumped out of him, his thoughts narrowed to a pinprick of pain and consciousness.

A hand reached from the aurora and took his soul from the body. A spirit in the form of the polar bear followed. It opened its mouth and the roar shook the skies. The hunters below took no notice, chatting as they made their way to the body of the bear.

The anger remained with Tyson. Sure, men needed to eat. He knew that, and why would these men have any motive other than feeding their families? But something still felt wrong. A brief, searing pain went through his elbow, then faded to nothing. He reached a hand across to touch it, but couldn't feel anything different.

They did not thank the spirit, a voice rumbled through him, immense and pulsing. It flooded his blood and pumped through his heart.

Who are you? Tyson asked, but his words came out as thoughts. *Why was I in the polar bear's body? Why did you bring me here?*

Silence. He felt no sensation on his skin, floating in the air, facing the glowing outline of the polar bear. He suspected his body lay somewhere without him. Was he dead, too? Was there a point to any of this?

The mysterious hand appeared again, pressing gently on his shoulder, moving him downward, toward the men spilling the dead bear's hot intestines across the snow. The stain of its was blood dark and filled Tyson with the smell and sensation of being sick. As he realized his destination, he balked. He did *not* want any part of that man's thoughts, of his actions, cutting into a creature that Tyson had been one with only moments before.

But he had no choice. A force beyond his power to withstand thrust him into the man's soul, taking up a tiny space in the back of the man's mind.

Satisfaction. Glee. Disgust. The man hated this part of his job, but it paid well—guiding elite, wealthy hunters through the Alaskan wilderness to get a kill like this one. They wanted polar bears, moose, and other large trophy game. Some of them hoped for creatures of legend. Others were intent on poaching the protected paranormals in this region. It all paid a handsome sum.

A shout from his companion alerted him to something. He turned. A young woman with short-cropped hair stood in the distance, a massive pair of wings grown from her back.

"Tyson!" she screamed.

He reached for his gun. A prize like those wings would bring in a hefty bounty with a few sellers he knew.

Harper! Tyson dragged himself out of the man's thoughts and pushed to the forefront of his mind. He beat himself against the wall between himself and the world.

The gun propped up on his shoulder. The body moved on the last order it was given. Aim and shoot.

Tyson yelled as the gun went off.

Harper's form faded before the bullet ever reached her. A hooking sensation grabbed his attention moments before he was dragged back into the sky, anger and fear coursing through him. They felt like heat, and he had none of the physical reactions he would have had if he'd been in a body. His own body, at least.

He glanced down at the hunter and shuddered at the murderous sensations that now flooded him. He wanted to stop the two men, turn those guns on them and leave their bodies to benefit the wild things that lived here.

Protection. From things both physical and spiritual. Can you accept that responsibility?

Who are you? Tyson shouted. No physical sound manifested, more like a vibration through the air. The polar bear spirit still hovered above him, joined by an eagle. But he hadn't seen an eagle. Did they represent something?

You are a dreamwalker. A realm skimmer. Understanding others'
experiences is essential for you to do the work before you.

Is this a job interview? The thought broadcast without Tyson
intending it. He wasn't sure he could have prevented it. *It'd be*
great to know what the position is.

You were born into this position, as you call it. This is merely a test.

Frustration built inside of Tyson. *A test for what?*

For your readiness to build a bridge between worlds. The voice
resounded in every part of him, disembodied and somehow fully
embodied within Tyson. It was maddening, it was calming, it
was everything he didn't understand about the world.

A burning pain pierced his ankle. He gasped and bent to touch
it, but of course he wasn't in his body. Somehow, he could still
feel every sensation.

Tyson floated in the void. The darkness pulsed, drawing close
enough to suffocate and then withdrawing, as if it were breathing.

"Hey!" Tyson yelled as loud as he could. There was no echo.
The darkness swallowed his words.

A form drifted past. The bear-man who had forced him
through the gash between worlds he had cut with the *ulu* knife
sat cross-legged in a meditation position. One of his scarred
eyelids cracked open.

"Do not waste your energy. Here, it is best conserved for what
comes next."

"What exactly comes next? There's nothing here!"

"This is a womb. Only you determine if you'll be expelled or
absorbed."

Tyson didn't like the sound of either of those options. He
folded his arms, and then unfolded them, feeling like a petulant
child. "Is Harper okay?"

"Her journey is her own. Focus on your path in the here and now." The bear-man's form blurred and he turned into a bear, then some sort of seabird.

"I still don't understand what I'm doing here." Tyson rubbed his hands on his pants. At least he still had a form that he was aware of.

"You will come to understand, in time. This is a test all of those with dreamwalker abilities are put through. You are being tested for your suitability in connecting with the power of the Eternal Source." The seabird gained the head of a man. Tyson winced, wishing he could look away from the combination, but feeling he had to look at the same time.

"But how do I have these abilities? Neither of my parents do. Did. That I know of," Tyson insisted. To his relief the bear man regained his human form.

"When you were an infant, someone spoke a sacred ancestral name over you. His spirit came into you, lives in you. You are Nukilik." The bear-man spread his hands wide. "If you reject this path, you reject the spirit inside and so will die. If you accept, you must prove you are worthy."

"Or I'll die. Okay, I get it. Seems like I don't have much choice in the matter."

"You will not be forced." A piercing blue eye directed itself at Tyson. When the other opened, it was green. "Do you wish to proceed?"

Did he?

His Nana's face came to his mind. Her smile. Her stories. Her determination. Had she been the one to speak his grandfather's name over him? Had she expected him to accomplish something beyond his human desires and goals in this life?

"Yes." The word sounded foreign as it left Tyson's mouth of its own accord. *I haven't decided yet!* His mind screamed. But he took in a breath, and then another, and imagined Nana was here with him, her cool, wrinkled hand in his, and the *ulu* knife in the other. Strength surged through him and he straightened, though his hands remained empty.

The bear-man bowed his head. "Let it be so. This next challenge will reveal your inner turmoil. You must be at peace to access the ethereal powers of worlds beyond. Still yourself and you will still the chaos around you. In that stillness, you can control the elements and you will find yourself back here."

"What chaos?"

The void swallowed the bear-man, and he vanished from sight. The tendrils of darkness shot out from within the void and consumed Tyson, smothering his screams and suffocating him until he landed on the other side of some dark rift in the air.

The rift sealed and he stood, all of his clothes removed except a thin panel of fabric at his waist. A loin cloth. He wore a loin cloth and stood at the top of a moderately sized mountain. Beside him, a massive boulder towered at the peak of the mountain. The rocks below felt warm below his feet. Was there a hot spring nearby?

A natural vent in the ground off-gassed behind him and Tyson jumped, shrieking at the heat scalding the back of his legs. He stumbled down the mountainside and away from the peak, rocks stabbing his feet and sliding out from beneath his steps. He landed hard on his behind.

A high-pitched cackling echoed over the blackened slope. "That's not how it's done, is it?"

A lanky-armed, long-legged figure leapt to the top of the boulder at the peak. Its pockmarked face gleamed with flecks, like the shining mica or quartz bits found in common rocks. It could have been human, once, but the face was too wide, the eyes narrow like a cat's, the ears stretched and floppy. It seemed to have all the right parts in all the wrong proportions.

"Is your name chaos, by chance?" Tyson muttered, more to himself than to the being.

"I'm offended. My name is Lars. I'm your guide." Lars bowed.

"Who sent you?"

"No one sent me. I have a job here and I do it." Lars wrinkled his nose as if he smelled something bad. "Yeesh, nosy. Maybe you want to listen for me a moment before offending me. We are standing on an active volcano. Due for an eruption any moment."

Tyson cocked his head and scanned the boulder. "How can you tell? There's no seismic activity."

The being swung its arms and twisted its mouth into a mocking expression. "'There's no seismic activity.'" The voice that came out of its mouth sounded exactly like Tyson's.

Tyson blinked at the being.

Lars rolled his eyes. "Listen Mr. Earth Science, let me tell you how this works. You have to get down this mountain and to the nearest village. The kicker is," the being sprung off the boulder, mouth split as wide as it would go in some version of a grin, "you'll be blind."

A steam vent erupted between them as soon as the words were spoken and Tyson stupidly looked down. Instead of steam, however, this time it was a black cloud. It coated his eyes and sealed his eyelids shut.

Tyson grabbed at his face, fingers probing where the black smoke had touched. It didn't hurt, it didn't seem damaged in any way, and in fact, he could still pry open his eyelids with both hands peeling back the folds of skin, but his eyes could no longer see anything other than darkness.

"What did you do to me?" Tyson yelled. "What gives you the right?"

"I told you, this is my job." The disembodied voice floated from Tyson's right. "The sight you rely on most has been stripped from you. Learn to rely on other senses."

Tyson turned toward the speaker, hands and jaw clenched. The mountain rumbled below his feet, enough to jostle, but not upset. "What was that?"

"Your seismic activity. Are you coming?" The voice sounded farther away now, as if the being were moving.

"Do you at least have a name?" Tyson held his arms out in front of him as he took his first steps downward on the steep slope. "I can't keep calling you 'the being' in my head."

"Nicer than some things I've been called. You mortals are so forgetful. I introduced myself already, don't you remember?"

Tyson scanned his memories, still trying to keep his breathing even. The smell of sulfur burned into his nose and down to his lungs, making it hard to concentrate. Had it gotten stronger?

The being sighed. "Lars. It's Lars."

"And you're a guide, Lars? How do I follow you without my sight? If you're about to say by sound, we'd better think of a different plan." His mouth felt dry. He swallowed, but he couldn't bring the moisture back. His palms, ironically, were sweaty.

"You have an inner sight. You're meant to learn how to use it."

"So is this a simulation or..."

"The volcano is real. This is your body. If you do something foolish, you will die. If you do not learn to use your inner sight, you will die." The mountain quivered again, nearly knocking Tyson off his feet.

Tyson grimaced and rubbed his hands together. He didn't sign up for this, but it appeared he didn't have a choice. It put a whole new spin on the idea of 'trial by fire.'

"Follow me!" Lars sounded far too cheerful. It also sounded as if he had started running.

Tyson took several jogging steps forward, mentally trying to reach outside of himself, to extend his 'sight' beyond the darkness his physical eyes were smothered in.

Every step spiked Tyson's adrenaline. Without even trying, his pace increased. The pull of the slope brought his feet down with jarring thuds. He stepped on a rock and yelped.

"Open those eyes, dreamwalker." The voice had shifted to the left.

But I'm not a dreamwalker. I'm human. I can't do magic. It's the knife. Tyson focused on putting one foot in front of the other. He turned to the left, matching what he thought he heard.

"Not that way, idiot," Lars growled. His voice burst out in Tyson's face, clearly on his right. "The sound bounces off the rocks and echoes strangely here. You need to open that third-eye. Didn't you learn anything?"

"No one appeared to teach me, if that's what you're asking. This is the first I'm hearing about all of this!" The mountain heaved, and a massive boom shot through the air.

"There she blows!" Lars screamed. He grabbed Tyson's arm. "You have one minute, then I'm letting go."

"What happened?"

"Volcano top released. We've got toxic smoke and ash raining down on us and fiery balls of death flinging from the mountain's mouth. If we don't run, we're both dead."

"You can *die*?"

Lars made an indecisive noise. "Well, no, but I thought it might make you feel better if I implied that we were in this together. I do get in trouble if you don't make it, though. Don't get any dumb ideas. Also, stay calm." His footsteps told Tyson he'd taken off running again.

Stay calm?! Well, that's simple enough. Tyson breathed in through his nose and out through his mouth. He counted to five and took off jogging. He didn't have the senses developed for this. He relied on his eyes to show him where he was going, and his feet were clumsier than usual as a result. There was no feedback telling him where he needed to place his feet.

And none of his psychology knowledge was helping. He had dozens of tools for helping paranormal clients visualize to improve their lives, but none of them seemed appropriate right now. He physically couldn't see, not just figuratively.

Picture the end result the way you want it. A common phrase he had used time and again. It felt pathetic now, but as fear crept through his limbs, stilting his stride, Tyson knew he had to try.

The way I want it. Unharmed. Or, whole, at least. And... In his mind's eye, he saw the Alaskan wilderness. And Becca standing there, smiling, and Quinn next to her. And next to him, Harper. With her brown eyes that were always charged with determination, her ebony wings flaring out from her narrow shoulders, and her smile... well, that was different. She rarely smiled around him, but in this visualization, she beamed as if seeing Tyson was something she had waited for, even anticipated.

Tyson's foot caught a stone and sent him skidding and rolling several yards. Blood trickled down his face from a sharp point of pain on his forehead. He'd received a cut, not to mention dozens of bruises on his limbs and ribs. He groaned and lay face-down, listening to the mountain rumble beneath him.

A flare of pain burned in his back. Had an ember struck him? He didn't bother touching it to see if his back had burned. He squeezed his eyes, then widened them as far as they would go, feeling the uselessness of it all. Silly dreams wouldn't help him succeed at this impossible task. He couldn't go any farther like this.

It's like dreaming. Open your inner eye.

The male voice sounded vaguely familiar to Tyson, but he couldn't put his finger on who it would be.

How could he dream while awake? He went limp and let his mind wander. It wasn't easy amidst the ground shaking and Lars running up, yelling his name. A red-hot pain seared between his shoulder blades, yanking him out of his nearly-relaxed state. He bit back a yell and breathed in and out rapidly until the pain dulled. He let his breathing fall into a rhythm, in time with his heartbeat, in time with the pulsing throbs from the points behind his elbow, ankle, and back.

A click resounded in his mind, and his breathing shifted, becoming less forced. His mind drifted until it aligned with his subconscious mind, and an expanding sensation filled his head.

Tyson opened his inner eye and Saw.

At first the image made no sense. A jumble of angles and curves, swirling with color.

"You're about to be swallowed up, my man!" Lars shouted.

Tyson focused on the bobbing image that seemed to be the creature's face and his vision cleared. The facial features never settled fully, which was dizzying, but he could *see*. Rivulets of lava flowed down narrow crevices around where Tyson lay on a more raised portion of the mountain.

Tyson reached a hand out to Lars, who took it without question. He grinned at Tyson, who nodded, and the two took off down the path, a path that to Tyson's inner vision glowed blue. Could Lars see it? Or had he taken the path enough times to know it was the right one?

The heat barely touched Tyson now. Geometric shapes appeared in the smoke-filled sky and the red-hot lava, shifting, changing, warping Tyson's vision. But if he kept his eyes on the sapphire-lit path, he had no trouble keeping his feet.

Ahead, Lars dodged a flaming boulder that bounced past them and rolled down the mountain, setting fire to the tree line ahead. "Is there anyone who might bear you ill will, by chance? A jilted lover, a sworn enemy?"

"Why do you ask?" Tyson hollered. He racked his brain. Possibly some clients he had pissed off from his time at Camp Silver Lake. But more than likely, if anyone hated him enough to cause turbulence in his subconscious, it was...

A symbol shaped like a fox flashed briefly across Tyson's vision, like those bright spots he saw when he stared at the sun and closed his eyes. A figure stood at the cliff edge that marked the end of the path Lars and Tyson ran down. Her red hair streamed behind her as if made of living flame. Tyson's feet slowed.

"Whoa, whoa, whoa, no stopping. That's a rule, remember?" Lars slowed briefly before wheeling his gangly arms and legs harder to regain momentum.

"You didn't tell me about any rules except don't get killed," Tyson murmured. He pointed. "Who is that?"

Lars looked at Tyson as if he'd lost his mind. "If you're seeing people, this is about to get worse."

Tyson looked again. The woman was still there. He hadn't expected to see anyone other than James or Violet. As soon as he thought of them, they were there, standing next to the woman with the flaming hair. They came forward first. The forms they wore now were somehow different than what they'd been in life. Tyson took a subconscious step backward.

"We should run straight through and ignore them," Lars said to Tyson, eyeing the images warily.

"Are they hallucinations?" Tyson asked.

"Er, no. I don't think they qualify as that. Here, they could kill you."

Violet's hair flowed behind her, and her feet floated above the ground as she came forward. "Tyson Miller, you have blood on your hands."

"I didn't kill you," Tyson shot back. "*You* tried to kill me, if you remember!" He didn't know if this spirit, or whatever she was, if she would remember.

The spirit cocked her head and let out a throaty laugh. James' masculine chuckle joined her.

"Oh no, this isn't about us. But we are tied to it, and therefore we are here," James said. He and Violet floated aside in concert, gesturing toward the young woman with the fiery hair.

Tyson blinked.

Lars nudged his side. "We go now."

"But that's..." He swallowed. "Reya?"

The woman turned a fiery gaze on him. She held something that glinted in the dim light of the flaming mountain. She tossed it at him.

Tyson fumbled the catch at the medallion-like object rolled away from him. Without thinking, he took off after it.

"Stay on the path!" Lars yelled, just as Tyson's foot left the sparkling blue line that marked the path he was supposed to take.

The mountain blew again with a thunderous crack. The rumbling threw Tyson off his feet. He slithered on his belly toward the coin, which glinted innocently a few feet away. His fingers scrabbled in the dirt and he managed to grasp the coin. A 'V' shape was raised on the worn brass surface. He turned to face Reya. The mountain was blank where she had stood. James and Violet stared at him without moving.

Tyson held up the coin. "What does it mean?"

"It won't matter if you die here." Lars hauled him up by the arm and dragged him back to the path. "From my experience, we have exactly one minute before the village is destroyed, and us with it."

Tyson clenched the coin inside his fist and pumped his arms and legs. His steps were out of control fast, skidding and slipping over rocks and ledges. The ridged edges of the coin bit into his skin, but he couldn't think about it now, or what it could mean.

His lungs burned with smoke and exertion. Ahead, through the sparse trees, he saw lean-tos and smaller fires. The villagers sat peering out of the entrances of their tents, staring toward Tyson and Lars. They didn't move. It was as if they didn't see the mountain spitting fire from its peak.

Tyson waved his arms. "Run!"

"They cannot. You must protect them."

Why? Tyson's mind screamed the thought. *Why me?* He couldn't protect anyone. Not Fletcher, not Violet and James, not Harper. Not even himself. Who had thought it a good idea to put him in charge of a whole village?

He gazed into their faces, sweat pouring down his brow. Rivers of lava flowed past him faster than he could run, curving around him, then in toward each other to meet in front of him. He wasn't going to make it in time, but he had to try.

The lava met and pooled into a thicker stream that spilled in the direction of the village. The people watched it coming with wide eyes, holding children close, not a single sound escaping any of them.

Tyson closed his eyes, which did nothing to block his inner sight, and jumped.

He soared in an arc, and for a moment his vision split and he saw from two perspectives—one from his own perspective, high in the air, higher than he'd ever jumped before, somehow defying the law of gravity, the laws of his own biophysics.

The second was that of someone watching him from the village, his face set in determination, his eyes shut tight, his feet angling to land. Despite the filth on his arms, body, and face, Tyson cut an epic image. Something he might have seen on a movie poster.

Then he landed. Rocks spewing, dirt filling his eyes and mouth, forearms, chest and knees scraping the surface of the mountain. He laid face down and waited for the lava to reach his legs and burn him alive.

Instead, a buzzing sound filled his ears, and the silence was broken by the whoops and hollers of the people who were emerging from their tents, clapping and leaping into the air. His eyes blinked open and the geometric patterns faded. His real sight was back.

The peoples' faces and forms changed. Tyson recognized past clients, friends, family—including his parents with tears streaming down their faces. Even Becca and Harper stood in the midst of them.

Tyson sat up, bewildered. A vivid blue dome, like a force-field, surrounded the village. Lava poured around it, an orange-red river that hadn't touched a single tent or being within the circle.

A less-familiar, but still-smiling face emerged from the crowd. His face glittered with tiny rainbows, and his lanky arm reached down to pull Tyson up.

"How are all these people here?" Tyson asked.

"Oh, they aren't really here. But this is how they would feel if they were, I assure you. A fabrication of the test to celebrate your accomplishment. I'm supposed to tell you two things now: the first is, you are not finished here. Clearly, your life has more purpose and meaning than this moment. And second, by surpassing the barriers in your mind to achieve what you have today, you've unlocked a number of abilities, only a fraction of which you've discovered. You may be surprised by some of them. But do not worry, a guide will be sent to you to help you on your path."

"It won't be you, then?" Tyson asked. After everything they'd been through on this mountain, he hoped...

Lars shook his head. "No, I have a job already. I'm flattered, though." And the man winked before loping off and disappearing through the force field. Tyson could barely see his outline as he waded *through* the pooling lava outside.

The crowd around them grew sparse as, one by one, the people Tyson knew and had known blinked out of existence. His parents, Harper, and Becca were last, in addition to a red-haired little girl standing at the edge of the protective force field. As soon as Tyson spotted her, the little girl faded. Why was he seeing Reya? Was this some manifestation of his guilt over her death, or was he supposed to be gaining some new understanding?

His hand cramped and he opened it, looking at the worn coin he held. The 'V' stared back at him.

"Are you what comes next?" he muttered to himself.

When he looked back up again, the figure of Harper stood alone in the center of the clusters of lean-tos. Her wings flared, flapping twice as if to get his attention, and then she pointed down.

A rift stood open in the earth at her feet, just wide enough for a person. Tyson approached her. He looked down, and a faint blue glow emanated from the depths. He drew in a breath.

"Am I supposed to go in there?" Tyson took in Harper's face. It was hard to believe this wasn't her. She looked so real. His hand reached up automatically, touching her cheek. It felt real enough. But the real Harper would have never smiled at his touch the way this image of her did. He let his hand drop. The image blended into the air and disappeared like the others.

Tyson squeezed the coin tight in his fist and knelt down, putting a hand on either side of the crack and sliding his legs into the opening. His feet met nothing but air. He couldn't see whether there was a ledge he was meant to land on, or if he had to drop and trust.

His arms trembled as he hesitated. He took one last look around at the village and the shield he'd somehow created to protect people he thought were strangers. He wanted to sit and ponder the meaning of everything that had happened so far, but the next part of this test awaited him.

"Any last advice?" he said aloud, not sure if the voice would return or not.

"Don't fight it."

"Who are you?" Tyson managed to grunt past the exertion of holding himself up.

"I am he who is in you. I am Nukilik."

Tyson's muscles caved and he released his arms, thrusting them upward and dropping into the crevice. The grey light darkened and turned to a brilliant aqua color. Stalactites made of glittering white crystal hung like icicles from the ceiling of a deep underground cave Tyson plummeted past. Some instinct told him to straighten his legs and cross his arms over his chest, so he did, bracing for an impact.

He struck ice-cold water and went fully under. A current swept him away, dragging him in the undertow. He fought the urge to struggle and try to swim, the words of his grandfather ringing in his ears. *Don't fight it.*

He rushed along with the current, toward whatever fate awaited him.

∞

CHAPTER FIFTEEN

HARPER

HARPER'S FINGERS RAN ALONG a set of claws clamped on her hair. She looked up and to her left. Standing off the path was an impossibly tall woman with rams' horns coming out of her bald head. Her too-wide mouth grinned as a second spindly arm wrapped around Harper and hauled her into the air. She made a guttural clicking sound and glided across the forest floor.

Harper thrashed and squirmed, but the ram-woman adjusted her grip, tightening Harper's position in the pit of her arm. The smell of death mixed with the acrid notes of sweaty socks assaulted Harper's senses so strongly she passed out for a brief moment. At least, she hoped it wasn't longer than that.

The creature muttered and cackled to herself. Around them, the forest was a flurry of distressed bird calls and darting shadows as creatures fled from the long strides of this inhuman thing. A splash resounded on the next step, and the next. Heavy droplets of water struck Harper's legs and face. A dark wide gash in the earth rose ahead, surrounded on either side with stone walls.

The creature hauled Harper into the cave and slammed her on the ground—no, a stone slab—near the center of the cave. Harper cried out at the impact. One of the creature's long claws dug into the center of her chest, as if she were pressing a button to stop the sound, stop Harper's breath, stop her heart.

Harper gasped for air. The tight point in her chest unraveled and her wings unfurled of their own accord, scraping against the rock as they opened, flapping helplessly against the creature's strength. The she-ram had a single finger on Harper, and yet it might as well have been a metal rod through Harper's chest. She stopped struggling, gasping for air. Tears burned in her eyes. She couldn't move. She could hardly breathe. She was never going to get out of here.

The creature chanted in garbled tones, and torches on the walls lit up, giving the cave a dim, flickering light. Mad shadows danced. Harper blinked. The shadows weren't on the walls, they were in the air, flittering creatures making yowling sounds. Shadow beings. She closed her eyes. She was going to die.

She wouldn't see Tyson again, and her death meant he, too, would fail. Their lives had meant nothing, her sacrifice to the Beryllium orb to free the occupants at Camp Silver Lake was a pittance in a world that would never accept her kind. And maybe they shouldn't. Maybe, like this skeletal woman with her inhuman form and her dark magics, there were too many paranormals who wanted to harm rather than live in harmony.

Jars clinked together. Harper squeezed her eyes shut, not wanting to see the end of her life coming. Her wings hung limp, draped over the edges of the stone table. The sensation of a rod in her chest had lessened, but only because she'd grown used to it.

The rock beneath Harper crackled. She opened her eyes to a brighter glow than before. The yellow-orange light hovered around and over her, and heat emanated from below. Harper squirmed, still locked in place despite the fact that the ram-woman's claws had retracted, stroking jars and bottles as she added the contents to a giant stone tub with fire licking the sides.

It was getting uncomfortably hot. The moisture in the air dried up, and the fire at the oxygen almost before Harper could draw it in. She hyperventilated. She was going to suffocate. She turned her head from side to side, gasping for air, her vision spotting. She saw the ram-woman, the fire, the stone tub, and the blueish grey light at the entrance of the cave, ten feet away but it might as well have been miles.

She couldn't move, her arms and legs locked to her sides as if she were bound by invisible cords. She felt like a fish out of water, her wings the only part of her that could fully move, but it hurt to flap them as the bones of her wings scraped and twisted against the stone slab behind her.

The creature heard her pathetic struggling and glided over to her with a single stride, stroking her hair and clicking, the milky white orbs of her eyes visible through her transparent, veiny eyelids when they blinked. She clicked, a guttural sound from the back of her throat, almost as if she were trying to soothe Harper.

"Please, let me go!" Harper meant to yell, but it came out as a raspy gasping attempt to speak.

The ram-woman smiled her too-wide smile, revealing pointed teeth, and stood, leaving Harper feeling as if her flesh were melting into the stone. The heat had grown to a nearly unbearable point. A point near her elbow seared, smoking slightly as the heat bit into her flesh. Harper gritted her teeth and her vision flashed, first dark, as if she'd passed out, and then bright, as if she saw into another world.

Tyson stood in front of her and turned. Could he hear her?

"Tyson!" she screamed. His eyes widened, and then he faded. Harper slumped onto the stone, her energy spent. The spot below her elbow throbbed. Another spot seared against the back of her ankle. Harper groaned, turning her head. Sweat trickled down her brow and sizzled on the stone. The acrid smell of burning feathers reached Harper's nose, and in her blurred state of consciousness it took her a moment to realize *her* feathers were burning.

She thrashed and screamed deep in her throat until her limbs refused to move any longer, and the heat stole the air from her lungs. The ram-woman ignored her.

Delusions took over Harper's mind. Her throat was parched, she couldn't speak, but she whispered.

"Quinn,"

The ram-woman ran a finger along Harper's forehead, then brought the finger to her mouth and licked it. Harper shuddered, feeling feverish. The stone table branded a spot near her shoulder blade, below her wing. A trail of smoke went up into the air above Harper's head, and her ears filled with the sound of feathers rustling.

"You nearly took too long. You have the ingredients?" The low-pitched voice came from the ram-woman. Harper didn't know if she was hallucinating again or if the woman had been able to speak this entire time, but had chosen not to.

"It's overcooked," the light, airy female voice said with disdain. Harper's head rolled to one side. Her eyelids slitted open and she saw white figures like angels, snowy wings spread, noses pointed like beaks, hands and feet black and scaled with talons instead of fingers. The four of them stared at Harper.

"Black sister," one of them murmured. A third figure handed a bundle to the ram-woman.

"You serve me," the ram-woman hissed, stretching to her full height. Her head scraped the ceiling, and her white eyes flashed blue. The four angelic bird-women huddled together and hooted anxiously. The ram-woman snatched the bundle and tore it open, dumping the contents into the stone tub. Harper heard liquid bubbling, and the slick sound of a knife on stone being sharpened. Her stomach clenched and heaved.

The ram-woman raised the knife, admiring the edge. She aimed it at Harper's mid-section, and a pointed tongue slithered along her lips.

Harper felt the Song build before it released. She opened her mouth and launched the notes into the air, but her voice was merely a hoarse keening, nothing like the vibrant melody she'd woven before.

A screech interrupted her attempt, like an owl's, and two of the white bird-women launched themselves at the ram-woman. Their talons gouged at her milk-white eyes. Harper's shut her eyes. Talons scraped her sides, and one plunged into her chest at her sternum.

She gasped, eyes shooting open, and she bolted upright, grasping at the blood that flooded from her torso. Claws gripped her shoulders and lifted her, pushing her to the floor. She lay there, sprawled helplessly, her skin burning against the cooler stone. Her hands pressed against the floor, but her muscles gave out under the slightest amount of effort.

Talons on her shoulders again, and another pair scraped her low back as they dug into the waistband of her jeans. Wingbeats accompanied the shrieks from the ram-woman, blood-curdling yells and curses spilling into the cave. Harper lifted into the air, her wings fluttering uselessly as they dragged in the dirt.

The bird-women soared with her into the cold Alaskan night. Harper shivered and trembled so much she thought the women might drop her. They flew and flew, the trees and ground a blur below. Harper passed out and woke to the ground drawing nearer and nearer, and then the women did drop her, and the skin on her face felt as if it peeled off as she skidded to a stop.

A figure in white crouched beside her. "We will tend your wounds, but then we must leave you. We have broken our contract with the sorceress and she will hunt us. We have sent a signal to the Raven, he knows of your survival."

Harper groaned in response. Gentle hands removed her clothes, rubbed a substance on her burns and scrapes, coating her face. Every touch made Harper want to scream. She withdrew deep inside her mind, to a place where she went when she dreamed. It only masked the pain.

Leaves pressed into her wounds, wrapped deftly by experienced hands. Four kisses marked Harper's brow, and murmured apologies, before the sound of beating wings filled the air, and then silence. Crickets chirped, and beneath their melody the land thrummed.

Drums?

Harper drifted into sleep, her pain momentarily soothed. She thought she heard wings again, and a croaking, low voice inquiring, but she couldn't muster the energy to understand the words, much less respond.

When she woke, the ground still throbbed with a far-off rhythm. Her limbs felt stiff, her skin stretched sharply, as if it were splitting. Gasping, Harper paused. She drew her wings in, then rolled over with a sudden motion, her yell startling birds from their nighttime roost. Her eyes took in the barely visible stars. The sky was brightening to a washed-out navy blue, almost grey, with pink tinging the edges. Dawn was coming. She would fail in her task.

Blank shadowy faces surrounded her. Long, transparent fingers trailed on her face and arms, and murmurs filled the air. Shadow people. Friends or foes?

A red gash opened in the face of the one near her head, and a half-dozen rows of teeth gleamed at her. It chittered loudly and leaned in toward Harper.

Near-death or not, her survival instinct was intact. Her body screamed for her to run. She managed to bolt upright, scattering the short shadow men. The nearest shadow bit her arm and she yelled, beating the creature against the ground until it let go, her blood coating its rows of teeth. She released her wings against the pain, though it was much less than before.

Something the owl-women had done to her had accelerated the healing of her wounds. Most of them. Some of her feathers had melted together, others fell out and drifted to the ground as she flapped her wings. Could she fly? There was only one way to find out.

The shadow men had scattered when her wings flared out, but now they crept forward. Harper ran at them, yelling and beating her wings. They fled back a few feet and she leapt, her wings catching the air. One side dipped dangerously. She fought to stay upright and failed, crashing to the ground in a gasping heap. She pushed to her feet again. Hands tugged on the edges of her wings, dragging her back down. She knelt, head lowered as she breathed.

What was the point of this whole supposed quest if she was going to die now? One of the men approached her, the one with blood still staining its teeth, the only feature visible on its dark, oblong face. It stroked her face, her nose, her brow, and then it transformed before her eyes.

Its shadow skin paled, became fleshy, grew in a blobby, disproportionate way until the features rearranged into something Harper recognized.

Her own face.

The body changed too, mimicking her crouch, getting every detail accurate down to the wound marks and scars and the fact that she wore no clothes. Brown eyes stared into hers. It reached a hand up, touched her forehead, and then phased through her skull. Harper's eyes rolled back. She felt the shadow creature sifting through her memories until it found what it wanted, memories of her parents she barely remembered herself. The mentions of the tribe she sought in order to be reunited with her people.

The shadow-Harper removed its hand. Harper's vision returned to normal, watching the other version of herself grin and launch itself into the air while its companions swarmed her. Where was it going? Did it know where the tribe was? Would it reach them before her?

Harper dug her hands into the ground, small rocks and dirt tumbling between her fingers. She clenched her teeth, and as the shadow form of herself flew away, becoming no more than a dark speck against the brightening sky, she faced the demons that surrounded her with the determination that she would either defeat them and follow the one that had stolen her image, or she would die here, in the land of her ancestors.

CHAPTER SIXTEEN

QUINN

THE FIRE STILL FLICKERED behind him, distant now. Quinn knelt at the edge of the clearing, his wings pulled tight to his back to keep the cold from creeping under his skin. He'd come out here to breathe—to think—but the weight of the vision he'd seen still churned in his chest like molten stone.

Washington D.C. burning. Himself, a stranger with bloodied hands. A war he didn't understand.

He rubbed his face, palms cold against his eyes. How could he lead anyone, let alone the Tulukaruq tribe? How could he make choices about life and death when everything inside him screamed that he wasn't ready?

A sound made him freeze. Twigs crackled softly in the near-darkness.

He dropped his hands and looked up. At first, he thought the figure stumbling toward him was a trick of the twilight—a shadow that didn't quite belong. Then the shape solidified, and his breath caught in his throat.

"Harper?"

She emerged from the dim light, ghostlike. Her dark hair hung limp, tangled across her face, and her shredded clothes fluttered around her in strips. She moved unsteadily, arms wrapped tightly around herself. The firelight from the distant bonfire barely touched her, but Quinn saw enough to know something was wrong.

"Quinn..." Her voice was a whisper, hoarse and thin, as if it had been scraped raw.

He scrambled to his feet, closing the distance between them. "Harper! You—" He stopped just short of touching her, his gaze sweeping over her appearance. "What happened? How did you—? Your clothes—"

"Shhh." She raised a single finger and pressed it to his lips, her skin colder than ice.

Quinn flinched at the contact, blinking rapidly. She wasn't acting like herself. Her movements were slow, deliberate, too calm.

"I'm here now," she said softly, that insipid smile curving across her pale lips. "That's all that matters, isn't it?"

"Harper, where have you been? Are you hurt? You—"

She swayed slightly, and instinctively Quinn reached out to steady her. "Come on. Let's get you out of the cold. I'll take you back to the fire."

She nodded faintly, her hair slipping over her face like a curtain. Quinn hesitated, feeling that same strange unease twist his stomach again, but pushed it aside. It's Harper, he told himself. It has to be Harper.

She let him guide her forward, shuffling as if walking pained her.

As they neared the tribe, the pounding drums and flickering firelight grew louder. The music felt almost jarring now, too alive and celebratory compared to the hollow quiet of the clearing Quinn had left behind. He led Harper toward the fire, feeling eyes turn to them as they entered the ring of warmth.

Chief Aguta was the first to rise. His sharp gaze fell on Harper, and Quinn worried the chief might see what Quinn hadn't yet grasped—what gnawed at him beneath the surface.

"Is this her?" The chief asked.

Quinn swallowed past the tightness in his throat, glancing at Harper before responding. "Yes?"

He hadn't meant for it to come out sounding like a question, but the chief didn't seem to notice.

Their grandfather's face softened, and he lifted his arms. "Welcome, granddaughter. You've returned to us."

Harper straightened slightly, her lips parting into that same eerie, too-bright smile. "You must be hungry," Aguta continued.

"Famished," she replied, her tone light and cheerful as she slipped into a seat on the chief's right.

Quinn blinked. That was quick. Harper looked like she'd crawled through hell, and yet she beamed as if this were the most natural place in the world for her to be. He remained standing for a moment longer, watching her as food and water were brought before her.

The tribe resumed their music and dancing, the fire roaring high into the night sky, but Quinn couldn't shake the strangeness settling like a stone in his chest.

Harper ate with a fierce, ravenous energy, tearing into the food before her. Quinn turned his head away quickly, embarrassed for her. Harper had never been one to care much about propriety, but this—this wasn't like her. None of it was.

He dropped into his seat near the chief, still watching her carefully, the fire reflecting in her storm-gray eyes. Why wasn't she asking about Becca? And where was Tyson? Why wasn't she furious, or sarcastic, or... anything that felt like Harper?

Something in his gut whispered that the sister sitting before him wasn't quite right.

But he didn't want to believe it.

Quinn picked at a bowl of berries, listening to Chief Aguta tell her many of the same things he had told Quinn earlier. Harper nodded and smiled at the right places, but none of her strong opinions surfaced, and she never mentioned Tyson once. Had the man been killed or had they separated? How had she found the tribe?

"I have a gift for both of you." Chief Aguta stood and kissed his wife on the cheek when she brought him the wooden box Quinn had seen him with earlier. He opened the lid, then gestured for Quinn and Harper to stand. They obeyed, Quinn glancing at Harper from the corner of his eyes. Something about the way she stepped out of the firelight and into the chief's shadow unnerved him.

"I have gathered these pieces from all over this land. Each one represents what I hope you will have in your life among our people: Prosperity. Honor. Love. Belonging." He drew out black cords, on which dangled a few beads, and stones.

On one cord, a tiny skull charred black. On the other, a raven's inky, clawed foot. The chief placed the skull one over Harper's head, and the foot one over Quinn's. The amulet rested on Quinn's bare chest, clunky and awkward. The claws scratched against his skin.

Quinn fingered a turquoise colored stone. "Thank you," he murmured.

"I do not know which of you will step into my place. Only you know if you have been called by Raven to lead his warriors and protect his people. But I know you will both make me proud." Chief Aguta smiled at them both, but his eyes lingered on Quinn.

"Now," Chief Aguta spoke again. "For the final part of the ceremony. Should you choose to remain among us, you will be named, loved, and celebrated all of your days. Should you choose otherwise, your names will be forgotten, never to be spoken among us again. Accept the name which we offer, and you will be one of us."

"Stop!" A hoarse voice cried from the darkness. A bedraggled figure from beyond the ring of villagers dragged itself forward. The crowd parted to let it through.

Wings trailing over dirt and rock, feathers sticking up or missing, blood trickling from wounds on her wings, arms, legs, torso and face, another Harper rose to her feet. As she stood, she drew her wings in close around her to cover her naked body. She shivered and swayed. Her hair matted to her face with blood on one side. She raised an arm between her wings and pointed at the doppelganger standing beside Quinn.

"That's... not me."

The other Harper smiled again, and Quinn knew without question this couldn't be his sister. She dropped the blanket someone had given her to the ground and laughed.

Claws grew from her hands. She shortened, then lengthened into a tall, skinny shadow with a red gash for a mouth.

"Shadow walker!" Someone screamed, and pandemonium broke out. The shadow walker reached for Chief Aguta. The chief raised one piece of the amulet he wore and bellowed a word that rang with power. A blast of white light expanded from the carved bone piece. The shadow walker hissed and slunk away, circling around. It swiped at a woman, its claws catching her wing and tearing into the feathers. The woman screamed and fell.

Quinn mustered his strength, beating his wings and leaping into the air. He aimed his legs at the shadow creature, expecting to go through its intangible flesh, but he made contact and the creature stumbled, falling away from the injured woman.

Harper reached the fire and took a burning branch from the pile in the pit. She raised it up for Quinn to see and he soared over to take it from her. She looked so thin, and her injuries were extensive. How had she survived the journey to the tribe this way?

"Fire will kill it, I think," she muttered. She sat on the ground in a heap of feathers and flesh, eyes squeezed shut in pain.

"Ahnah!" Quinn yelled. The woman left the group of younger women she had been herding away from the monster. Her hand flew to her mouth at the sight of Harper.

"I am so sorry. I should have attended her. I will make her safe. Go!" his grandmother insisted. She knelt at Harper's side and spoke in low tones. As Quinn turned away, he heard her bark instructions at a passing man who held a spear in his hand.

Quinn saw others gathering, amulets in hand, wicked-looking spears in their other. Some had amulets attached to their spears as well, and they sprang toward the shadow walker below Quinn, jabbing into its legs and sides with sparks of light.

Quinn adjusted his grip on the branch Harper had handed him and flew at the monster. It turned as he came and batted him aside with its massive clawed hand. Quinn soared through the air, managing to catch himself mid-flight. He had dropped the branch, but he still had the amulet Chief Aguta had given him. He just didn't know how to use it.

He grasped the raven foot, then dropped it as if it had burned him. It felt... wrong. He tried another, a marbled stone bead, and it, too, felt wrong. He didn't feel anything when he touched the bone, but when his hand brushed a carved bit of wood, a surge of power entered his body. That one.

He dove for the shadow walker. It had shrunk to half its initial size, but it still had an insane amount of strength, and each blow and claw sent another warrior to the ground. Quinn held out the amulet and closed his eyes. He collided with the shadow walker.

A beam of greenish-blue light shot into the shadow creature's chest and it exploded. The ribbon of light shot into the air, painting an iconic picture in the Alaskan night sky that Quinn had seen many times in books, but never in person.

The colors danced. Quinn swore he could hear someone singing. The ringing in his ears faded and the light vanished. An object fell through the air, and Quinn swept down and snatched it. The amulet meant for Harper.

He tilted his wings and flew to meet the two small figures beside the dying fire below.

"How is she?" he said breathlessly as he landed.

Ahnah's round face held a frown. "She is not responsive. I need to get her to our healer's tent."

"I'll carry her," Quinn offered. They wrapped a blanket around Harper and Quinn picked her up, placing the amulet on the blanket over her chest. She felt like nothing in his arms, but positioning himself around her injured wings was awkward. He tried not to step on them as they dragged on the ground. Ahnah led them to a more dome-like tent and gestured for Quinn to follow.

He ducked through the entrance, letting his own wings draw inside his body to create more space inside the tent. Ahnah, too, did not wear her wings out, though the woman who greeted them inside did.

"Lay her down here. Roll her onto her stomach. Hold the blanket."

Quinn knelt beside a bed of furs and carefully turned Harper over onto her stomach, his own clenching at the sight of her wounds. He winced when he saw her back. Faint burn scars, including three darker circular marks at her back, elbow, and ankle in rune-like shapes. Quinn bit his lip and touched one, ever so gently.

"I will tend to her," the woman said. She had owlishly large eyes, and to Quinn's surprise, glasses. She held a pot in her hand and a rag in the other, a look of determination on her face.

"Where should I go?" Quinn asked.

"Get some sleep, perhaps? I will send someone to wake you when she wakes."

Ahnah cleared her throat. "We've prepared a space for you in our family tent."

Quinn stood, dragging his eyes away from his sister's wounded body, and left the tent with Ahnah, the sound of the healer-woman's chants fading behind the closed tent flap.

Quinn scrubbed at his eyes. The sun had risen high above the mountain top in the distance.

"It's morning?" Quinn asked, confused.

Ahnah nodded. "Meriwa will heal your sister. Her hands are deft and her knowledge wide. She has studied with some of the greatest dreamwalkers in the land."

"Can I visit Becca?" Quinn asked suddenly, his eyes landing on the tent at the far edge of the community, barely visible through the haze that seemed to settle in front of his eyes.

Ahnah's hands rested on his shoulders and steered him in the other direction.

"You should rest first, I think. There will be time for that."

"You won't let the chief decide anything now?"

"No, I will not. My husband is resting also. Nothing will be decided until rest and food have been offered." The woman exuded calm, her hands relaxed at her sides, her gaze steady.

"Thank you." Quinn's eyes suddenly filled with tears. Ahnah's head tilted and she smiled at him in a grandmotherly expression he had never known before. She stepped forward and embraced him.

He felt like a giant compared to this small woman. He worried he would break her, but she squeezed him tightly without inhibitions and he hugged her back.

"Now, then, get some sleep." She sniffed and wiped a tear away. Quinn let his arms fall away from her and backed up, ducking inside the tent.

It was empty but for a bed of firs on the fresh dirt floor, the surface stamped down and hardened with clay. There was a large clay jar, like a pitcher of sorts, with water inside, and a wide flat bowl. Perhaps for washing. Quinn ignored it. He kicked his shoes off and collapsed into the bed, burrowing beneath the covers and falling asleep the moment his head rested.

A rustling sound woke Quinn. His eyelids cracked open, crusted and heavy. His head pounded.

"The virtue of Raven is not so easy to handle, is it?"

"What?" He groaned and put a hand to his head.

"You drank and you channeled Raven's power through your amulet." Through cracked eyes he recognized Ahnah placing a tray beside him on the floor. She handed him a cup. "Only water. Drink."

He had so many questions about what she'd said about using Raven's power and the amulet he wore, but he needed to drink first. Quinn sipped experimentally. None of that sour brew from the night before. He gulped down the freshest, coldest water he'd ever had, and lay back on the pillow for a second before sitting up.

"Harper?"

"She is well enough. Eat." Ahnah passed him a flat, pale brown bread that smelled fried.

Quinn picked it up and felt something sticky. "Honey?"

Ahnah smiled and indicated a bowl on the plate. "Also some blueberries picked this morning. And the cooked meat for strength."

Quinn ate as directed. "I will say, your food is the best here."

"Most years, it is. We trade for some things, like flour." She indicated the bread he was biting into.

Quinn nodded, his mouth too full to respond. He licked his fingers and finished the rest of the food, energy returning to his limbs as the food settled. He followed Ahnah out of the tent and stretched his wings and arms.

"Would you like to see your sister?" Ahnah asked. Quinn noticed her wings were not in view, which surprised him. Nearly everyone kept theirs out all the time here. It would take getting used to, having to hide his wings his entire life.

"Of course. Is she awake?"

"I believe so."

They made their way through the village. Women crouched by fires, stoking them to life so their breakfast would cook. He even spotted a few gas stoves and other modernizations. They even had a small row of outhouses at the edge of the village, which Quinn visited before they reached the healer's tent.

"Her mind is a bit muddled from the herbs she's been given for the pain," Ahnah instructed. "Be gentle with her."

"I will," Quinn promised. He moved the tent flap out of the way and stepped inside, bringing his wings tightly against his back to avoid knocking anything over. The healer knelt on the floor beside a low stone table, mixing herbs and putting them into jars and bowls, grinding them with a rounded stick made of stone.

She adjusted her wide-brimmed glasses and gave Quinn a friendly smile, then looked to Harper. "You have a visitor."

Harper stirred, turning her head to face Quinn. Her expression didn't change. He knelt and took her hand in his, but confusion crossed her face and she tugged the hand away.

"Harper, it's me."

"You know Becca," she said, her voice a quiet croak.

"Yes, I do." Quinn's brow furrowed. "How do you feel?"

"Terrible."

Quinn couldn't help smiling. "So much happened the past few days, it's hard to know where to start."

Harper shook her head. She reached up to touch it, and her frown deepened. Her brown eyes stared Quinn down with a hard, determined expression. "Look, am I supposed to know you?"

Quinn rocked back on his heels, his wings flaring out to balance himself. "What do you mean?"

Harper looked at the far tent wall, fingers picking at the blanket over her. "There's a... hole in my mind. All the memories are gone. I just...I don't know what or who is supposed to fill them." She turned back to Quinn, and the vulnerable version he had known when she was a child peered at him through her gaze. "Is it you?"

Quinn's head jerked, as if he'd been slapped. His breathing constricted. He had to focus on a bundle of dried herbs that dangled from the ceiling before he collected himself enough to answer. He licked his lips. "I'm your brother. Our parents are Mick and Anna."

"I was an only child," Harper insisted.

"No," Quinn whispered. He licked his lips and put his hand back over hers. "No, you weren't. You're not. We have always had each other. I don't know what happened, but I swear to you, we are family."

Harper's eyes filled with tears. She looked to Ahnah, who stood behind Quinn, then to the healer. "Do either of you know if what he's saying is true?"

Ahnah moved forward, standing next to the bed. "It is. I am the mother of your father. You have a family, Harper. We are here with you now."

"I don't know how to be part of a family." And at that, Quinn's bold, fearless sister burst into tears. Her entire body shook with hoarse sobs. She sat up, thankfully clothed. "I'm sorry. I'm so sorry."

The healer rushed over with a clean rag and handed it to her. Harper blew her nose, wiping it. She looked at Quinn with red-rimmed eyes.

He did the only thing he could think of. He reached out and embraced her. Her shoulder blades stuck out beneath the leather vest she wore. She seemed so small and frail, and yet, from what he'd witnessed last night, she was stronger than anyone he knew. The part of him that had protected her through their childhood and never stopped searching for her when they got separated, it relaxed. He felt at ease. He would help her remember. They could create new memories here in the safety of the village. Everything was right in the world. Everything except—

A faint scream split the morning air. Quinn released Harper, whose eyes had widened. She threw off her covers, but the healer laid a firm hand on Harper's thigh. "You will stay here. We have plenty of able-bodied warriors who can investigate the sound." Her brow creased, and she looked toward the entrance of the tent.

Another scream. And a yell. A clatter of logs falling. A tent collapse, perhaps? And then a word Quinn had heard before.

"Namigiak!"

He scrambled to his feet and bolted for the door. At Ahnah's cry he turned around. "It's Becca. I'm sorry, I have to—"

"Go," Ahnah urged him. His last glance took in Harper's confused and frightened gaze.

"I'll be back," he said.

The tent door disintegrated before his eyes, sizzling with an acrid stench as a thick grey substance dripped from it. Becca burst through, her long, serpentine body writhing and smashing into the walls. The beams creaked.

"Get Harper out of here!" Quinn shouted, backing up. His wings flared out, blocking them from view. "Becca, it's me."

She hissed in response, fangs dripping, eyes narrow and yellow. Nothing human left in her gaze. Her entire body was covered with scales. Her shirt hung in tatters around her torso.

Quinn crouched, ready to spring and wrestle her to the ground if she moved. She slithered to the left, then darted to the right underneath his wings and struck.

Ahnah called out. Quinn pivoted and grabbed Becca around her middle, the scales sliding out from under his grip as she twisted and writhed. He threw her to the side, barely able to manage her full weight with his supernatural strength. She wound herself up, ready to strike again, spitting acid.

Quinn dodged and surged forward, and Becca struck at him. He jumped, crashing into a shelf of medicines against the side wall. The serpent's tail whipped around, catching his legs and he fell. Becca raised herself to the full extent of her height possible in the tent, tongue flicking out.

Behind Quinn, Ahnah groaned and lay slumped on the floor, a deep bite wound in her shoulder trickling blood and a grey liquid.

"Enough, pet," a male voice came from the ruined entrance. Quinn glanced over and saw the middle-eastern photographer, Avaan, stride in holding a blue flute in his hands. He smiled when he noticed Quinn.

"Ah yes, excellent. We've been looking for the chief, but you'll do nicely. He's sure to come here when he realizes his grandson and heir is in danger."

"What do you want with him?" Quinn growled.

"Only to petition for our freedom."

"He would have given it to you without violence."

"Perhaps. Perhaps not. The thing is, even you don't know what the chief is thinking about our friend here." Avaan gestured to Becca.

Ahnah moaned again. Her color had paled, and her breathing appeared shallow.

"What part do you have in this?" Quinn demanded, climbing to his feet. "Did you agitate her? Force her to turn?"

Avaan walked over to Becca and stroked her scales, an admiring look on his face. "My ancestors have ruled over the lamia for centuries. I am merely reclaiming my birthright. Together we will rebuild the serpentine empire that was lost when her kind were hunted nearly to extinction."

He looked to Quinn. "You're fortunate that I hold the means to controlling the deadly specimen before you. This ability had all but disappeared as heirlooms became artifacts and the graves of my ancestors were pillaged by archaeologists and cryptozo-ologists. Their skeletons were stolen in the name of science, put into museums, ravaged. I thought they were gone, and I mourned the loss of our power, our position in society as the strongest warriors, the most respected leaders. Until I met her,"

Becca's tongue flickered. She lowered down, her tail coiling until she stood at a more human-height.

Shouting grew louder outside the tent.

"The warriors are coming. You'll never withstand all of them," Quinn said.

"You underestimate the power of the lamia. A single one in the hands of a charmer can take out armies. We will walk out of here unscathed. You and your people?" Avaan clicked his tongue. "It's a shame, truly. How about you go out to meet your grandfather? I'll come with you to make sure you don't try anything, and Becca will keep these women company. You can help me negotiate for our freedom."

Quinn's mind reeled, searching for a solution. How to inca-pacitate Avaan and take possession of that flute without making Becca go mad and hurt anyone else? Nothing came to mind. If only he had more time.

Avaan gestured and Quinn reluctantly followed, the two men emerging from the tent at the same time.

Avaan spread his arms. "Welcome. You are just in time."

"What have you done?" Chief Aguta snarled.

"I have awakened the bond between a lamia and her charmer. I am the only one who can control her."

"Then we will kill you both." The chief took hold of the amulet on his chest, and the others did the same. "Raven will protect us."

Avaan scoffed. "Your heathen god will not interfere. Even if he does, I have gods with me as well, and the power of the lamia at my side. How many of your men must die today? I will tell you the answer: none."

"What of Ahnah?" Quinn hissed. His fists clenched. "She will not survive the poison, unless you have an antidote."

"Let us free and we will not harm another being on your land. Provisions and supplies to survive the wilderness, safe passage guaranteed. That is all I ask."

"What's this about Ahnah?" The chief turned to Quinn, his face paling.

"I do feel badly about that," Avaan said. "The lamia became overeager after being trapped so long. I let her out on too long a leash, perhaps, but now you can see what we are capable of."

The chief stood straight-backed, his tone firm. "The antidote, or you die where you stand."

"You may kill me," Avaan said, smirking, "but she will destroy many lives in her madness when you do. Lamia cannot control themselves, they can only be controlled by one of my blood with an instrument of power." He patted the blue flute hanging on the cord around his neck.

"We will carry you both into the sky and watch your entrails paint the rocks unless you provide an antidote," Chief Aguta threatened. Quinn shifted.

Avaan visibly swallowed. His voice took on a less haughty tone. "I never intended for anyone to be harmed. Listen, in my bag I have an antidote—an attempt at an antidote. I made it as a precaution for myself, should things go wrong, but I would be willing to give it to you for the woman if you will hold to your end. My things, provisions, and your word we will travel safely."

"We can't just allow you to leave with her. With Becca. Let her go," Quinn said.

"Quinn," the chief barked. Quinn tore his eyes from Avaan. His grandfather shook his head. "This is the best option for everyone. She is beyond your help now."

"She deserves to be with someone who sees her as human, not as an animal to be controlled," Quinn clenched his fists.

The chief's face softened. "She deserves to be understood for what she is. She is no longer human. She is no longer the human she was when you met her. Can you bring yourself to see that this will be best for our people and best for the lamia?"

Quinn looked at Avaan, hating the desperate tightness in his chest. "What will you do with her?"

"I will take her back to my country. She will live a luxurious life, I assure you."

"But as a prisoner."

Avaan shrugged, as if there were nothing he could do about it. As if he had no choice. As if he had any right to make that decision for Becca. "I hope she will come to like me. Perhaps even love me. It is the way of our people."

"She will never love you, not after you've sought to control her. She deserves to be free." Quinn's voice rose. From inside the tent, he heard a hiss.

Avaan motioned with his hands for Quinn to lower his voice. "You will agitate her into attacking. I need to return to her. Our bond is new and relatively unstable, but I assure you, she will be happier with me, in time. There is no cure for the curse of the lamia."

Quinn looked away from him. He wanted to hate Avaan, wanted to blame him for what had happened to Becca. But more than anything, he didn't want to accept that his time with her was over.

"Bring the snake charmer's things," Chief Aguta commanded one of the warriors. He rushed forward. "I must see my wife."

Avaan nodded. "I will come with you. The serpent will not harm you, you have my word. Bring your warriors, if you wish."

A wild, screeching yell came from the tent. "Harper," Quinn murmured. The three men bolted into the tent. Quinn's breath came ragged. He saw Harper standing on her bed, throwing pots at the serpent. They exploded with clouds of herbs and dripping liquids. The healer lay sprawled on the ground, a bloody gash on her head. Quinn couldn't tell if she, too, had been poisoned or wounded.

Becca swayed and spat at Harper, who wielded a pot lid like a shield.

Quinn reeled around, spotting Avaan. "Do something!"

Avaan hurriedly put the blue flute to his lips and played a tune. Becca's eyes closed. She swayed, lowering to the ground until she had fully curled up and appeared to sleep.

Quinn rushed to Harper's side as she swayed, catching her in his arms. They both stared at the sleeping Lamia, and Quinn glanced at Avaan. A tiny smile played at the edge of the charmer's lips as they curved around the instrument that controlled the violent serpent Becca had become. Quinn hated himself for the relief he felt. He should have fought harder, should have found a way to help her instead of giving up.

Quinn turned away toward the opening of the hut, helping Harper walk steady. Behind him, the music stopped for an instant, and Quinn stiffened.

"She doesn't need you anymore," Avaan said quietly, the sincerity in his voice piercing Quinn's chest with the truth of his words.

Quinn straightened his back, walking out of the hut and into the sun. His heart clenched in a tight ball of pain that he tried his best to hide, but Harper looked at him and in her eyes, he could see that part of her understood.

CHAPTER SEVENTEEN

BECCA

BECCA DRAGGED HERSELF OUT of a stupor that coated her like a blanket. A thick, itchy blanket that she never wanted to wear again.

It wasn't a blanket, but a dress, made of animal skin pieces that scratched against her skin with every movement. She sat up from the ground and her head spun.

"Who knocked me out *that* time?" she said crossly, holding her head in both hands. No one answered, and she realized she was alone. It didn't last. A dark-haired, dark-skinned figure ducked through the hut entrance and smiled a familiar, alluring smile.

Avaan.

"Guilty," he said, waving a sheepish hand. "But to be fair, you almost killed Quinn's grandmother, so—"

"What?" Becca shrieked and stood up.

"Now, now, don't excite yourself. Stress-induced transformation is something we want to avoid. I don't want to put you under again. It's such a shame. Even if you are lovely while you're sleeping." Avaan stroked the flute against his chest.

"It was *you*?" She stepped closer, clenching her fists. "How come I don't remember? What else did you make me forget?" She couldn't remember another time she'd felt this furious.

"It was the transformation, love."

Becca recoiled. "Don't call me that."

Avaan reached for her, a concerned look creasing his face.

"Don't touch me, either. Where's Quinn?"

"With his sister."

Becca sat back down. She expected a bed, but realized before her behind hit the hard ground that there hadn't been one. Just a bundled up coat on the packed dirt floor where she'd lain moments before. She sat in the prison-hut she'd shared with Avaan before. Or had she been returned to it?

Avaan's eyebrows drew together. He reached down to help her up, but she slapped his hands away.

Becca put her hands over her eyes and rubbed them. "Let me get this straight. I transformed and tried to kill someone. Quinn's grandmother? And you...you used that flute thing to what, subdue me? Put me to sleep? Who are you?"

"I am Avaan Mansur. You might call me a snake charmer. We are the *Muluk Altheaebin*. For centuries my people bonded with the race of Lamia and made our armies, and our families, to-gether. Now we can renew the traditions and powers we shared in the past." He clasped his hands together over his chest, eyes wide and hopeful.

Hopeful that she'd share his perspective? That she'd rejoice at the prospect of slavery, even if it did mean some sort of status or wealth in his culture?

"You're nuts. I never wanted anything less than what you've suggested. I'm not going anywhere with you."

He froze, hands dropping, expression sinking. "You don't have much choice. If you don't stay with me, the serpent will consume you and you will die a violent death at the hands of your enemies." He spat on the floor.

Becca's stomach clenched. She shook her head. "No, there's another way. There has to be."

"He's right, Becca." Quinn's voice floated across to her from the doorway, more subdued than she'd ever heard it. "More people will get hurt if we don't... if you don't listen to him." His eyes were downcast, and he seemed to have trouble making eye contact.

Becca pushed off her hands, getting to her feet and crossing the room. As she neared Quinn, however, he flinched away.

"I see." Becca tucked her matted hair behind one ear and clasped her hands together. "What does that mean for..." She stopped herself from finishing her sentence.

"Becca, if things were different, if there was a way to fix..." He ran a hand through his long, beautifully dark hair in that frustrated way Becca had come to see as sexy. Now the sensation that pulsed through her was a heavy pain, like her heart was being squeezed. Whatever had happened, whatever she didn't remember, it had changed things between them.

"There has to be a way to break this curse. I mean, it was a mummy that gave me this stupid scratch," She gestured to her scaled arm. She had a full sleeve of scales now, all the way up to her shoulder. "Mummies have curses, and curses can be broken."

"The gift of the Lamia is not a curse," Avaan insisted. "There is nothing to break. You're perfect."

Based on the wounded look in Quinn's eyes, he didn't see it that way. He would never see it that way.

"I'm a monster," Becca hissed. It startled her how snake-like the sound was. She bit her own tongue, to make sure it was human. The tang of blood coated her mouth. She swallowed and straightened the animal skin gown she wore. "I won't stop until I find a cure, Quinn. You have to believe me."

He looked at her, the sadness in his brown eyes deepening the pain in Becca's heart. "If anyone could find a cure, it would be you. But I can't... I don't think..."

"You're thinking of staying," Becca realized out loud. "Aren't you?"

He sighed. "Not forever. But at first... probably."

"I guess having a half-snake girlfriend wouldn't fly. Especially..." She swallowed hard and licked her lips. "Especially after what I almost did. Is your grandmother going to be okay?"

"Avaan had a remedy. It seems to be working. We won't know for sure until tomorrow when she wakes up."

Becca heard the unspoken *or not*. Her palms felt sweaty. She'd never been responsible for almost ending someone's life. "Look, I'm sorry," she said desperately.

Quinn shook his head. "You couldn't help it. That's why you're leaving with him." He jutted his chin—that handsome, square jaw—toward Avaan.

Avaan shouldered the duffle bag he arrived at the airport with and gestured to Becca. "Come. With me, you can learn of your abilities and thrive in a place with people who appreciate you for all that you are and will become."

"I—" Becca looked to Quinn, who nodded once, then glanced away.

"He made a deal with the chief," Quinn said. "You're free to go. And I think you should."

"If that's what you think." Becca said haltingly, unable to keep the hurt from her voice. She took one step toward Avaan, and then another. She didn't know what she wanted. She didn't want to die, which she surely would here at the hands of the raven tribe. But she didn't want to leave Quinn, either.

"You found Harper?" she asked.

Again, that silent nod. Becca did her best to smile, emotion like a rock in her throat.

"I'm glad for you. What about Tyson?"

Quinn cleared his throat. "He wasn't with her. She mentioned something about a bear-man cutting a hole in the sky and pushing Tyson into another dimension. I don't know what that's about, and we don't know what's become of him. I'm sorry I can't give you better news."

"If..." She corrected herself. "*When* he shows up, could you tell him about me? And tell him hello for me, and that I'm sorry I couldn't be here?" Her voice wavered and Becca had to shut her mouth tight and breathe deeply to stay in control. She folded her arms tight over her chest, as if she could hold the bursting dam of emotion inside.

Faint shouting came from outside. Quinn opened his mouth to reply to her, and then her brow creased. He darted out, and Avaan and Becca followed.

A figure lay on the bank of the river running along the edge of the village. His nearly naked body shivered, only a scrap of filthy cloth at his waist.

"Tyson!" Becca shrieked and ran to him. Half a dozen men with spears sprinted forward and surrounded her, blocking her path.

"You don't understand! He's family. My cousin," Becca insisted.

"Let her through," Quinn barked. The men exchanged con-fused looks, but parted, and Becca ran to Tyson's side. His hair was damp and plastered against his face. Becca moved it aside, taking his face in her hands. His skin was like ice, but his chest rose and fell, so she didn't need to try CPR. She gave his shoulder a gentle shake.

"Tyson? If you can hear me, open your eyes. Do anything." The stress of the past few days broke past the dam inside and tears flowed hot down her face.

Quinn crouched beside her, examining Tyson. "He looks like he's been through a lot." He glanced at the women standing a short distance away, fishing baskets in their hands. "Did you pull him out?"

They shook their heads. A younger girl spoke up, her wings trembling. "He climbed out and collapsed."

Tyson moaned and tried to sit up. Becca reached for him, supporting his arms. She sniffed, rubbing her tears off on one shoulder.

"Wish I'd had a warning about that last drop," Tyson mut-tered, holding his head in one hand. He stared at the ground. No, not the ground. Becca's bare arm, coated with green scales. His eyes traveled up it to her face, and his wide eyes softened when he recognized her.

"Becca. What happened?"

She couldn't stand that pitying look on his face. She ducked her head and picked at the hem of the dress. "You know how I always wanted to be able to shift forms?"

"You wanted to be a werewolf. Or a bear," Tyson said.

"But I'm a snake. Or will be. Permanently. It's not everything I imagined it would be. Apparently, 'my kind' has to be controlled, and there's no fix. At least none that anyone here knows of."

She glared at Avaan. She wouldn't put it past him to withhold that information. If it existed, she was determined to find it. A solution that wouldn't have her enslaved to a charmer for the rest of her life, no matter how hot he was.

"I keep telling her it isn't a curse, but she won't listen. This is how it has always been. Charmer and serpent." Avaan gestured between himself and Becca. Tyson studied him, brow furrowed, but he didn't seem angry. Finally, he nodded.

"It makes sense. But Becca won't go quietly to a fate like that, not if I know her." He grinned and Becca's mouth stretched into a smile. Just like Tyson to cheer her up. "Now, I'd like to see a man about some clothes."

Becca laughed and even Quinn smiled. He stood, but froze midway up. Becca turned her head to see what— or who—he was looking at.

It was Harper.

Harper gazed at Tyson, face an indecipherable mix of emotions. Her mouth pursed and twisted one moment, then her face gave way to a look of utter relief.

Quinn quietly slipped away.

Tyson grabbed Becca's shoulder. "Help me stand."

Becca put her arm under his and they stood together. He released her after a moment and took a few steps forward. Becca expected a movie-style reunion, with running and crying. Her heart ached, even though she'd be happy for Tyson. But after a long pause, Harper folded her wings in and pushed back through the small crowd of villagers that had gathered.

Tyson put a hand up to the back of his head and rubbed his hair. "Guess that was pretty awkward."

Quinn returned, looking back the way Harper had gone. "What did you say to her?"

"Nothing, she's just being Harper." He shrugged. Was that a blush? Becca thought she saw his cheeks redden, but it could have been the cold. The goosebumps on his arms and legs were ridiculous.

"She'll come around." It seemed like a safe thing for Becca to say. "Probably overwhelmed."

Quinn eyed Tyson before handing him a set of clothes. "Might fit you. Wasn't sure about your size."

Becca made eye contact with Quinn briefly before they both looked away.

Quinn gestured for Tyson to follow him. "I'll show you a place to change."

"Thanks."

As they left, the crowd's murmurs turned from curiosity to dissension. A hand landed on Becca's shoulder.

"That's our cue to go. Before this group turns into a mob," Avaan murmured. He was probably right. But couldn't she have more time with Tyson before they left? Tell him what was happening to her, get some of his amazing advice? Hear his story and how he ended up naked on a riverbank in Alaska at the exact place he needed to be?

"I'm not ready to go."

"Sometimes you have to leave before you're ready."

Becca hated his poetic words and his soft brown eyes and how everything that she wanted to like about him was tainted with the knowledge that she didn't have a choice. At least, not a reasonable one. Not one that wasn't between slavery and death. But weren't all great choices impossible ones?

She squared her shoulders. "I'll come with you on one condition: we search for a way to end this."

Avaan laughed. "We will waste precious time, risking capture and the erasure of who we are. Why fight this?" He lowered his voice and leaned in, the flute dangling out of his shirt. "I could tell from the time we met that you were drawn to me." He raised his eyebrows. Becca felt like spitting.

Becca eyed the flute. It was within reach. Her fingers twitched. "Being attracted to a handsome man isn't the same as consenting to a lifetime of servitude."

He paused, and in that pause Becca took advantage of his proximity. She grabbed the flute, yanking the cord over Avaan's head. He shouted and lunged at her, but she hissed, letting her fangs emerge. Her eyes flashed with thermal colors. The snake coiled itself inside of her, prepared to take over her body and strike, but somehow, she managed to remain in control.

Avaan scrambled away from her, straightening his clothes. "Give that back," he whispered loudly.

Their spat was drawing attention from others. Good. She gripped the flute. It didn't feel like anything special. No tingly magic or weird sensations came from the wood touching her skin.

She pulled the cord over her own head and tucked the flute into her dress. "Now you can't coerce me. Do we have a deal?"

He pouted, which accentuated his handsome lips, but Becca did her best to ignore the twinge of attraction she felt. She tossed her hair and crossed her arms and waited.

Avaan sighed. "Very well. But we will give it a month."

"Two months."

"Six weeks," he said firmly. "Six weeks of my best efforts, using all of my knowledge."

"Can I read your notes?" Becca countered.

"If you can read Arabic."

"Drat. You'll have to read it to me, then."

He rolled his eyes and Becca nearly laughed at how ridiculous the expression looked on him. He gave her a pained look, but eventually held out his hand.

"You have a deal."

Becca moved to take his hand, but froze, noticing Chief Aguta's gaze locked onto her, sharp and unrelenting. His wings spread wide, casting a shadow that seemed to swallow the firelight.

"What have you done?" His voice was a low rumble, quiet but far more threatening than a shout.

Becca's fingers twitched against the flute hidden beneath her dress, its shape pressing cold and solid against her skin. "I stopped Avaan," she said. "He would use me. He can't now."

Chief Aguta's expression darkened, his wings rustling like a gathering storm. "Foolish girl," he said softly, "Without it—without him—you are an unchained weapon. A serpent untethered."

The words sent a chill through Becca, but she squared her shoulders. "I won't hurt anyone."

"You may not intend to." His gaze bore into her. "But you have hurt others, and you will again."

The murmurs of the tribe swelled, a low hum of unease that crawled over Becca's skin like static. The warriors at the edge of the crowd began to move, stepping forward with hands resting near their weapons.

"Stop." Quinn's voice cut through the tension. He shoved past his grandfather, standing between him and Becca, his wings flaring wide as if to shield her.

The chief didn't look at him, his focus fixed on Becca. "Are you so sure you control it?"

Becca opened her mouth to answer, but the words stuck in her throat. The serpent stirred deep within her, coiling tighter, listening. It wanted to be released.

Becca clenched her fists, trying to steady her breathing. "I can control it," she said, though her voice wavered.

The chief's expression hardened. "You are dangerous whether you wish to be or not. I will not allow you to bring ruin to my people."

"Then what?" Becca shot back, anger breaking through her fear. "You're going to kill me?"

The chief didn't answer, but his warriors advanced another step, their feathers whispering through the air like a thousand drawn knives.

"Becca, run!" Quinn hissed, grabbing her arm.

But she didn't move. She couldn't. She could feel the serpent uncoiling inside her, eager, alive. Her pulse roared in her ears, and the world narrowed, her thermal vision making the firelight flare, glinting off of the weapons as the ring of warriors closed in.

Becca's breathing slowed. Her fear twisted into something else—something darker, more primal. She lifted her chin and took a step forward, breaking free of Quinn's grasp.

The crowd murmured, startled. The warriors hesitated.

"Becca, what are you doing?" Quinn's voice cracked, but she ignored him.

Her fingers brushed the flute beneath her dress, and she exhaled slowly, letting the tension bleed from her limbs. The serpent surged in response, heat spilling through her blood, her vision fracturing further into thermal colors. She swayed, half-expecting the transformation to consume, but she held on—barely.

"I don't want to fight you," Becca said, though her voice was laced with a growl that didn't sound entirely human. "But I will."

The chief's wings snapped open fully, his face hardening into a mask of resolve. "Then you leave me no choice."

The warriors stepped forward, weapons glinting. The fire roared louder, its light throwing dancing shadows across the clearing.

The serpent's presence surged—hungry, eager—as Becca braced her legs and spread her arms, her muscles coiling tight as if ready to strike.

The warriors rushed forward.

And Becca let go.

∞

CHAPTER EIGHTEEN

HARPER

THE WORLD SLOWED AS Chief Aguta raised his hand. The warriors tensed, poised to strike, their feathers rustling like blades unsheathed.

"No!" Quinn shouted, stepping forward. "Stop—"

Too late. A pulse of energy shot from the chief's palm, aimed straight for Becca.

Before Harper could even react, Tyson lunged in front of her. His arms shot up, and a shimmering shield—jagged and translucent, like fractured glass—manifested between Becca and the attack. The force slammed into the shield, exploding into a blinding flash of blue light.

Harper stumbled back, shielding her eyes with her arm. A rush of heat and wind blew through the clearing, throwing snow into the air. When she blinked the spots from her vision, Tyson was still standing, arms spread wide, the shield dissipating into a faint shimmer of light.

The chief lowered his arm, his expression thunderous. "This is what happens when you bring outsiders among us. Chaos. Power unchecked. The serpent stirs, and you shelter it in your midst."

Becca raised herself on a coiled serpent's body, panting, her fingers curled as though holding something invisible.

Harper could see her trembling, see how hard she was fighting not to lose control.

A hum started among the warriors, their mouths opening. They would Sing, and this time, their Song would kill.

She had just arrived at the tribe—the family she had searched for her entire life—but this was wrong.

"Stop!" Harper screamed, darting forward to stand beside Quinn, wings outstretched.

The chief turned on her, gaze sad. "Has it truly come to this, Raven's daughter? You would deny yourself the chance to know your lineage, your power?"

"No, I wouldn't. There has to be a peaceful way to resolve this," she pleaded. She would know her grandfather. She wanted to know him. But if he insisted on killing Tyson's cousin, maybe even killing Tyson, she would accept the consequences of protecting them both.

"I will not tolerate such blatant disregard for the safety of my people. You and your brother must decide now. Will you remain with this tribe, honor its ways, and protect it from outsiders? Or will you go, taking this danger with you, and never return?"

The words hit Harper like a stone to the chest. "You're banishing us?"

"I am giving you a choice," Chief Aguta said gravely. "I hope you'll choose your tribe. Choose your family. Like your parents could not bring themselves to."

A chill swept through the clearing, sharper than the Alaskan wind. A hum still held in the air.

Harper's pulse thundered in her ears. She looked back toward Chief Aguta, trying to summon the words to argue with him, to fix this, but before she could speak, a new sound tore through the clearing.

A scream. A terrible, echoing scream that seemed to come from everywhere at once.

The crowd stiffened, heads snapping toward the dark line of trees at the clearing's edge. A sudden gust of wind blew through the camp, whipping the long dark hair of the watching tribe members, rustling the feathers of their outstretched wings.

"Whatever you are doing, stop it this instant," Chief Aguta demanded, his own wings flaring as he stepped back behind his line of warriors and scanned the horizon for the danger.

"What's happening?" Tyson whispered, stepping closer to Harper.

Harper's wings shifted uneasily. Her heart hammered in her chest as she scanned the darkness. "I don't know."

A low, guttural hiss rippled through the air.

Becca's eyes widened, snapping toward the sound.

The shadows at the base of the cliff moved. No—they writhed. Something stepped out of the darkness, a figure that shouldn't have been possible. Her shape was tall, feminine, but warped, her limbs too long, her body twisting unnaturally as if it were only barely human. Even with the inhuman shape, Harper recognized the witch's face.

Lilith.

Harper's stomach dropped. The air seemed to thicken, pressing down on her chest. Lilith's violet eyes gleamed as she smiled, her sharp teeth reflecting the faint firelight.

"There you are," Lilith purred, her voice sliding like oil through the crowd.

The tribe scattered. Warriors shouted orders, spears raised, but Lilith moved too quickly. She blurred into shadow, appearing suddenly in the center of the camp. Her dark claws lashed out, sending warriors sprawling.

"Protect the chief!" someone screamed.

The clearing erupted into chaos, but Harper couldn't move. Her legs, and her wings, were frozen as she stared at the horrifying figure of Lilith's transformed self.

"Go!" Quinn grabbed Becca's arm, shoving her towards the man behind her.

Lilith's head snapped toward them, her smile widening. "Leaving so soon?"

Harper's breath caught in her throat. "How did you find us?"

Lilith tilted her head, her smile sharp and predatory. "Did you really think I wouldn't? I've been waiting for this, Harper. You knew I would come."

"I—" Harper's words faltered. "I didn't think you'd... follow me. Not here. Not after—"

"Not after what?" Lilith's voice dripped with amusement, though her black eyes blazed. "Not after I let you leave the camp? Or perhaps you thought I'd grow tired of my little raven and forget you entirely?"

Harper swallowed hard, her hand trembling as it brushed against the faint scar on her palm—the mark Lilith had burned into her skin back when Harper had trusted her. Trusted her lies.

"You don't need me," Harper said, squaring her shoulders, though her voice shook. "Why are you really here, Lilith? What do you want?"

"What I want is simple," Lilith purred, taking a step forward. The snow hissed and melted beneath her feet. "You. Your brother. And perhaps a few others to sweeten the deal." She smiled, her teeth gleaming. "But most of all, I wanted to see the look on your face when you realized what I've already taken from you."

Harper's stomach dropped. "What do you mean?"

Lilith clucked her tongue, her smile widening as if savoring the moment. "That poor blue jay boy—what was his name? Fletcher?"

Harper's heart stopped. "Don't."

Lilith's grin turned cruel. "Oh, but you must know the truth. You assumed he took his own life because of weakness, because he couldn't fight his demons. But I am the demon that whispered in his ear. I planted the thought, fed his despair. His death was your motivation to use the orb, and in using the orb, you freed me to take over the camp, and from there, I'll raise the most powerful coven of witches the world has ever seen and take our freedom back by force. You will be hailed as our hero, when we're through. You should thank me."

Harper staggered back as if struck, the truth of Fletcher's death sinking like a stone in in the pit of her stomach. "You... you're lying."

Lilith shrugged, feigning boredom. "Believe what you wish, but you know the truth. And you know that resisting what's coming is futile. There are other rebellions, but their pitiful efforts pale in comparison to the power I will use to consume the humans of this world and replace them with more of our kind. You want that too, don't you? Or you did, once." Lilith's slitted eyes narrowed, still glowing with an eerie violet light. "Perhaps now things have changed, now that you've fallen in with humans."

Harper glanced at Tyson. Lilith still didn't know that he had awakened to his own kind of power, no longer entirely human, but a bridge of sorts between the two.

"I still want freedom, but not the kind you offer. You would slaughter millions to create the world you want. I won't take part in that," Harper said. Her hands clenched into fists, strength surging through her limbs at her conviction.

Lilith laughed, a high-pitched, grating sound. "Tell yourself that as much as you want, but you have blood on your hands, Harper King. And that mark on your hand? That's proof of your desire to serve me. Now, be a good little raven and come home."

The X on Harper's palm flared to life, burning like fire under her skin. Harper fell to her knees, clutching her hand as violet light pulsed through the veins of her arm.

"Harper!" Tyson cried out, frantic.

Lilith loomed closer. "Let me in, Harper. You belong to me."

"No!" Harper shouted. She staggered to her feet, the mark on her hand searing like a hot brand, but she shoved the pain down. Inside her, a voice rose unbidden, erupting raw and guttural from her throat, shaking the air itself. Her Raven Song.

The sound burst from her chest like a war cry, primal and defiant. She jumped with all her strength, flapping her wings so she hung in the air. The dirt at her feet whipped up in violent spirals with the force of her wingbeats and her song.

Many voices joined hers, the tribe's raven warriors joining her song until it climbed louder, higher, until even Lilith staggered.

"Enough!" Lilith snarled, the shadows around her boiling like smoke. She extended her hand, and the mark on Harper's palm flared hotter.

Harper screamed, her song breaking as the witch's magic surged through her body. She fell out of the sky, crashing to the ground where she lay gasping for breath. Her vision filled with pulsing dark spots and all of her strength bleeding from her limbs.

"Foolish girl," Lilith said softly, kneeling before her and grasping her chin. "Did you think you could win?"

Tears streamed down Harper's face as violet light flooded her vision. The pain in her hand spread through her arm, then the rest of her body. She didn't even have time to resist before her mind shattered.

"Harper?" Tyson's voice sounded like an echo, distant and afraid.

Harper stood slowly, arms and legs jerking, her wings twitching as another force controlled her every movement.

She tilted her head, smiling faintly, a smile she didn't feel. She didn't feel anything. She was nothing.

"She's mine now," Lilith said, her voice echoing through Harper's mouth, and then she laughed.

CHAPTER NINETEEN

TYSON

TYSON'S BOOTS SLAMMED AGAINST the frozen ground, his breath ragged as he sprinted away from Harper. She dove down from the sky, her eyes a violent purple color, her free will stolen by Lilith. He tried to summon a force field to block her attacks, but failed, his focus too scattered.

Lilith's laughter followed him. "Run all you like, Tyson," she cooed. "You'll come back for her in the end. They always do."

Tyson didn't look back. He couldn't—not with Harper's violet-glowing eyes burned into his mind. Not with the image of her face twisted, her wings a dark blur as she crashed into him.

He shoved her off, barely avoiding her scratching fingers as he scrambled away. How could he fight her without hurting her?

He had no direction now, just away.

Chief Aguta's voice barked an order in the Inuit tongue, and though Tyson didn't understand, he caught the gist of it. They were evacuating. The tribe scattered, chaos breaking out as the people panicked, gathering items and fleeing on foot and on wing towards the cliffs surrounding the village.

A desperate shout pierced the air. Tyson turned just in time to see Quinn approaching, his wings unfurled and wild. Behind him, Lilith emerged from the clearing, her silhouette wreathed in shadow, her smile terrible and triumphant.

Quinn stumbled to his knees, clutching his head. "Get... out of my head!"

"Poor boy," Lilith crooned. Her voice was soft now, almost motherly, though it dripped with venom. "Why resist me? Your sister didn't."

Quinn's wings spasmed, his entire body trembling. Tyson watched, helpless, as the violet glow began to seep into Quinn's dark eyes, spreading like a stain.

"Quinn!" Becca cried, starting forward. Avaan caught her arm, holding her back.

"Let him go," Avaan said sharply. "You'll only get yourself killed!"

"Stop!" Quinn shouted, his voice strangled. His hands clawed at his head, his wings beating wildly. "Don't let her—"

He froze. The violet light solidified, flooding his gaze. He lowered his hands, his expression smoothing into something vacant. The Quinn they knew was gone.

"Much better," Lilith said, her smile gleaming. "Now, my raven prince, bring me the others."

Quinn turned toward them, his wings rising menacingly.

"We need to run," Tyson said to Becca, his mind racing. "Now!"

"But where?!" Becca yelled, panic rising in her voice.

Tyson clenched his fists, his pulse hammering in his ears. He had no plan. No escape. But deep inside, he felt something stir—a memory of the trials. The power he'd glimpsed. He didn't know if he could do it again, but if they stayed, they were dead. Or worse.

He closed his eyes and reached for that power. He didn't even know if he could do it, only that he had to.

Come on, he thought, heart pounding. You can do this.

"What are you doing?" Avaan's voice cut through the noise, sharp with alarm.

Tyson ignored him. He let the world around him blur, focusing on the image in his mind—an image of home. His apartment. Oregon. The ripped-open wall where Quinn had once burst through the window, back when life had made a shred of sense.

Something tugged at his chest, pulling from deep inside. His skin prickled with heat, his vision pulsing.

"Tyson!" Becca screamed.

He opened his eyes.

A swirling vortex of silver light had split the air before them, shimmering and alive. The edges rippled like torn fabric. Tyson staggered back, sweat dripping down his temples.

"It's open! Go!"

Becca didn't hesitate. She grabbed Avaan's arm and pulled him toward the portal. "Quinn, come on!" she shouted, as though her voice alone could pull him free.

Quinn's glowing violet eyes snapped to them, expression blank. His wings beat once, twice—then he lunged.

Tyson dove for the portal, feeling the rush of cold wind as Quinn's outstretched hand grazed his arm. For a split second, their eyes met—Quinn's lit with Lilith's power, Tyson's wild with desperation.

Then Tyson hit the vortex, and the world shattered into light.

CHAPTER TWENTY

TYSON

TYSON HIT THE FLOOR hard, landing in a heap on cheap linoleum. His head spun, and the air around him crackled like static before going still. Silence swallowed him, broken only by the sound of Becca gasping beside him. Avaan sprawled out across the kitchen floor, groaning softly.

Tyson pushed himself upright, heart racing. The familiar smell of his apartment—stale coffee, old wood—hit him all at once. He was home.

Becca sat up, her serpent scales fading, her hands trembling. "Where are we?"

Tyson swallowed, looking around the dim room. The hole in the wall stared back at him. Someone had taped a sheet of thick construction plastic over the opening, and it flapped loudly, becoming taught, then slackening as the wind passed.

A laugh escaped him, breathless and hollow. "We're... we're in my apartment."

Becca's eyes landed on the broken wall, and her lips twitched in an almost-smile. "This is where Quinn busted through the window, isn't it?"

Tyson nodded, a lump forming in his throat. "Yeah. Back when all you wanted was my help busting Harper out of Camp Silver Lake."

Becca huffed softly. "Simpler times."

Tyson didn't answer, the irony not lost on him. He leaned back against the wall, staring at the hole, noticing the lights of the town filtering through the plastic as darkness fell outside. Everything felt unreal. Like they'd stepped out of a nightmare and into a world that hadn't yet caught up to the truth.

But the truth was still there—burned into his memory. Harper's face, glowing violet, turning on him with claws that weren't her own. Quinn's eyes, empty and lost. Lilith's laughter. Her plan to eliminate humankind and put herself in charge.

Becca's voice broke the silence. "We left them."

Tyson flinched. He turned away, his fists clenching. "I left them," he whispered. "I left Harper behind. I didn't even try to save her."

"You couldn't save her, Tyson," Becca said, her voice gentler now. "None of us could."

"But I ran," he shot back, the guilt clawing at his chest. "I ran like a coward."

Becca crawled over to sit beside him, her knees pulling up to her chest. "You ran because we needed you to. Because you're the only one who could get us out." She glanced at him. "That doesn't make you a coward. That makes you the reason we're still alive."

Tyson stared at the broken wall, noticing that tiny wet spots now covered its surface. A gentle pattering sound filled the apartment, the only sound in the silence. It was raining.

He didn't feel like a hero. He felt like a hollowed-out shell, filled with guilt and exhaustion.

"We'll go back for them," Becca said softly, as if reading his mind. "We'll find a way to save Harper. And Quinn too."

Tyson closed his eyes, her words washing over him like a promise he wasn't sure he could keep.

"Yeah," he murmured, his voice rough. "We'll go back."

Outside, rain fell silently on the lush Oregon landscape, far from Lilith's reach. But Tyson knew it wouldn't last.

Lilith was still out there. And Harper and Quinn were hers.

Not forever, he promised himself. Only for now. Until he was strong enough to get her back.

∞

Can't wait to find out what happens next? Keep reading for a sneak peak at Lost Souls Book 3: Coven Bound!

SPECIAL THANKS

Writing a book is no easy task, and I could never do it alone.
Thanks to my writing group for trying to keep up with my
lightning-fast pace, for cheering me on when things got hard,
and for being there for everything else. Here's to another seven
years writing together!
Special thanks to Amanda for making it all the way through and
re-reading the ending like four times. You're my hero.
As usual, I owe so much to my husband, who takes over the
house and kids when I need to escape and write. You're the best
partner I could ask for.
I want to thank my faithful readers, especially those who have
stuck with me since my first book was published. You've kept
me going with your help with my launches, beta reading, and
general support.
Thank you.

EXCERPT FROM COVEN BOUND: LOST SOULS BOOK 3

MANDI

DEEP, SLOW BREATHS.

Visualize. Keep thoughts positive.

The coven was meeting tonight in the astral realm, and Mandi was determined to make it. No one would have to take notes for her.

She'd figure out how to separate her spirit from its mortal cage and fly through time and space to the purple tree with a starlit canopy and blue algae growing on its trunk. A place where the witches could discuss their private coven matters with confidence that no one, and no thing, would be listening in.

The others talked about astral projection like others talked about breathing or walking. If that was the case, Mandi was the infant who hadn't figured it out yet. A late bloomer, as Violet would say.

Blobs of color floated in Mandi's vision, and she couldn't help but feel resignation instead of excitement. That was how it started. Her usual sea of darkness, lit by strange, wavering clouds of color. Sometimes she saw faces, a random blip of an image, but she'd been blind too long for her subconscious to keep populating her dreams.

The colors faded. That was how it always ended. She'd enter a deeper sleep state, now. Her mind grew heavy and sleep crawled in, despite her fighting it. No astral projection. No flying over cities, no creating new worlds, no meeting spirit guides or coven sisters. No Sight. No one was sure why, but as a blind witch, Mandi seemed barred from the limbo realm. Why should one need working eyes to See the different planes?

The unmistakable sound of glass breaking shattered the nothingness. Shouting echoed as if from the inside of a tunnel, and a werewolf howled. Not Zeke.

Footsteps. They came fast, the thudding, rustling, muted steps of several people running over grass. Panting.

"...Merry meet and Merry part and Merry meet again. You may all step forward and say a few words, as moved upon. I only ask that you respect the dead and each other in the utmost." Violet's voice drifted through the air. The words she would speak at a funeral. Someone coughed.

Feet pounded and a sound like wings unfurling caught the air.

Gasps and cries. A bellow came from the direction of the woods. Fire crackled nearby, but instead of heat it let off a strange, whispering energy.

Violet. What had happened to Violet? Were her other friends there?

"They're dead!" a voice cried. It sounded like Honey. Honey was there. Mandi tried to speak, but her voice didn't work. She reached out to touch someone, anyone, but despite the nearby voices her fingers grasped nothing. It was like she was there, but a ghost, only to observe with her limited senses.

It sounded like an action film, the battle scene, a cacophony of sound with no way to ground herself in what was happening.

A dragon's bellow split the sky. Mandi crouched, terror pounding in her heart.

The story continues in Coven Bound! Get it on Amazon today!

Bree Moore lives in Iowa with her husband, seven children, and two cats. When she's not busy homeschooling or folding laundry, she sneaks off to write more fantasy.

Bree writes urban and epic fantasy to explore different worlds with amazing creatures and magic systems. She enjoys giving her readers a story that is both entertaining and emotional, with a healthy dose of romance. When she's not writing, Bree can be found foraging for edible plants, watching fantasy shows and movies, or hanging out with her husband and kids.

Published works include: *The Shadowed Minds* series, the *Lost Souls* series, and *Shadows of Camelot* series. She's currently working on *The Plague King Chronicles*.

Visit www.authorbreemoore.com for a FREE fantasy book!

♪ tiktok.com/@breenovels

⊙ instagram.com/breenovels

Shadows of Camelot
The Lady's Last Song
The Queen's Quiet End

Shadowed Minds Series
Prequel: Thief of Lies
Thief of Magic
Thief of Aether
Thief of Bones

Wings of Rebellion Series
Prequel: Raven Blood
Raven Born
Serpent Cursed
Coven Bound
Serpent Turned
Siren Called
Rebel Sworn

The Plague King Chronicles
The Keeper of the Well
The Quill and the Vial
The Arrow and the Ivy
Of Dusk and Dawn Collection
Sacrifice for the Standing Stones
Vows Beneath the Frozen Stars